By Disha Bose

Dirty Laundry
I Will Blossom Anyway

I Will Blossom Anyway

I Will Blossom Anyway

Anyway

A Novel

DISHA BOSE

Ballantine Books
New York

Ballantine Books
An imprint of Random House
A division of Penguin Random House LLC
1745 Broadway, New York, NY 10019
randomhousebooks.com
penguinrandomhouse.com

Hardback ISBN 978-0-593-87532-2
Ebook ISBN 978-0-593-87533-9

Printed in the United States of America on acid-free paper

2 4 6 8 9 7 5 3 1

First Edition

BOOK TEAM: Production editor: Kelly Chian • Managing editor: Pamela Alders • Production manager: Jane Haas Sankner • Copy editor: Pam Feinstein • Proofreaders: Allison Lindon, Megha Jain, Barbara Jatkola

Book design by Virginia Norey

The authorized representative in the EU for product safety and compliance is Penguin Random House Ireland, Morrison Chambers, 32 Nassau Street, Dublin D02 YH68, Ireland. https://eu-contact.penguin.ie.

For Ellora

I Will Blossom Anyway

Chapter 1

BENGAL HAS ALWAYS BEEN RULED BY GODDESSES.
According to Hindu mythology, the all-forgiving Goddess Durga, pure of heart, became ensnared in a losing battle against a demon who was set to destroy all of humankind.

When Goddess Durga stopped to look around the battlefield, she found nothing but death and destruction. She became frenzied with fury, at her own weakness against the demon, at the futility of this battle.

That was when Kali appeared. Durga's other form, her dark alter ego. Kali emerged right out of Durga's forehead wielding a sword, wearing nothing but a sari made of a tiger's skin.

Kali was invincible. By the end of the battle, she had not only defeated the demon but had a garland of men's skulls around her neck. She was on the warpath now, and in her anger couldn't distinguish between good and evil anymore. So enraged was she that she wanted everyone and everything dead.

So, while Durga gets her own ten-day celebration, we worship Kali in Bengal too, with hibiscus flowers and offerings of sweets. Durga is worshipped for the victory of good over evil, while Kali is worshipped for her strength. My parents named me Durga, perhaps in the hope that I might embody the Goddess's virtues of integrity and goodness. But I yearned to feel the full force of Kali, for her to make my toes tingle, straining to be let out.

My mind seems predisposed to expect decay too, the way Kali did. For instance, in autumn, all I notice is how leaves are so exhausted with life that they give up and fall to the ground. That animals begin to panic; gathering their food, hiding it, preparing to hibernate. The seasonal lattes are only a distraction; the hollowness of winter is forever looming in my background. I've always been an overthinker, allowing the possibility of complications to dampen my mood. I stopped getting manicures because I'd worry about chips and lifting from the moment I walked out of the nail salon. I'd spend all of Sunday feeling gloomy, anxious about sleeping through the Monday morning alarm. I found it impossible to enjoy the changing colors of autumn, or the relief of the crisp air after a muggy summer, only agonizing over a dark winter ahead.

For my walk in the park that autumn evening, I was bundled up, cursing the wind. My body hadn't adjusted to the sudden drop in temperature. I was freezing in a lemon yellow scarf, a black beret the color of my hair, and a big coat that engulfed me. Autumn isn't for people like me, who are unsettled by change. Today, as I soldiered on through the park, I could sense Kali stirring. I was here with a purpose.

I wouldn't have wandered outside at this time for no reason, when the sun was disappearing fast, shooting neon jazz hands from behind a veil of clouds. I longed to be home, safe in my comfort zone, pining for Jacob from afar.

Besides, the sun would set soon and I carried the primal ancestral fear of darkness everywhere with me. Even in bed with all the lights turned off, in the absence of a sentry guarding the cave, I required a source of light to lull me to sleep. This was a good excuse for why I scrolled through my phone until my eyelids drooped. A light on my bedside table would've been an easy solution, but I found comfort in dreaming about the twenty second cat video I'd watched last. A satisfactory way to end the day.

At the park, I noticed my boots were speckled with mud from stepping over puddles, and I stopped to retrieve a baby wipe from the pack I always carried in my bag. While I was bent over, giving the smooth leather a clean, my phone chimed in my coat. It was Joy.

Sorry. I'm late. Be there in a few ticks.

Joy was my flatmate, and best friend. The woman I shared my pizzas and hot-water bottle with. I trusted her to not use my razor in the shower, and to cancel Friday night plans if I didn't feel like going out. In her, I'd found my ride or die.

She was one of those millennial unicorns who forgot to check her phone, didn't post on social media anymore, and didn't feel the need to wear a watch. She rarely knew what day of the week it was. It wasn't that she was an irresponsible person, not like some other people we knew—Maeve, Joy's childhood friend and on-and-off flame, for instance, was the poster child for Millennials Who Never Learned to Adult.

Joy paid our bills, scrubbed the baseboards, remembered to lock the flat at night, kept herself sufficiently hydrated. However, she forgot all her friends' birthdays and was never on time for work—a small price to pay.

Being Jacob's sister was also a particular kind of problem, given the change in our circumstances. My relationship with Jacob, the big love of my life, had ended after two years of bliss. But since his sister had become so inextricably bound to me, there was no hope for him ever disentangling from my life. Something we would both have to learn to live with. I didn't know how to, yet. How to not see Jacob when I saw Joy. How to not notice the way she threw the tea towel over her shoulder while emptying the dishwasher, exactly the way her brother did.

In Joy's last-minute absence, I considered leaving the park. My nerves were getting the better of me. I wasn't comfortable with the voice rattling inside my head. It may all boil down to having grown up in a large family, sharing my room with a sister, and not having much opportunity for a silent thought.

India is noisy in general, but it wasn't just the blaring horns and the electric sound of life outside. Somebody was always shouting *inside* my home too. My mother spent a lot of time barking orders from the kitchen or on the phone with old relatives who were hard of hearing. My father had the news perpetually turned on, which synthesized with cricket updates on the radio my brother was glued to. My sisters quarreled incessantly, with one another or with our mother. While my grandmother scolded the maid for not cleaning under the cupboards. If I had an inner voice, it had remained muffled since my birth.

My first night in the overpriced flat I'd found in Cork two years ago was also my first night away from my family. I'd got a promotion at work and been offered a transfer to their offices in Ireland. I'd jumped at the opportunity to move away, to finally find that voice I'd missed hearing all my life.

Joy and I hadn't met yet. I didn't have a flatmate at first. While I was desperate for company from the moment I walked into my new abode, dragging my bags behind me, I didn't meet her until later.

Alone in my new home, I'd turned on all the lights and sat on the couch with my legs crossed, listening for a voice, any sound.

I could hear the fridge whirring and the sporadic sound of an engine outside. For years I'd wanted this—the freedom, the absence of the overbearingly loud intrusion of my family. I thought I'd find some peace with the continents and large bodies of water between us, but the voice in my head, which appeared suddenly, was whispery and alien. It was telling me I was alone, that there were purple monsters under the bed, and they liked nibbling on feet. That the branch thumping my windowpane was actually the severed arm of a hairy ghoul, and it would continue tapping until I opened the window and allowed it to come in and suck my soul.

My life had changed so drastically in these two years though, that I didn't recognize that subdued woman anymore. The woman who'd arrived here as a girl, really. Who didn't know how to live alone.

I made my way around the park slowly, stepping to the side for every runner who passed me by. Six o'clock was a popular fitness slot for the office-going types. They were in high-vis tops and shorts, squeaky sneakers, a podcast in their ears, braving the cutting cold for their daily dose of adrenaline. I felt a moment's anxiety for having consumed nothing but a donut for lunch. This I quickly suffocated by reminding myself that I'd leave the running to my thirties. What were my twenties for, if not to skip breakfasts and make up for it with fried dough and pistachio cream?

You made me come here and now I'm by myself.

I typed a quick text to Joy, then made my way toward the pebbled bank of the river that ran alongside the park. It wasn't the best idea because the wind, which was stronger here, blew straight into my face with its icy claws. I was sure my cheeks would bleed.

After I was done fussing with the scarf and looping it tighter around my neck, I saw a man throwing a stick into the river. He was making a big show of it. He bent far back into the shape of a croissant and then whipped the stick into the water, whistling urgently. My eyes were drawn to his mouth, a nice mouth, and when he looked over and smiled at me, it was surprising how vastly it took over his entire face.

The splash of a dog hurling itself into the water interrupted my staring, gave me something to look at other than at him. The dog paddled toward the stick, drifting with the strong current, and I worried that it mightn't be able to make it back safely. I'd watched videos of dogs paddling in swimming pools, but I had no idea of their prowess in a gusty river at high tide.

But the man appeared untroubled, and slid his hands into the pockets of an oversized fleece jumper. A square of a man, I thought. He must have a hard time finding clothes that fit him correctly because he was so tall and broad. Slender at the same time. The jumper hung off him as though on a hanger. I immediately guilt-tripped myself for objectifying a man's body, especially at a time like this. When the only man on my mind should have been Jacob. I was here to fix the mess we were in.

"I apologize if Dusty is ruining your quiet time," this man said.

We were standing some distance apart, so he had to shout to catch my attention. He was right, I did want some time to myself to compose my thoughts.

"It's fine. I'm enjoying watching him," I replied.

I would never admit to being inconvenienced anyway. I once nicked my finger in my aunt's kitchen while helping her chop onions. Instead of letting her put a Band-Aid on, I was more concerned with blotting out the drops of blood on the floor. I insisted fervently that I felt nothing while my finger throbbed from the sting of the onion juice on my hand.

But I wasn't really inconvenienced by this man today; in fact, I welcomed the distraction.

Dusty was expertly paddling toward the bank, the stick held in his mouth above water, like he'd won an Oscar.

"Good, because it would be impossible to take him elsewhere now. This is his favorite spot," he said.

Dusty jumped out, shaking and splattering water all around him. Then he bounded over to me and dropped the stick on my shoes, startling me. I didn't know what to do with the stick at first, my interactions with dogs had been minimal thus far. I'd only ever admired them from a distance, wary of lolling tongues and their heavy, meaty breath.

The man whistled, trying to get him to come over, but Dusty sat down, cocking his head to the side expectantly. I picked up the stick and made a weak attempt at a throw, trying to emulate what the man had done. It landed on the bank, missing the water by an inch, but Dusty ran after it nonetheless.

"There's nothing like a dog to brush up the ego," I said, chuckling to hide my embarrassment.

It was obvious I'd never thrown a stick before. In my twenty-six years of life, how had I never been faced with a stick-throwing opportunity?

"You shouldn't have done that." His tone was serious as he came toward me. "Now you'll be stuck here throwing the damn stick into the river all evening."

"I could use the practice."

"It's a useful life skill."

"For when I need to get rid of evidence of a crime."

"Just make sure you don't bring any dogs, because they'll fetch it all back."

"Not much danger of that, I'm a cat person."

His eyes grew big, as though in horror, then he made a face like he'd smelled something funky in the air. It was cute and it made me giggle. I was instantly charmed.

"I won't apologize for it," I said.

I was only pretending to take a stand. If he even hinted at being offended I would have immediately backed down. I didn't like the idea of anyone being mad at me, especially not a handsome stranger.

Dusty was at my feet again, his shaggy bronze coat was soaked, and his bubblegum tongue hung out like a wet rag. I threw the stick again, making a bit more effort this time so it actually landed in the water.

"It's okay. There are all kinds of people in the world. Some reply to texts with emojis. There's space for everyone. I'm Niall, by the way."

I chewed on my bottom lip. There were strings of conversations between Joy and me on my phone that were only a series of emojis. The more obscure the better.

"Right. You're one of them," Niall said. "So you're a cat person and an emoji aficionado. What else don't I want to know about you?"

I hoped he couldn't see my face flushing in the quickening darkness. I wasn't well practiced in sustaining conversations with handsome strangers. But this man had put me at ease and I was enjoying his company. Also, I was chicken. My uneasiness over meeting Joy and then Jacob far outweighed the discomfort of making small talk with a stranger. I would've done anything to delay the inevitable.

"If you really want to know, I can't take a bite out of a burger in public. I just can't open my mouth wide enough, not in front of other people," I said.

He laughed at that, lightly scratching his chin while he looked me up and down. "So you eat your burgers in the toilet at a restaurant?"

"It's nice in there. Nobody interrupts my chewing with small talk. I can take as big a bite as I want and get ketchup all over my clothes in peace."

He nodded, as though making mental notes. "I get the feeling you're the type to ruin a perfectly good burger with ketchup."

The sun was setting directly behind Niall, making it difficult to discern the exact shade of his hair. If Joy were here, she would've seen right through me. She would've taken one look at me scraping my thumb cuticle and known I liked this man. This breezy Niall with his happy dog. The lure of an easy out.

"I wouldn't diss ketchup if I were you. Tomatoes help your body fight against the sun's UV rays," I said.

I was instantly reminded of where I'd got that nugget of information from, and I pushed against the descending gloom. My brain was already revisiting the image of Jacob, stretched on my couch, one long leg looped around my thigh, both of us lazily scrolling on our phones at opposite ends. I could smell the shea butter cream he used to keep his hands moisturized, and my eyes watered.

"Sorry, I don't mean to get emotional about ketchup," I said, when I saw Niall looking. I was making a fool of myself.

"Hey, you won't get any judgment from me. I still cry when I watch *The Lion King*," he said.

He was sweet. There was no comparison between Mufasa dying and my interest in ketchup, but he didn't want to embarrass me.

"The cold makes my eyes water too. It's really chilly by the river."

"Durga Das," I supplied my name quickly.

"Hi, Durga."

Dusty returned to Niall and they played a quick game of tug, until he whistled and Dusty dropped the stick obediently. After it was chucked back in the water, he straightened up and looked directly into my eyes.

"Want my jumper?"

There were two reasons why I wanted his jumper. I'd be warm in it, and I wanted to watch him removing it. But even I, as shameless as I was feeling, with adrenaline coursing through my veins, couldn't bring myself to accept this chivalrous offer.

"I wouldn't want you to freeze to death," I said.

Niall already had a hand bunching up the bottom of his jumper, getting ready to pull it off. I saw a flat stomach, with a dusting of dark hair going down his navel, disappearing into his loose-fitting jeans.

I didn't know they still made men like this, who were willing to make grand gestures for a woman they wanted to keep talking to.

I looked over at Dusty, who was wading back toward us. The sky was set in an apricot and aubergine glow, the two colors not quite mixing, like in a lava lamp. Niall whistled again, having noticed Dusty running off in a different direction.

"He's obsessed with birds." We looked up and saw a flock of them flying in a V formation. Dusty was looking up too, wagging his tail, spinning around in circles. "He wishes he could fly."

"He was literally chasing his dream," I said.

Our eyes met and we broke into a laugh. I liked the way he gave his nose a quick pinch and sniffled when he was done laughing, as though marking its end with a ceremony.

I heard my phone ding in my pocket and pulled it out to check Joy's latest excuse.

I'm traffucked, but I'm on my way. Promise.

At least she was keeping an eye on her phone. When I looked up, I found Niall staring. He had that easy confidence of not being ashamed when caught looking.

"This is not make-or-break, but can you parallel park?" he asked.

"I don't actually know what that means. I don't drive. I grew up in India." Which was not a self-explanatory statement. I should have detailed the anxiety of driving in India. How there is only one road rule to follow—which is to forget all rules, instinctual or otherwise.

"That answers my next question. You're Indian."

"Please don't ask me how hot it is there. I can't come up with any more ways to describe it. The heat is relentless in the summer, and we all just wait patiently for monsoon."

"I was going to ask if you miss the food."

I saw a slim vein throbbing in the center of his forehead as he smiled.

"Oh . . . You know, what I really miss is a good cup of loose leaf tea."

"I could arrange one, I know a place. It's an Indian joint, in Bishopstown, and I've seen it on their menu. I just need to drive Dusty back home, and I could meet you there? I don't want to creep you out, but I'm happy to give you a lift. If you don't mind being in a car with a smelly wet dog. You could tell me all about the weather in India."

Niall's shoulders shook as he laughed. He'd spoken slowly, and didn't appear nervous. He was interested in me, but not invested, and this gave him his self-assuredness.

I watched him pull a ropy lead out of the pocket of his jeans and he was beginning to absentmindedly twist it around his palm. Another gust of wind blew into our faces, ruffling his hair and making me grateful for my scarf.

"That sounds great," I said. Niall was clipping the lead to Dusty's red collar while looking up at me. "But I'm meeting someone here."

My hands sweated inside the pockets of my coat, and I wished I had the courage to offer him my number. It was a confusing psychological block. Even though he'd technically asked me out, I couldn't bring myself to reciprocate. I didn't want to seem too eager. Or maybe it was the minuscule chance of rejection that scared me. I was already thinking ahead—picturing myself pacing at home, waiting for him to call. Besides, there was Jacob. It was not over yet.

Niall didn't look surprised, almost as though he was expecting this response. "Right. No bother. I better take this one home. He gets hungry after he's been swimming."

This was a man who knew how to take a rejection.

"Of course. Poor Dusty. I won't keep you."

"You wouldn't want that on your conscience."

"I'm a cat person, not a monster."

Niall waited a beat. I pulled out my phone again, in an awkward show of not being affected by his impending departure. But my heart sank when he started to walk away. I didn't know his surname. I knew nothing about him, other than the name of his dog and that he had a driver's license. He'd asked all the questions.

Niall was already on the walkway, with Dusty pulling at the lead, and he gave me a quick wave.

"Bye!" I shouted, but he mustn't have heard because he didn't turn to look. It made the whole thing worse. It felt like a missed opportunity, like I'd led this nice man on and then embarrassed myself.

I felt even colder as I stood there. Without Niall's jumper, without his number, not knowing if he could parallel park. It wasn't even winter yet. There were still leaves clinging to trees, making a last-ditch effort for life even as they changed color. One cold breeze and they'd be on the ground. That was how I felt, like I'd already lost everything. Typical Durga, with no Kali in sight.

My phone pinged in my hand. It was Joy.

I'm here. Where are you? Have you met Jacob yet?

I wished I could tell her how much I didn't want to do this.

Chapter 2

JACOB WAS LIKE A BEAUTIFULLY TAILORED DRESS ON A mannequin in a display window. Admirable, but far from aspirational. I wouldn't put on the dress, in fear of what I might look like in it, that it wouldn't fit me, that I might ruin the clasps. The dress was made for another woman.

Firstly, I couldn't afford the dress, so I knew it would be an exercise in futility. Secondly, if the dress looked as beautiful on me as it did in the window, then it would ruin all future dresses forever because I could never want another.

Jacob was too handsome for me, and my fear of rejection had motivated me to avoid all contact with him. It was my defense mechanism. I'd repeated this pattern with Niall today.

Jacob I admired silently at the office, like my other co-workers did, but I kept my thoughts to myself. Following tradition, I was the quiet one in the cafeteria, having never done well in social group settings. I was new to the job, new to the country, and still getting used to the local accent.

Everyone I'd met thus far was friendly, and they'd invite me to sit with them. Fiona was the most vocal in the group. She complained about the quality of the food, the weather, dished out TV show recommendations, and had an obvious crush on Jacob. The rest of us giggled when she talked about him, and she brought him up nearly every day. What he was wearing, how he'd pulled out a chair for her, how she'd seen him waiting patiently in his car at the pedestrian crossing for everyone to walk and hadn't beeped once. That was the thing the women most gushed about—Jacob's good manners.

I assumed my interest in him was mob mentality—Fiona's doing. The other men in the office weren't worthy of my admiration, not with Jacob around, but I thought this because Fiona told us so.

Jacob had never spoken to me, he'd never given any indication he was even aware of my existence. I was simply the new girl from India.

Then one day we were the only people in an empty corridor, walking toward each other from opposite ends. It was like I'd been thrown into the deep end of the pool. The closer he got, the more I felt like I was thrashing in the water, like I'd forgotten to float.

He was watching me, and I sensed he was preparing to speak. I couldn't think of one thing to say. What did people use as greetings? *Hello? Mornin'? What did you eat for breakfast?*

I thrust my hands into the pockets of my jeans and kept my head down as he approached. Sinking now.

"Durga, right?" he said, stopping in front of me.

"What?" I shouted.

He looked a little taken aback and pushed his glasses up his nose.

"Sorry, did I mispronounce your name?"

He knew my name, and that was enough for me to panic. Pull the shutters down, turn off the lights, pretend like nobody's home. Crickets.

"You're Jacob," I said, failing miserably at playing it cool. I was barely meeting his eyes, flushing.

"That's me." He smiled, and I realized I'd never seen his smile before.

I had been so shy about looking at him directly before this that I didn't have a clear idea of what he actually looked like. I had a vague impression of a tall, athletic man from the rare occasion that he walked past. I knew what he sounded like—gravelly and serious, like the voice-over for a religious doomsday video.

I'd based the rest of my knowledge of his good looks on Fiona's description of him. She was right, he had a supremely symmetrical face, and when he smiled his chin narrowed.

I'd mistakenly thought that he was clean-shaven. When in fact, now that he was so close to me, I could see a dark stubble. His eyes were a light shade of brown behind his glasses. I was unquestionably drowning.

"Breakfast?" I said. Absurdly, it was the first word that spilled out of me.

"Just wanted to introduce myself," he spoke at the same time. "What? Breakfast?"

I panicked and looked behind me. Thankfully, the door to the cafeteria was just there.

"It's nearly time for lunch, isn't it? I was going to grab a snack. Haven't you eaten yet?" he said.

Jacob held an arm out, as though allowing me to lead the way. I'd just eaten some toaster waffles, but I couldn't say no to this, not to him.

I managed a smile and we headed into the cafeteria. Fiona and her gang were still at the table I'd left a few minutes before. They all turned to look when I entered with Jacob. I saw Fiona's tinted eyebrows twitch and rise, and some of her pals leaned in toward her, as though waiting for her reaction before they made theirs. This was a high school scene from a Hollywood movie about a teenage love triangle.

Jacob had walked ahead to the table laden with waffles, cereal bars, jars of nuts and dried fruit. I thought of my childhood swimming lessons, how scared I was to jump off the diving board. I'd already sunk to the bottom of the pool now, breathless. Could they all see me losing air underwater?

Before Jacob could turn around, I whipped away and practically ran out the door. What was I thinking, trying to swim in the deep end?

I'D COME A long way since that day. We went from that first awkward interaction at the office to falling into a secret relationship, full of hopes and dreams. Jacob was the kind of man who greeted me with flowers after work. A flowering plant in a pot actually, because he knew it made me sad to watch cut flowers slowly dying in a vase.

We'd been together nearly a year, but nobody at the office knew about our relationship still, other than his best friend, Dennis. Jacob waited for me in his car so he could drive me home. Eight hours of sitting at my desk, and I was finally back to Jacob, to the way he enveloped me and kept me still. Along with everything else, he'd brought this stillness to my life. "Stop moving," he'd say when he was holding me, and it became meditative—the simple act of hugging.

I practically skipped to him across the car park on one of those days, a memory that seemed like an old faded Polaroid now. He'd kissed me with one arm around my waist. The terra-cotta pot was in his other hand, which he must have bought on his lunch break. It was drizzling lightly, but it didn't bother me anymore. I was grinning like I'd just been greeted by the sun.

"You shouldn't have waited, I could have taken the bus," I said, even though I had wanted him to.

Jacob gave my butt a small pat in response. He hadn't stopped touching me. We'd spent the whole day within earshot, starkly aware of each other's presence on the same floor, sometimes crossing paths. Jacob stared at me openly at work, confident he could take the heat if anyone else noticed. While I knew that if I met his gaze I'd burn slowly the rest of the day.

"You have no idea how much I've missed you," I said.

He placed my backpack and flowerpot on the backseat and pushed his glasses up the bridge of his nose. Jacob had one of those faces, precise and unflustered, the kind that makes you self-conscious of how frayed you probably look. When I was with him, I studied my appearance in every reflective surface that crossed my path.

We kissed again when we were sitting together in the car. I slipped my fingers between his shirt buttons so I could feel his almost-smooth chest. He kneaded the small of my back and held me close, and even then, while I was living it, it felt like a dream. A familiar feeling of foreboding crept in, like something terrible was about to happen.

"Hungry?" he asked, starting up the car, snapping me out of my apprehension.

"Just take me home," I said, and then immediately bristled. When had this become home? I was being disloyal to my real home, to my family.

My silence gave me away and as Jacob started the car, he squeezed my knee.

"Durga, you *are* allowed to have two homes."

It had been raining when I left the office, but as is Ireland's nature, the sun was shining brilliantly by the time we were on the road. The car was flooded in a sepia light, refracting off the drops of rainwater that clung to the windows. It was as though we were sitting inside a suncatcher.

It was ridiculously perfect. Like a staged photograph posted on social media.

We were quiet, listening to the radio for a bit. I was thinking about the string of texts in the family group chat I'd received the last few days. My parents were talking about arranging my marriage, again. It was all jokey. Ma and my sister had mentioned guys I was familiar with, who they knew I wouldn't dream of marrying. But underneath the humorous comments about finding it impossible to make me a match was a more serious undertone about how my time was running out. I didn't want to think about it, mainly because I was a coward. Not only had I not told my parents about Jacob—they couldn't have conjured up the idea of a black boyfriend if they tried—I also didn't discourage their arranged-marriage talk.

As though he'd read my mind, he said, "So, how's the husband hunting going?"

"Huh?" I mumbled.

"I saw your phone last night, while you were in the shower. I didn't mean to look, your screen lit up next to me."

"Jacob!" My embarrassment instantly turned into indignation.

"So they've found a guy for you? They actually have a few men lined up, from the sounds of it."

"You know I'm not taking any of that seriously."

"Yet."

Jacob was gripping the steering wheel so tight his dark knuckles had paled.

"I'll handle it when the time comes. I promise."

There was a beat of crisp silence in the car, and I wondered if he believed me. Did he think I'd give him up for them? For an arranged marriage?

"I'll tell them soon that I'm not on the market." I spoke softly through his thoughts, so as not to spook him.

He pasted a smile on his face, distractedly, like he hadn't heard what I'd said.

I touched his hand on the gearstick, while he stared ahead. I could feel him slipping from me, like a painting hanging crooked on the wall, annoying me to distraction. I wanted to put it right, but my hands were shaking.

Perhaps because I knew that this was the beginning of the end.

AND I WAS in the park now, and could finally see Joy in the distance.

"I just got asked on a date!" I shouted.

We were jogging toward each other. She, with her leather satchel swinging behind her, and my scarf, having come undone, was billowing around me.

"What? I thought you weren't meeting him until seven."

Any other person would have checked their watch, but Joy just looked up at the sky as though she could tell the time that way.

"Not Jacob! Someone else. Just now. He went that way."

I was out of breath and looking over her shoulder. Some embers of courage were licking at my breast, and I was half-resolved to run after Niall and say . . .

"What? I'm confused. Aren't we trying to get you and Jacob back together?" Joy's thick wiry hair was held together with carefully positioned clips, and the baby hairs were artfully swirled into kiss curls all over her forehead. I admired this about her, how put-together she appeared to be, even when she was utterly frazzled inside. I could never mask how I was feeling.

I nodded and let out a sigh. "I'm so nervous, I'm shaking," I said. I held a trembling hand out to demonstrate. "I want things to go well today. For us to go back to how it used to be."

She looped an arm with mine and began to lead me toward the skatepark where we were meeting her brother. I felt like a dog being gently coaxed to the vet with my tail between my legs. My limbs had turned to jelly.

"It'll be okay. It's only Jacob. You two have always been good at talking to each other. I hate seeing you both so miserable," Joy said.

I wished I could refute it, claim I wasn't that pathetic. But it had been two months of me moping about, sobbing in the shower, pretending they were happy tears from laughing too hard while we watched stand-up comedy on TV. I wouldn't be able to convince Joy I wasn't only half a person since Jacob told me he needed some time apart.

I stopped in my tracks as the anxiety mounted over. I was suddenly afraid of seeing him and that look on his face. He knew I wanted him back, and I was the reason things ended. He had the upper hand.

"Don't tell me you're having second thoughts just because you had a meaningless conversation with some stranger," Joy said.

"It wasn't totally meaningless, and it's not just that." I stopped and let out a breath. "This feels hopeless. Jacob hates me."

Joy let my arm go. "Is that why I've spied him listening to Lana every day? His Spotify sessions are public. I can see what he listens to during his commute."

"He's hooked on Lana, who wouldn't be? Means nothing."

Objectively speaking, even though Jacob was the definition of my perfect man, we hadn't shared the same taste in music. Lana wasn't on his radar before we met, and he'd roll his eyes when I'd put her on.

Joy pulled me into a hug, and I buried my face in her shoulder. The rough texture of her gray denim jacket was comforting against my cheek.

"He doesn't hate you, Durga, he's just very, very sad."

When I think about it, the stage was set a long time ago for my entanglement with Jacob and Joy. Brother and sister. Lover and best friend.

I'd always wanted to live in a bubble. In a self-sufficient ecosystem with inside jokes and secret handshakes.

Growing up as a member of a seven-person household, I'd only ever lived in a crowd and craved personal space. My childhood best friend was a girl from school who I was never allowed to have sleepovers with. I wore my sister's hand-me-downs. Meals were group decisions where the majority always won—fish at lunchtime and chicken curry for most dinners.

Being accepted into Jacob and Joy Cronin's world felt personal, like I'd been given the password to a secret club.

They'd grown up in Carrigaline, which might have been a village long ago but was a full-fledged suburban town now, twenty minutes from the city center via the Ring road. Theirs was a detached two-story home in one of the old housing estates. They had a small garden in the back, which their mother kept tidy, and a driveway in the front big enough for three cars. They'd bought the house during the boom, Jacob had explained, when everyone was flush with money and the banks were handing out loans like product samples at the mall. All you had to do was ask.

Fortunately for the Cronins, their father didn't lose work when the crash came later. He was a secondary school history teacher. No matter how broke everyone was, people still sent their kids to school. Eric Cronin had chosen a recession-proof profession.

THE FIRST TIME I was invited for dinner to the Cronin home, Naledi cooked bunny chow, a popular South African street food invented by Indian immigrants. She asked lots of questions and was genuinely interested in my answers, and only insisted on second helpings once.

She was good at sensing people's discomfort. She gave Jacob and me time to ourselves, dragging Joy and Eric away to the kitchen for extended periods of time, allowing me the opportunity to decompress in private. She knew how intense it can be to meet your boyfriend's family for the first time. Naledi was the next best thing to having my own mother around, and this too was all because of Joy and Jacob.

And I wouldn't have Joy either, if it wasn't for Jacob.

Chapter 3

IN MY FIRST MONTH OF MOVING TO IRELAND, I'D LIVED alone in the flat, paying full rent.

There were things I liked about living alone. Nobody told me to pick up my shoes from the hallway, I could play music as loud as I wanted, dirty dishes were piling up but there was nobody to see them. I was eating crap food every night. But I couldn't afford it, not for much longer, and it was too quiet when I woke up in the morning.

My co-worker and former friend Fiona, who seemed to no longer want anything to do with me after Jacob spoke to me in the cafeteria, snarkily suggested I send out an internal email advertising the other bedroom in my flat. I sent that email partly because I wanted Fiona to see I was capable of taking charge of my life.

I got a text that very evening from a woman called Joy, who I assumed worked in a different team at the company. We arranged a viewing for Saturday evening.

I spent the whole day cleaning, which was my first time doing it since I moved in a month ago. I couldn't figure out the dishwasher, so I washed everything by hand. I mopped the floor with a wet cloth and on my knees, the way I'd watched our maid, Kobita, doing it for years. I threw out all the takeaway containers.

Joy arrived, twenty minutes late, which I would soon learn was early for her. I opened the door to a tall, lanky girl with thick, coppery curls and a gap between her two front teeth. She was in oversized black cargo pants, a white crop top, and spotlessly white chunky sneakers. She'd winged her eyeliner perfectly and had a neon pink lipstick on, several shades too pale against her olive-toned complexion. She appeared effortlessly stylish. Like she could blindly pull out a few articles of clothing from her wardrobe and they just went perfectly together.

"Hey, I'm Joy. Here to see the place?"

I stepped aside, blushing, realizing I'd spent too much time scrutinizing how she did it—managed to look so good in wrinkled clothes.

Joy walked in, through the hallway and into the kitchen area, and did a full spin. "Looks good."

"Would you like to see the room?"

"Sure, why not," she said, like it was an afterthought.

The spare bedroom was the only space I hadn't touched since I moved in. It wasn't anything great, but it was pristine. The double bed was neatly made up. There was a chair and a small desk by the window, and a small wardrobe.

"We'll have to share the bathroom. It's here."

I went to show her and Joy followed me in. I'd scrubbed every inch of the bathroom and hoped it smelled okay. I tried to gauge her reaction from the corner of my eye as she gave the bathroom a quick cursory glance. She had a smattering of freckles on her cheeks and nose, large light brown eyes.

"Looks good. My share would be seven hundred a month?"

"With bills, yes. Is that okay?"

Joy seemed to consider it for a moment. I was waiting for her to ask me some personal questions. Where I was from, how long I'd been living here, my role at the company.

"Okay. Can I move in tomorrow?"

I wasn't expecting that.

"Umm. We need to have a cleaning rotation. Like, who cleans when, empties the bin?"

Joy was walking back to the kitchen and I followed her. She opened the fridge and I was embarrassed by how empty she'd find it. Nothing other than a carton of milk and a big bottle of Coke. Not one banana or a bell pepper in sight.

"I can clean up after myself. You don't have to worry about that." She spoke without turning around. "Jacob mentioned you'll probably want privacy, that you're not much of a talker. We don't have to become best pals."

"Jacob? Cronin?"

Our encounter from the week before flashed before my eyes. I hadn't run into him since I'd run out of the cafeteria that day.

"Yeah, my brother. Sorry, didn't I say?"

"Jacob Cronin is your brother?"

Joy was smirking, studying my face closely, as though mildly amused by this reaction. My voice must've been shrill and squeaky in alarm.

"Yes. He saw your email? I've been looking for a room to rent. I can't live with my mother one more day. Seriously, can I move in tomorrow?" Joy pulled out a barstool and sat down.

I could already see the looks Fiona and her friends would exchange when I told them. They'd made casual remarks about how I'd acted so cagey that day with Jacob. Fiona said I should have just eaten with him, when I knew she was secretly glad I'd chickened out.

"Sorry, I need to think about this. Your brother works at my office, and I want to keep my private life separate from my work life, you know?"

"But you advertised the room in an email blast to your coworkers."

Yes, yes I had. Joy and I stared at each other in silence. Too long and awkward for it to be a natural pause in conversation.

She drummed her sharp, pink acrylic nails on the kitchen island.

"Any other objections?" she said.

This was my introduction to her stubbornness, but it was my flat and I could be stubborn too. "There are some other people coming to see the room, and I want to give everyone an equal chance. That's all."

Joy made no move. "Is it Jacob? You two have something going on? I'm sensing a vibe here."

I didn't want to think about that. Perhaps she meant she got a whiff of ill feeling between us.

"Okay, how about this?" Joy stood up as she spoke. "I'll keep the whole place clean and cook on the weekends. I'll give you eight hundred. And best of all, you won't even know I'm here." She held out her hand for me to shake.

There was a part of me that wanted to spin in Joy's orbit from the moment I'd seen her. She was like one of those girls who'd kept me out of the loop all my life. One of the popular girls who'd been blessed with natural charm and good taste.

As would become the story of our friendship, Joy could convince me to do anything.

"Okay, move in tomorrow," I said.

When I shook her hand, she pulled me into a hug.

Chapter 4

A T TWENTY-SIX, I STILL CONSIDERED MYSELF A BEGIN-
ner in romance. I was brought up in a conservative country, in
a family that clung to tradition, surrounded by nosey relatives, and
an older sister who was about to marry a family friend's son. Their
marriage had been arranged between the families years ago, almost
as soon as they were born. Tia and I had grown up with the knowledge that one day she would be living in his home. The boy whose
family invited us to dinner once a month. She wrote secret love letters that she never gave him, and when we visited their home, she'd
inspect his room and later talk to me about how she planned on redecorating when she moved in. Tia would also have told on me if I
ever got myself a boyfriend, because she felt a fiery need to protect
me. They'd tried arranging matches for me too, in the hopes that I
would accept them as easily as Tia had, but I'd put up a resistance. As
much as I loved my family, I could never be completely honest with
them because they didn't seem to understand what I wanted. They
viewed my resistance as defiance. But now I can almost see how
being set up by a friend is not so different.

* * *

I'D BUMPED INTO Jacob a week ago, before this meeting at the park. Joy sent me to Dunnes for honey sriracha almonds, claiming a sudden craving.

I should have known she had an ulterior motive.

Joy was torn since we paused our relationship. Neither of us had given her the full picture, and kept details and specific reasons to ourselves. Joy had become accustomed to being the third limb in our relationship, a consistent feature of our nights in. She had tried every emotionally manipulative tactic to get me to tell her everything. Jacob had shut her out too, and I assumed he didn't want to tell her what happened out of respect for me. And Joy was the kind of person who needed to know everything about everyone, to quiet the voices in her own head.

I was the one to blame for what Jacob was experiencing, and in turn Joy too. This wasn't easy for any of us. And so I'd agreed to walk to Dunnes that day, just to get out of our flat, stop the constant barrage of questions from Joy.

At Dunnes, I had a four-pack of lemon muffins in one hand and a head of lettuce in the other. I was still looking for the almonds when I saw Jacob, about to leave through the automatic doors. He was tapping at his phone with his thumbs, while a half-eaten protein bar dangled from his mouth.

He'd always needed both hands to type.

Before I could think it through, I had blocked his path by jutting a hand in front of his face. Jacob looked up from his phone and, surprised, moved his mouth in such a way that the protein bar fell. He caught it just in time and my cheeks flushed. I was still impressed by everything he did.

He was in one of his trademark crisp linen shirts with the sleeves rolled up. Tan trousers and white sneakers. The sunglasses he wore hid his eyes and I couldn't tell if he was put off by seeing me.

"Hey, Durga. You're looking well."

I knew I was not looking well. I'd been lounging in front of the TV before this, in an old pair of joggers with my hair tied up in a bun. I wasn't even messy-chic because I hadn't showered or exfoliated my face. I wasn't leaving a trail of Tom Ford behind me, which he'd once claimed drove him to insanity. It reminded me of how different today would have looked if we were still together. Neither of us would have wanted to go outside, happy to stay in our pajamas all day. We would have ordered in and then forgotten about the food if I looked at him in our secret way. My eyes would glide over his half-naked body and the rest of his clothes would immediately come off.

But maybe he wasn't thinking about that then, and Jacob dragged the sunglasses off his face slowly.

"Thanks. You too."

I must have been drifting away from him because he reached for my hand and pulled me back in one smooth jerk. It was when his hand left mine that I realized we'd touched, that he'd scorched me in so many ways.

"Can we talk soon?" he asked.

Hope. Charging my whole body into action. Finally, he was willing to talk.

"I would like that very much," I said.

"I don't want to see you hurting. I loved you."

I was still in love with him, it wasn't in the past tense for me.

"We should talk, Jacob. Please."

Jacob was a controlled person, who chastised himself for breaking his self-imposed rules, and instead of giving in to the moment, he repositioned his sunglasses and nodded.

"The almonds are in aisle six," he said and began walking away. "We'll plan something. I'll text you."

While I related the Dunnes encounter to Joy upon my return home, she pressed her lower lip with her top teeth. She was anxious and I was hurt.

She eventually interrupted me. "He told me he thinks about you every day. I know he does. His heart is breaking, Durga."

"I don't care what he said to you, Joy. Did you send me there to cross paths with him? He knew I was there for your damn almonds."

She was sitting on our scratchy corduroy couch in the kitchen, and I was pacing around with my fingers in knots.

I sensed she was going to throw up a ridiculous argument because she couldn't meet my eyes anymore. She began sheepishly worrying a thread that was coming off the upholstery.

"But he wants to talk, he said he'd text you, right?" she asked. "What about dinner? Just the two of you. I'll text him."

I should have nipped Joy's idea in the bud while I had the chance. But I didn't.

"Umm . . . okay."

"That's what I want to hear!" She sprang into action while I chewed my fingernails.

She was already typing something on her phone, the tip of her tongue sticking out from between her lips, as it did when she was concentrating. I put down my bowl of barely eaten salad, beginning to panic now.

"What happens if he ends it for good?" I asked.

While we continued to not speak to each other, there was still hope, I thought.

Joy looked up from her phone, tipping it forward. "It's been two months, Durga. You both need this. I can't watch you disintegrate, while Jacob self-destructs. You don't know how much more he's been drinking. Whatever is going on between you, I'm sure you can get through it. Just talk to each other."

She was right, because I wanted that too. If I could just explain myself to him, I knew he would understand.

Joy arranged a date, mediated the whole thing for us, and booked a table at Oregano in Ballincollig. Now here we were, walking toward the skatepark, where Jacob was already. All three of us had come directly from work. He had his tie loosened and jacket thrown to the side. He was speaking with two younger guys at the top of a deck, both of whom were dressed for the sport—in baggy trousers and beanies. Joy called out to her brother, and when he saw us he waved and then slammed his skateboard down. He swooped over the ramp, soaring like an eagle into the bowl.

I glanced at Joy, who was smiling proudly. I would be too, if he was still mine to be proud of.

After Jacob was finished showing off his skateboarding skills, he came up and playfully nudged his sister with his elbow. Both siblings were tall but Jacob towered over us both. I'd always felt petite in his presence, which used to stir up those pesky butterflies in my belly. Now it just made me feel like I didn't deserve to be in his lofty presence.

"So what do you have planned for us this evening?" he asked, a little suspiciously.

Joy stood leaning toward him with her ankles crossed and one hand on a hip. She was the kind of sister who would take any opportunity to spend time with her brother. Even back when Jacob spent whole weekends at our flat, he'd have to physically push her out of my bedroom so we could be alone.

"I want the two of you to talk. I've booked a table at Oregano. They make the best pizzas. Order some wine and tiramisu, take it easy." She looked encouragingly at both our faces.

Joy served as the buffer space for now, giving us somewhere to look while we avoided looking at each other. I did glance at his hands though, at his perfect half-moon clipped nails. I didn't expect Jacob to let himself go, but some evidence of subpar personal hygiene would've soothed my soul. Instead, his thin-rimmed circular spectacles were spotless, and his black leather Derbys were glassy in the evening light.

"We're all adults here, Joy. You don't need to babysit us," he said, and finally, his eyes flickered in my direction. I melted immediately. I couldn't bring myself to be malicious toward him, as painful as this forced separation had been. His face had a student-artist's touch. Too proportionate, no blemishes, smooth skin, and a sharp hooked nose.

I stood back and listened to the exchange between brother and sister. They were having a friendly argument over which pizza joint in Cork cooked the best crusts.

"Will you be okay?" Joy asked me, suddenly directing her attention to me.

"We're all adults here," I said, echoing Jacob.

"Fine. I know when I'm not needed. I definitely won't be sitting at home waiting for an update," Joy said.

"Don't turn this into a sitcom, Joy. I'm parked this way." Jacob was already walking away.

I gave Joy a parting look of pressed lips and wide eyes, like I was expecting disaster, and she shook her head.

I followed Jacob to his car, keeping a distance. I'd suddenly forgotten how to be comfortable around him. Before, we couldn't stop touching when we were in each other's presence. A hand on his bicep, fingers brushing when we walked. We were that couple who always sat next to each other at a restaurant table, heads bent low over the food.

Now, wordlessly, he held my door open and waited until I'd buckled in before gently shutting it.

Sitting inside his Golf led me, unbidden, down a quick journey of feeling disjointed. Up until now, from when my eyes landed on him at the skatepark, it was like I was traveling in a spaceship, hurtling ahead in a quiet temperature-controlled cocoon, waiting for ejection. And now, in his car, which still smelled of Yankee Candle's Black Coconut, I was spit out into space. It was dark and bottomless, and I should have been in a protective space suit instead of this flimsy coat.

Jacob settled in beside me and turned the heat up as soon as he started the engine. I was floating around, untethered from my spaceship now, staring at the air vent that blasted warmth at my face and smelled of wet grass and coconuts.

This was how it always smelled in here, and now this felt like a very bad idea. I was reminded of those long weekend drives when we'd stop at filling stations along the way. Of the seat covered in sandwich crumbs, which stuck to the backs of my bare thighs when we parked at scenic viewing spots to make out.

Our first kiss, that was what I was thinking about now in the car. If Joy hadn't basically forced herself into living with me, that kiss wouldn't have happened.

I hadn't wanted a flatmate but Joy was holding up her end of the bargain. I barely saw her. Other than her toiletries in our shared bathroom, there wasn't much personal evidence of her around the place. I hadn't even mentioned her to Fiona or the others at the office. The conversation about finding me a flatmate had died a natural death at our lunch table. Fiona's new boyfriend had taken precedence.

On a Friday evening, two weeks after Joy moved in, I got home from work and saw her leaving her bedroom. She was in a leather miniskirt, a crisp white shirt tucked in, and silver high-heeled clogs. I could see she'd spent time on her hair. The curls were looking moist and well defined, framing her face with a shimmering cinnamon cloud.

She slipped a tube of lip gloss in her small silver purse. "Going out. Wanna come?"

"I think I'll stay in."

These were our first words exchanged in days.

"It'll be grand. Just throw on something. I'll wait. We're only going to the pub."

At the pub Joy didn't even ask and left me with her friends Lorna and Billy, then returned with four pints of Guinness, all carefully carried with fingers like pincers.

I absolutely detested the taste, nearly choking on the froth and bitterness. Joy, whose elbow grazed mine on the table, noticed and gave a shrug. Like she knew exactly how terrible it must be for me.

A live band was playing rock covers very loudly in one corner. Lorna and Joy shouted over the music, exchanging gossip about one of the bartenders, who they seemed to know.

When they'd all finished their round of drinks, Joy left the table and returned with more. A cider for me this time. I sipped it tentatively and was pleased to find I liked this much better.

"You don't have to finish it if you don't like it," Joy whispered in my ear.

I smiled at her gratefully, just when I saw Jacob approaching, weaving through the crowd. Another co-worker of ours, Dennis, was close behind him.

The smile dropped from my face and I sat up straight, suddenly becoming very aware of my bitten-down nails.

Joy had caught the change in my expression, and she spun around in her seat. "Jacob!" She leaped out of her chair and hugged him.

It was my first time seeing them together, and I witnessed how much she adored her brother. This would be her level of enthusiasm every time she saw him. Like she couldn't believe they were related.

He kissed her lightly on the cheek and then turned to me.

"I thought you weren't going to make it," Joy continued.

My initial impression of Joy was that she was an extremely confident person. Like she could trip and fall flat on her face right here and wouldn't care who saw. In her brother's presence, however, she was a giddy teenaged girl looking for an autograph from a heart-throb.

"Dennis made me come," Jacob said, referring to the friend who'd been left forgotten to hang about the fringes of the group. "It's nice to see you, Durga."

I could have done with Kali making an appearance right about then, but I couldn't summon her.

"Mind if I sit down?" he said, glancing at Joy's empty chair, and I knew I'd already fallen for him. As quickly as candy floss dissolving on a tongue.

I'd tried to join in their conversations but didn't have any of the backstory. Billy and Joy were telling tales about the time they worked in a hotel together as teenagers. Their job was to sort out all the empty beer bottles for recycling and they used to get drunk off the dregs. I tried to not look horrified while the others laughed.

Jacob had leaned toward me and said, "Very different from your teenage years in India?"

When I nodded he'd said: "Tell me about it."

How could I possibly begin? I told him about how my evenings were spent doing homework and then helping my younger sister with hers, and Jacob listened intently.

"Does that sound boring?" I'd asked, worried his thoughts were drifting.

"Were you bored?"

"I didn't know any different. I didn't know teenagers in Ireland were getting drunk on the job."

He laughed at that. His laughter was deep and throaty, like he'd truly enjoyed himself in that moment.

Not a lot of people had found me interesting before. Not interesting enough that they wanted to sustain a conversation with me. I was too geeky and meek in school, and even in a college full of tech students, I was the quiet one. I had a brother and two opinionated sisters at home who occupied all my thoughts, and I never had the time to go out with my classmates. There was always somewhere I had to be—the market, some cousin's house for tea, walk Parul to evening tuition classes. By my second year in college, they stopped inviting me altogether.

But Jacob wanted to keep talking. "I was doing my homework too. Only difference is my parents weren't making me do it. My dad wanted me to go out and play rugby, I wanted to be a gymnast or hang out at the skatepark. Staying in my room and studying was easier," he said.

He was so close our lips could have touched, but they didn't, not yet. After we'd spent an hour speaking only to each other, exchanging notes on our teenage years, Dennis had clapped a hand on Jacob's back.

"Ready to go? We have to go meet the lads, remember?"

Maybe Dennis was offended he'd been ignored so long. He looked at me suspiciously, even a little disapprovingly. I could sense Joy watching us too, suppressing a smile.

"You go. I'm going to stick around," Jacob said.

Dennis looked at his watch uneasily. "You sure, pal?"

Jacob stood up, picking up my empty glass. "Yeah, go on. It's my round here."

He waited for Dennis to leave and then bent down to me. "You want another one of these, or something else?"

The cider had made me more fluid, lubricated my tongue. The alcohol and Jacob's unerring attention had given me confidence in my choice of outfit too.

I wanted another cider. Then another one. I told Jacob about my best friend from school whom I hadn't spoken to in years because I never met her outside school hours. She was married now, with a baby on the way. He told me he'd gone to school with Dennis. They didn't have much in common anymore, but Dennis knew him longest and best.

The music had become louder. The band was gone and pop techno was playing in the pub now. Billy and Lorna were dancing. Joy had disappeared. Gone smoking, Jacob said. We were the only ones sitting at the table, but a crowd of drunk dancers were pressing in around us.

"Should we leave?" he said.

And I'd left with him, to walk around the cool night streets. To pour my life out to him, to kiss him for the first time under the bright glow of a lone streetlight, like we were center stage.

Chapter 5

IN THE CAR NOW I REALIZED THAT JACOB HADN'T STARTED the engine yet.

"It might be safe to make an escape, if you want to," he said. Jacob wasn't the type to fiddle with buttons or keep his hands busy, even when he wasn't enjoying an experience. He had one hand on the gearstick and another on his knee, as though awaiting further instructions.

"Is that what you want?"

"No, I want us to talk," he said.

"Then let's go try these pizzas."

Jacob smiled and shifted gear. When we were finally moving, I felt like I'd passed a test.

Every little thing reminded me of how it had been before. The way he flipped the indicator with a flourish, how he sat leaning on his window, his body half-turned to me while we idled in traffic.

Since we both worked at the same company, we had enough small talk to fill the awkward spaces. I was tech support and he was sales, and we'd spent two years together without anyone at work finding out.

It wasn't Jacob's idea to keep it coy; I was excited by the secrecy of it. I used to look nonchalantly the other way when we passed each other. If we were in the lift together, we'd stand close but apart in one corner, thrilling in the stolen moment of public intimacy. I enjoyed eavesdropping on conversations between my female co-workers about what a thirst trap Jacob Cronin was, with his big hands and deep voice, in his tight white T-shirts.

There was no real reason to hide it. One quick email to HR would have done the job, and nobody would have batted an eyelid. But keeping it a secret was more fun. And now, post-breakup, I wished everyone knew why I was struck dumb every time he entered the cafeteria. Why I had gooseflesh if I heard his booming laughter at the end of the corridor. I couldn't grieve openly.

In the car, Jacob asked me if anything interesting had come up at work recently. He was either being polite or obnoxious, because he knew exactly how uneventful my hours at the office were.

"Yesterday, this guy called in to complain that his wife's phone wasn't playing music loud enough in the shower, and it was ruining her routine."

"Why's this madwoman taking her phone into the shower?" Jacob asked.

"Well, technically, the phones are waterproof, right?"

He rolled his eyes. "Jesus. Did you cut him off?"

"I couldn't. He is one of the guys from Lokomotif, and we've been given strict instructions to make ourselves available at their every beck and call."

"Is there even a solution? Other than don't take your phone into the fucking shower?"

"We told him to mess about with the Dolby Atmos setting, and it worked. He called back a few hours later to say his wife had an enjoyable showering experience, and that he was most grateful."

"He sounds like a suspiciously happy customer. His wife must have given him some bollocking when she couldn't listen to Taylor Swift over the sound of gushing water," he said.

We shared a laugh just as Jacob drove into the tiny car park at the back of the restaurant, and I allowed myself to hope that we could go back to where we'd left off. The day Jacob suggested we take a break, we'd gone for a walk in Crosshaven. He'd collected me from the flat and I noticed the frown on his face immediately. Other than accepting a peck on the cheek, he didn't seem interested in physical contact. I assumed he was hungover from his night out with friends, or had words with his father that morning.

When we'd hardly spoken, even after we got out of the car and were greeted by the blue and green of the river walk, I asked him what was wrong. I stood with him in the carpark, lingering near where he'd parked.

"You asked Joy to go to your sister's wedding with you, but you haven't asked me. You obviously don't want me there."

I tried to explain, but he was already back in his car. We hadn't even walked a few paces.

"I don't want to complicate my sister's wedding. When I introduce you to my family, I want it to be all about you. About our relationship, not my sister's."

"Do you know how insulting that is to me? That you would take my sister to a family event, and leave me out? You didn't even tell me you invited her. I had to find out about it from Joy."

"I was going to tell you. I was waiting for the right moment because I knew it would hurt your feelings."

Jacob held a stony expression the whole drive back to Ballincollig, where we lived, while I did most of the nervous talking. He stopped outside my flat and I had refused to get out. He wasn't going to physically push me out so all he could do was drive to his house, only a few minutes away, and then get out himself.

"Please, Jacob, let's sit down somewhere and talk. I can come in with you," I'd pleaded, following him to his house.

He'd stopped at the door, blocking my way in. My desperation was so intense that I couldn't feel embarrassment. It was an out-of-body experience—I was detached from my physical self. It was as though I was watching someone else—a crazy woman with no sense of dignity, imploring a man to save her from herself.

"You don't want me coming to your sister's wedding because you're too ashamed to introduce me to your family. How do you think that makes me feel? They're still looking for a husband for you."

He was right. I didn't know how they would react to Jacob and I was too nervous to try to find out, not without some preparation. I'd based my trepidation on a throwaway comment my mother made when I was planning my move to Ireland. "Don't bring home some foreigner, Durga," she'd said. After that, every time I'd thought of telling them about Jacob, I remembered her comment and was filled with guilt.

"I told you how I feel about you, Jacob. Doesn't that count for anything?"

He'd shaken his head, even more resolved.

"Two whole years, Durga. We've been together two whole years, and you haven't even mentioned me to them. You went on a holiday to India, you spent time at home. They're clueless about me, whom you claim to love. And now you've invited Joy to the wedding and not me. You're willing to introduce her to your parents, but not me."

I'd pasted myself to his front door.

"I do want to introduce you, Jacob. I just need it to be the right time."

"I'm going in. You should head home."

I'd refused to budge.

"Don't do this, Durga. You're embarrassing yourself."

Shame. A gut-wrenching contraction of the body. I still remembered that sensation, like I'd disappeared into my clothes, the shoes had slipped off my feet. I was too horrified to say a word after that. This was what two years' worth of bliss was reduced to.

I'd stepped away from the door and Jacob quickly pushed it open.

"I'm sorry. I just need some time to think about this, us. You should too," he'd said, before shutting the door firmly.

The suppressed shame and mortification had rushed into my bones then. I had practically stumbled to the closest newsagent for a bottle of Coke, but that didn't help the loss of feeling in my fingers and face.

* * *

"I'VE MISSED YOU," he said now, when we sat down at our table in the restaurant. "How have you been?"

"I've been lost without you, Jacob, but I've been giving you time like you asked. I want to explain."

"About why you don't want your family to meet me?"

"Jacob, you know that's not true. I just don't think my sister's wedding would be the right time for an introduction."

"To introduce a boyfriend, or a black boyfriend specifically?"

He'd stumped me with his quiet accepting tone. He didn't need to shout, the truth of his words were icy enough to pierce me.

In his silence I could see him contemplating how to best break it to me—that my family wasn't as virtuous as I viewed them. That I was ridding them of blame and guilt against my better judgment. The silence yawned between us. I entertained the idea that if we remained silent long enough this would all be forgotten.

"Durga?" he finally prompted me.

"I want us to go back to how we were."

"Then make a choice now, Durga. Take me to the wedding with you. Introduce me to your family."

He'd said it, the thing I feared most. I'd had two months to closely consider this idea and I was still hesitant. Afraid of the consequences, and what that scene would look like. How my parents would react when they saw Jacob, witness the ease and comfort between us. They'd know instantly, without me spelling it out to them, and what would happen then?

Jacob's eyes were on me, and before I could even answer, he was shaking his head.

I wanted a fresh start, but that wasn't what he wanted. He wanted me to take action, make amends, show him I was willing to choose him over my family. And he deserved that.

It was eventually the server who put an end to it. He came to ask if we were ready to order.

Jacob looked like he'd been delivered some terrible news.

"Do you need more time?" The man was confused, waiting for one of us to give him a clue.

I managed a smile in his direction, which prompted him to back away.

"You can't do that, can you? Or rather, you won't do it," Jacob said. He'd pulled out his wallet, preparing to leave.

In my panic I spoke too much, too quickly. "I will. I want to do it. Come to the wedding with me, Jacob. You and Joy can both come."

He took a tenner out of his wallet and placed it on the table. "I shouldn't have to convince you, Durga. I thought enough time had passed. I was hoping you'd invite me yourself. The last thing I want is to force myself on you and your family."

I stood up when he did, not knowing what I could do to stop him. The server was watching us from across the room. Other diners had looked up too.

"I want you there, Jacob. I'm sorry."

He came over to my side of the table and took my hand. I was self-conscious of people looking, but he wasn't.

"No, you don't want me there. Maybe I was your act of rebellion and you've come to your senses now."

His mouth was close to mine, his voice was almost a whisper. I met his eyes, and only a breath escaped my lips. I didn't care who was looking anymore. I just wanted him to kiss me.

"I want you to be happy, Durga."

"I was happy with you."

Jacob smiled a sorry smile, then raised a hand to brush a lock of hair away from my eyes. "Maybe it's not our time yet."

With my hand in his, he led me slowly but inevitably out of the restaurant. It was his last act of kindness toward me. After the scene we'd just made, he didn't want me leaving the restaurant alone and disgraced.

Outside, he let my hand go and it felt like falling.

"Goodbye, Durga. I will always love you."

I had to let him go.

Chapter 6

"WHAT DID HE SAY?" I ASKED JOY.

She was lying on the couch in our kitchen, her phone held up above her head, not typing just scrolling.

She'd eaten a baguette for dinner, the crumbs of which were strewn all over the floor. I wasn't the hoovering type; in fact, I knew practically nothing about household chores or how to look after myself. I'd grown up with a maid, every member of the Indian middle and upper classes does. Joy would inevitably be the one cleaning the kitchen later that night before bed, and I'd follow her around, taking direction.

She looked intent on reading something on her screen, avoiding my question. This made me nervous because she was never afraid of speaking uncomfortable truths. She was the kind to interrupt a conversation to point out that my breath stank. Instead of meeting my eye, she had her eyes narrowed at her phone, pretending like I wasn't even there.

"Just tell me!" I yelled.

"He told me it's over between you. That's all he told me and hasn't been replying to my texts since then."

I sat down on a barstool at the kitchen island, with a glass of Coke in front of me. The bubbles soothed my stomach.

"Did you guys talk at all? I mean, it was the perfect opportunity," she said.

"We talked a little, but not long enough to even order food. Joy, I can't come to your birthday party."

"We can discuss that later." She was looking bleary-eyed. "Shit. Maybe you needed me there. Do I have to do everything?"

It wasn't funny and neither of us were laughing. She wasn't completely off the mark either. Maybe having Joy there would have kept us more upbeat, the conversation more lighthearted. Maybe we would've been more inclined to remember the good times. But we wouldn't have been able to talk about the hard things, and what kind of relationship would that be, if we needed his sister to make the boo-boos go away.

I slid the glass back and forth between my hands, struggling to choose what to say, because the floodgates had burst when I met Joy. I found it impossible to keep anything from this woman. The first night we got drunk together, I'd told her I was deeply envious of my teenaged sister, Parul, because she was going to be the ruler of Silicon Valley in a few years' time. She'd rubbed my back and said: "I know how it feels to love your family so much you hate them."

Joy was waiting for me to give her something now, to be honest. It had been so hard keeping the truth about our breakup from her.

"Maybe if you told me exactly what happened . . . I don't understand why neither of you want to tell me."

"I don't think he wants you to know," I said.

"Why the hell not?"

"Maybe he's protecting you," I said. "From me," I didn't add.

"Protecting me? From the harsh realities of a romantic entanglement?" Joy rolled her eyes.

"The point is, I don't think we can come back from this. He's made up his mind," I said.

I wasn't crying anymore because I wanted to put up a brave front for Joy. I'd taken a long way back home from the restaurant, crying my eyes out in the rain as I walked in circles around the housing estates. I was all cried out now.

Joy sat up, rubbing her eyes. "Jacob seems angry. He's a sensitive soul. He obviously still has feelings for you. If I knew the truth, maybe I could help."

I'd taken Jacob's cue and left Joy out of our fight. When she told me what Jacob had said—that we'd had an argument and were taking a break—I'd refused to give her more. I told myself I was only respecting Jacob's choice, when in reality I was ashamed of myself. Of admitting to Joy how much of a coward I'd been.

But maybe now it was time I took some accountability.

"You told Jacob about going to Tia's wedding. I hadn't invited him. He thinks it's because I don't want my family to meet him. And he's right, I've been shit-scared of doing it. My family has no idea I've been dating, let alone I was in a relationship with a black guy."

Joy's mouth hung open. I expected her to scream but she didn't. "We're mixed. Doesn't Daddy being white buy us some brownie points?"

"Joy, please."

"And you want *me* to go to your sister's wedding with you. Will they let me in? I'm as black as Jacob is."

I put my head in my hands. I could force one foot in front of the other and get on with my new life without Jacob, but only because I had Joy. If she turned against me now too, it was game over. I was wrong when I first left India, thinking I wanted my space and needed to be alone. I would never make it without Joy.

"They will love you, Joy, I know they will. I know they'd have eventually loved Jacob too, after I'd broken it to them gently. It would be the same if he was white. My parents would be just as shocked. It's all too foreign for them. I wanted time, to break it to them when they're not fussing over Tia. Everyone is stressed back home, Tia needs things to be perfect. If I bring Jacob in the mix, it will all erupt."

Joy sank back into the couch. "Have you told him this?"

"I've tried to, but I can't blame him for not accepting it. He deserves better than this, than my bullshit insecurities about my family."

"Yeah, I don't blame him either."

Joy's words were harsh but true. A strong silence lingered between us, while I waited for her to make her choice. Side with her brother entirely and leave me friendless, as I deserved. Or see that I regretted it, understand that I was working through the clutches of familial duty I'd been bound to for so many years.

"But he knows about your family, how they are. You're right, the wedding isn't the best time to introduce him."

"Joy, I don't want what happened to come between you and your brother. It's our problem and shouldn't become yours."

"Too late now. I love you both," she said.

Before I met Joy, I didn't think there was more to life than family, a career, and procreating. Since having her around, I could enjoy a book on the couch and be lazy on a Sunday, because I didn't feel the need to rush around trying to overachieve anymore. I was content with my life because I had her.

"It's our mother. He's reacting this way because of her," Joy said. "Her family was too proud to accept the relationship when she started seeing Daddy. They are a proud Zulu family, determined to keep the bloodline pure and uphold their traditions. A gangly Irish boy with meager prospects didn't cut it for them. They were ashamed of her."

Joy and Jacob had both talked about this before, about the history of their parents' relationship and the circumstances under which they found themselves living in Ireland. Naledi spoke about it too sometimes, making passing comments about how she was one of the few people of color in these parts back when she first arrived. It had been an uncomfortable and long journey for her, to finally arrive at contentment in her life, to make true friends.

"There's a history of family hostility with us. Mum was disowned by her family when she became pregnant with Jacob. They wouldn't support the marriage. Mum hasn't been back in South Africa since she left. Jacob and I have never met them. So, your family's misgivings trigger him. He feels like everywhere he turns he keeps hitting these brick walls."

Joy got up to go empty the dishwasher, to keep her hands busy while we talked about a subject that made her uncomfortable too.

She had the tea towel thrown over her shoulder the same way as Jacob, and I wondered if they'd picked it up from their mother. There was evidence of Naledi everywhere in both their lives. They were both more inextricably bound to her than they would've cared to admit. More than just the melanin and long slender legs, which made the three of them tower over every person in a room. It was in the way they bounced their feet when they sat, as though they had a tune playing in their head. Or how they had a taste for rooibos tea and liked to keep a clean house.

"I'm really sorry to bring this all up again."

"It's not you, it's us. If Mum hadn't been through all that, Jacob might be reacting differently now."

I went to help her, and dried the bowl she picked out of the dishwasher. When she saw the tears in my eyes, she caught my fingers and pressed them.

"You did well, Durga. You've apologized, you've given him time. You've both done everything you could. It's time we tried to create a different dynamic between us. I mean, I'm not going anywhere, you'll always have me. But it doesn't mean you have to be around my brother."

I felt a sudden irrational urge to admit to her how much I missed the Sunday lunches with her parents.

"I miss what we had. The three of us," I said instead.

"Yeah, it sucks."

"I'm sorry," I said.

"Don't do that, Durga. I know you feel guilty, and like this is all your fault, but stop apologizing. Especially to me."

We hugged and I told her I wanted to go to bed. Joy and Jacob already had tons of familial complications between them, so I'd probably be nothing more than a blip in their story. I, on the other hand, was the one who needed distance and time to station this in the past and label it a minor occurrence. Jacob had been in other relationships, but he was my first serious one. It didn't feel minor, nor like my first. It felt like it would be the only one, because no other man would give me the space and silence I needed, or fill my head with interesting facts he'd read online, or replace my toothbrush when he noticed the bristles fanning, or carry me to bed when I fell asleep on the couch at night.

I took that feeling to bed with me. I wouldn't be experiencing this, all those memories revived, if I hadn't agreed to meet Jacob today. I should have gone for tea with Niall instead: I spent a moment picturing Niall throwing the stick in the river, with the sun setting behind his square shoulders. He'd smiled so easily, laughed at my feeble attempts at being funny. I was filled with regret.

My fingers shook as I scrolled through my phone. I tapped in and out of various apps. Games I didn't want to play, social media posts I didn't want to look at, an e-book I'd forgotten I was reading. Anything to keep myself from looking in the folder on the Cloud labeled "Do Not Open."

If I looked at one photo of Jacob, any evidence of how happy I'd been with him, I'd live in the past forever.

In my hand, my phone rang. Tia was calling from Calcutta, to gush about her wedding plans, no doubt. Somehow it was two A.M. here, which meant Tia had just woken up. I shuddered at the thought of still living at home. Arjun and our father arguing about cricket. The maid massaging our grandmother's feet with warm mustard oil, while they watched soaps on TV. Our mother on the phone with one of her sisters or the charity she spent her mornings working with, or at the door chatting with a neighbor, or trying to bribe Parul to attend the dance lessons she'd signed her up for. I did miss them.

I let the phone ring and stop, knowing Tia would sense something was wrong with me. We'd already had the conversation, months earlier, when I'd made her promise that she'd leave if she ever realized she'd made a mistake marrying Bikram.

She thought I was being ridiculous because she believed he was the only man for her, but she'd sworn to not remain in a bad marriage.

Since that conversation, I'd joined in her excitement about the wedding. My lack of enthusiasm today would arouse suspicion in her. My family didn't need to know about Jacob just yet.

Especially not the fact that I'd been dumped.

Chapter 7

THE REALITY OF MY LIFE WITH JOY IN IT WAS THAT I would still have to see Jacob. Joy's twenty-fifth birthday dinner had been planned in advance, for two days after we'd officially broken up.

Joy probably harbored hopes of reconciling us, and wanted me to attend. Like us, she too had fallen comfortably in sync. It had worked so well while it was still working. She'd been able to keep her two favorite people close to her, be an active and constant part of our lives. She was still in denial of the breakup, in denial of how she truly felt toward me because of it. The fact that she hadn't yet blamed me was akin to a child covering their ears and pretending they can't hear their mother's calls for bedtime.

But it felt too soon for me. I tried to skip the dinner, making claims of having work calls, then being struck down by food poisoning, then pretending to be asleep when Joy came banging on my door. Nothing worked. She dragged me out of bed, threw clothes at me, literally knelt at my feet and put my shoes on, and then pushed me out of the door. "I'm your best friend, you can't avoid Jacob all your life," she said. "Besides, our parents don't know you've broken up yet, you need to keep up appearances."

This was the night their father drunkenly announced to the table that he was divorcing their mother. Naledi Cronin raised her glass of wine casually and took one dainty sip before saying she would love to watch him try. She was right in her prediction that he would fail miserably.

Joy said her mother was always right. Their father would never leave the family home. He was already sleeping in Jacob's old room, but shared the en-suite with his wife. He would always wake up and find his clothes ironed and laid out at the foot of the bed. According to Joy, this would be one of the biggest reasons why he'd never leave his wife. So none of them were shocked when he stood up and declared his plans of divorce. They'd heard it before.

But Joy was embarrassed. She forgot to blow out the candles on her cake and dug chunks out with her hand instead of slicing it with a knife. Eric, her father, was still standing, swaying a little, and making declarations of how he was in the process of purchasing a caravan. This he was going to use to get as far away from his wife as he could. Behind her lips Naledi moved her tongue over her teeth. She tapped her wedding band gently on a wineglass while she smiled up at her husband, as though enjoying the performance of an orchestra. Her only intrusion to his speech was an apology to the table for her husband's inebriation.

I didn't know how to feel about what I was watching. I couldn't help but feel sorry for Eric, for how nobody in his family was taking him seriously. He may have been drunk but wasn't alcohol the elixir for truth? And then when I looked at Naledi, really looked, there was sadness behind her long lashes. Her pearly pink nails shook a little as she tapped a tune on her wineglass. Maybe she was afraid, just like I was, that she wouldn't be able to go on if her relationship fell apart.

Joy continued eating cake through it all. In fact, she was the only one eating it. There was chocolate icing on her mouth and fingers. Eric had stood up with the intention of toasting Joy on her birthday, and we were expecting a heartfelt speech to mark this milestone.

We were at an upscale restaurant Naledi had picked for the occasion, and Jacob sat across from me. We both stared worriedly at Joy stuffing her mouth with cake. Other than casual pleasantries, we hadn't spoken much yet. Eric and Naledi mustn't have noticed the lack of intimacy between us. Joy and I regularly arrived at their house together, Jacob joining us later. They were accustomed to seeing Joy and me as one unit, and their son as the third party. But I knew we wouldn't be able to keep this up for long. Someone would have to break the news to them eventually, but tonight was not the night for it. Everyone was too drunk.

This was what Jacob looked like that night:

Brown chinos rolled up at the ankles. Brown, the color of a rich mahogany desk. Jacob had a knack for purchasing perfectly fitted trousers. His trick, which he'd disclosed to me, was that he sized down, instead of relying on the less risky loose fit. He also had on a white V-neck, and a lightweight blue jacket with a buffalo plaid lining. He wore his Afro with a fade and a sharp hairline on the top half of his forehead. The rest of his hair was left to look casually thick and lived-in.

The first impression Jacob made on anybody was that he dressed well. You paid less attention to his straight teeth, the kind eyes behind spectacles, but focused entirely on his almost formulaic ability to know exactly how to match color, pattern, and cut to his build. I wondered what he'd ever seen in me.

I tried to catch his eye in moments of weakness, and despised myself for it. He looked up at me on one such instance and his eyes warmed, as though he knew exactly what I was thinking: I wanted him to forgive me.

"What did you get Joy?" he asked.

I'd already looked away, trying to focus on the tender but firm way Naledi was tugging at her husband's arm, coaxing him to sit back down and stop making a fool of himself.

I had given Joy two tickets to a cabaret show in Dublin, and was planning to fund the whole trip away for us—two nights at a hotel and a weekend of brunches. Jacob said he'd bought her a birdhouse, which was part of an inside joke between the siblings.

"She'll love that," I said.

"Your present is better."

The wounds were still fresh and every word exchanged felt like a knife turning under skin.

"How have you been?" I asked, in a rush, while I still had his attention.

Jacob sipped his pint, taking a luxurious length of time to answer. Perhaps he was enjoying the way I was sitting on the edge of my seat, leaning over the table to hear him above the music, waiting breathlessly to see how he'd answer this question.

"Miserable. You?"

"Same," I said.

We smiled weakly at each other. Neither of us wanted to be there, in such close proximity just days after we'd said our final goodbyes.

It had ended badly, even though I'd thought it would never end. I should have paid more attention to that foreboding feeling I experienced every time I saw him waiting in his car for me, searching for me in an approaching crowd. I shouldn't have told him he was the only man I could ever love because he used to lie on top of me like a weighted blanket. He always went to the door to receive deliveries when he was at our flat, because he knew I disliked small talk with strangers.

All of that had lulled me into believing it would go on forever, that we fit too well together to be pulled apart. But the end was my fault.

Before I could say anything more he stood up abruptly. His beer sloshed and dribbled down the side of the pint glass.

"Come on, Dad, time to go home."

I caught the look exchanged between Joy and Jacob. There was relief on her face.

Since the grass is always greener, it didn't seem to me that Joy needed rescuing from her family. I'd always wished I had a family like hers, that I'd grown up in Ireland, had a less claustrophobic childhood.

It was difficult for me to fully sympathize with Joy and her clawing compulsion to leave home. I had always felt welcome there. Naledi was a gracious host, their home was decorated in good taste—in a theme of gray and mustard yellow. Delicious meals and leftovers in the fridge. Fresh free-range eggs in a wire basket shaped like a hen. I adored the big distressed farmyard table that consumed most of their kitchen. The gingham tablecloth and how their bathrooms always smelled of eucalyptus.

But Joy didn't like to spend a minute longer at the house than absolutely necessary. Every time we returned home after seeing her parents, she regaled me with stories from her childhood. She complained that Naledi resented having to live in Ireland, that she was a cold mother devoid of affection, that she drank too much and cared more about matching upholstery patterns than her own children.

I hadn't witnessed this version of Naledi, and Jacob seemed to remember his shared childhood a little differently. He spoke about how he wished his mother had returned to South Africa, visited her family at the very least so she had some closure. He mostly praised her. For her determination to make Ireland her new home, for raising the two of them the best way she knew how. He glorified the very things his sister criticized. According to him, Naledi wasn't harsh like Joy claimed. She was a woman who had a precise perception of what was morally right or wrong. She made no excuses. He rejected Joy's claim that their mother punished them too hard and often. How else were they going to learn?

Jacob embraced his love for his mother, while Joy fought it. She struggled against the tight restraints of Naledi's straitjacket hold on her. She said she'd never felt comfortable being in the same room as her parents. Her mother trying so hard to please, her father hoarding his words like he had a quota he couldn't go over. The silence in their house deafened Joy, suffocated her. So she moved out of their home the first chance she could afford to.

And now I had this knowledge about them, the opposing views on their parents' marriage that the siblings shared. My relationship with Jacob had ended, yes, but that didn't mean I didn't know him anymore. I knew how painful this night was. To watch his father embarrass himself, wishing his mother would just let the marriage go. The way he'd released me.

Jacob left the dinner with their inebriated father. Perhaps he had tried to get out of attending the party like I had. We were both here for Joy's sake and now her brother, her savior, had come to her rescue.

I decided then that I wouldn't allow Joy to force Jacob and me together again. I hated being reminded of what I'd lost.

Chapter 8

O N SATURDAYS, WE BRUNCHED, AND AFTER JOY'S birthday dinner the previous night, we both needed to eat all our feelings.

Joy and I had a list of restaurants we were eager to try, but week after week we returned to the same place in the city. Perhaps it was the comfort of a familiar menu, knowing exactly what we wanted, ditching the effort of deciding. We placed the usual orders: Eggs Benedict and a cappuccino for me, American-style fluffy pancakes with bacon and orange juice for Joy.

We invited Lorna and Maeve today.

Lorna was a fast-talking, petite snap of a woman. It came as no surprise to me that she and Joy have been close since primary school. They complemented each other well, but they could be a handful to be around when together. As much as I enjoyed their company, I usually found myself needing a midday nap after we brunched. Maeve was characteristically quiet, sitting close to Joy and not saying much. If there was one thing Maeve and I had in common it was that neither of us got the point of Lorna.

Maeve and Joy had an unusually stress-free relationship, given that they'd made out a few times as teenagers. While I was in the trenches, nursing open wounds Jacob had left on my heart, I wished

Maeve and Joy would just figure it out and make it official already. I knew Joy was in love with her.

"I'm a good judge of character, aren't I, Joy?" Lorna said, ripping a French toast apart.

Joy nodded. "She clocked Colin McEwon, the creep, even though all the girls were jelly-legged for him in secondary school." She popped a maple-syrup-soaked blueberry in her mouth, then washed it down with some orange juice. "He's a registered sex offender now."

Lorna honked a laugh, which turned into a loud burp. This made Maeve shift uncomfortably in her seat. Sober Maeve had very little patience for bad manners. At a party, she was a whole other story. "He'd been grooming his last girlfriend's fourteen-year-old sister. That dirty bastard." Lorna seemed to know all their friends' secrets, and Joy's gossipy side appeared whenever she was around.

Joy shook her head. "Disgusting."

"Anyway, Durga, my point is, Jacob is one of the good ones and you should go down on your knees and beg him to take you back," Lorna said.

I could sense Joy's eyes on me. I was exhausted from discussing him the last few days. Joy and I had talked about little else since the park, picking apart every moment of our interaction. We'd dissected the situation from every possible angle, weighed all my options, considered all future scenarios. There was nothing left to suck on.

However, there was no working around this.

"I mean, all this over a wedding invitation?" Lorna continued now with a shrug, while toying with the big silver hoop in her ear. "I wonder what your parents would do if you just showed up with him at the wedding. Like, *Here you go. This is my boyfriend and he's black. Deal with it.*"

Maeve coughed into her hand and glanced at Joy.

"They'd be in shock. Then my sister's wedding would become all about me, and how I've been keeping this big secret from them."

I looked at Joy, but she wasn't looking at me. Maeve was stroking Joy's shoulder as though she needed emotional support. I wasn't

Maeve's biggest fan, subconsciously fearful that she'd take Joy away from me one of these days, but today I really disliked her. I had to wonder what Joy and Maeve were saying about the breakup behind my back.

I didn't want to explain this to Lorna, that I was fearful that my family had race *reservations* that would bubble to the surface if I told them about Jacob. In fact, I was expecting there to be some awkwardness upon meeting Joy too. I'd shared photos of Joy and me, but only to the private chat with my siblings. They had to have noticed Joy wasn't Caucasian, but they hadn't commented on it. But it didn't fill me with as much positivity as it should have. I'd wondered if they were being polite, if they'd shown my parents the pictures, or were they so clueless they didn't realize Joy was half-black.

I'd spent my life experiencing a particular blend of feelings toward them: tenderness, comfort, reverence, annoyance, and amusement. This emotion of discomfort about their feelings toward Joy and Jacob was a new one.

"Well, how will they react when they meet Joy?" Lorna said, smirking because this wasn't her family.

When I said nothing, Joy placed one piece of crispy bacon on my plate, as a sort of peace offering. "I'm sure they'll be fine. I'm just a friend."

Lorna put down her cutlery. "I'm stuffed. I always eat too much when I'm with you."

"We were going to get bubble tea," Joy said.

Lorna stretched out in her chair, rubbing her belly and sticking her neck out repeatedly like a pigeon, in an attempt to burp. "Well, I'm done. Laters, langballs."

She left a twenty-euro note on the table and gathered herself and her bag. "Same place next weekend?"

None of us responded. She was leaving us all with a bad taste in our mouths.

"Is Jacob open to seeing other people?" she asked, just as she was about to go.

"Geez, Lorna, it's not going to happen with you two. He's genuinely still hung up on Durga."

Lorna laughed. "Let him know I'm here if he needs help licking any wounds." She winked at me, and stuck out her tongue to slurp the air.

"Just get outta here." Joy gave Lorna's shin an aggressive kick and Lorna chuckled, hiking her jeans up as she went.

"She likes to push things far to see where it gives," Joy said, after she was gone.

"Why are you still friends with her?" Maeve asked.

I could have said the same about Maeve. I knew Joy had feelings for her, and she insisted she was happy keeping things casual between them, but I couldn't understand why.

I toyed with the sticky, crusty mess of yolk on my plate, scraping it off with my knife. Joy hadn't abandoned me, regardless of the way I'd hurt her brother. I needed to make more of an effort with Maeve.

DESPITE BEING FULL of food, we'd made our way to the Bubble Tea shop, without Maeve, who had taken her leave soon after Lorna left.

"Maybe we should just stop talking about Jacob. Pretend like he doesn't exist. It's not helping either of us," Joy said.

I shook the tall plastic cup of coconut tea, to make the black tapioca pearls swirl around in the cloud of sweet milk.

"Yes, no more Jacob talk." I sucked on the chunky straw and got a mouthful of boba, which I chewed through. "The worst part is that he's hurting too. It might be easier if I knew he hates me now."

"I said no more Jacob!"

Joy had this remarkable quality of being able to compartmentalize her thoughts and cater to her audience. I could bet money that she was pandering to Jacob in my absence, agreeing with his side of the story, about how I'd gravely wronged him. I couldn't hold it against her. She was caught in the middle and deeply felt how we were both affected by this.

I was worn-out by now, bone weary of having had to listen to Lorna for over an hour.

"Can we go home? I think I want to nap," I said.

On the bus ride, while Joy listened to a podcast through her earpods, I took the plunge and scrolled through my old conversations with Jacob. I hadn't looked at them in over thirteen days; my personal best streak. But we'd spent the whole afternoon discussing him and it triggered me to look.

Jacob had a pet habit of making unsolicited reading material recommendations. I'd always been interested in people's habits.

When Jacob and I began spending entire weekends together, I was excited to learn some things about him through silent observation. A personal thing or two that we would never have to discuss, which I'd carry with me forever.

One sugar and a splash of milk in his coffee. An aversion to runny eggs. A mild case of tritanomaly, which didn't seem to affect his ability to choose the right colors in his wardrobe. An obsession with cleanliness. Reading the acknowledgments section of a book first. This was all information he'd offered up willingly. I needed something more. Something he wouldn't know I'd noticed and noted.

And then one day when we were alone together, I had it. I'd complained that my feet hurt. We were snuggled on the couch together, trying to pick something to watch. He reached for my feet and while massaging them, recommended an "interesting article" he'd read on the history of female shoe designs, and how it had evolved into a means of subjugation, how it affected the way women held themselves in the world. I smiled at that, finally recognizing a pattern. Telling me what to read was his love language.

We were in the shower together one other time, about fifteen minutes after we had sex on his bed. We were holding each other under the warm stream of water, and while I was enjoying the moment, safely imagining what our life together might look like in ten years, Jacob interrupted the image with another "fascinating study" he'd chanced upon. This one was about how sexual intimacy is possibly the easiest way people know how to connect. Emotional intimacy, the far superior medium, is a foreign skill set to most.

A few days after our walk in Crosshaven, when Jacob told me he needed some time away from me, my sixteen-year-old cat died. My father called to give me the news and I'd cried bitterly over the phone. I'd come so close to telling him why this was affecting me so hard. My cat had been a special part of my childhood, and losing her at the same time I'd lost Jacob felt like all the good things about my life were disappearing. It was just one blow after another.

That evening, Jacob texted me, to ask if I was okay. We'd exchanged monosyllabic messages since our last encounter, when he'd asked for a break. He had been cold and remote, like we'd never been more than friendly co-workers.

Joy must have given him the news about my cat and he reached out.

Upon receiving the text from him—a genuinely heartfelt message—I was overcome with grief and loss once again.

You should read Goodbye Mog came his response.

I hadn't replied to that because I'd fallen into another bout of crying, and by the time I'd composed myself again, it was too late to respond without it seeming like I'd been thinking about him for hours.

I did, however, wander into a bookshop the next day. I found the book, which was part of an older popular children's series about Mog, a cat. I bought the omnibus, and delighted in discovering the sweet stories about a forgetful, loving, scaredy family cat. By the time I arrived at the final story, the one Jacob had recommended, an older Mog, done with this life, was ready to leave the world. I was soothed into an acceptance of her death. I shed some tears, smiled at the parts where I was supposed to, and shut the book and put it in the box with Jacob's underwear and other things.

I looked at that message on the bus.

You should read Goodbye Mog

Joy put her head on my shoulder, her eyes were closed.

I regretted rolling my eyes all those times he talked about what he'd read, a strange fact he'd chanced upon, a scientific study he'd scrutinized. I'd complained to Joy about it and thrown cushions at him to stop him from boring me. But I don't know if I'd have been able to accept the loss of my cat if it weren't for Jacob, and for that too I was grateful to him.

Chapter 9

O N SUNDAY, THE DAY AFTER BRUNCH WITH LORNA and Maeve, I woke up groggy with what felt like a hangover. In fact, there was no alcohol involved the previous night, and I'd slept an incredible eight hours. I was hungover from feelings and from feeling them too deeply.

I heard my phone ringing, not sure what time it was.

"It would be nice if you answered the phone sometimes."

It sounded like Tia was running on a treadmill. Pumped-up workout music was playing in the background.

"I just did!"

"I've been trying to get ahold of you all week, Durga."

"I've been busy. You always ring when I'm at work or cooking dinner."

"Since when do you cook?"

"When will you get the hang of the time difference? It's been two years."

Tia was huffing and there were unnaturally long pauses in our conversation as she tried to collect her breath enough to speak. Eventually, I heard the beep of the treadmill speed being slowed.

"This is important, Durga."

"What's happened?"

"Ma wants me to speak to you about Surjo Sengupta."

"Who?"

"That guy who lives in London. You know, Bikram's friend. He's friends with Arjun too."

A brief conversation with my mother sparked in my memories. "Ma told me about him months ago. I thought it was forgotten and done with."

Of all the things for my sister to call me about, did it have to be the thing that had made Jacob most uncomfortable about our relationship? He never did get it—how I could allow this to carry on, why I didn't discourage it.

"Durga, these things take time to set up. Ma had to speak to Bikram's mother first, and she connected us with the Senguptas." Tia had regained her natural cadence because she was only lightly jogging now.

I didn't fancy any of Bikram's friends. The few I'd met briefly all came across as spoiled brats. It was bad enough that Tia had this misplaced notion about Bikram's worthiness of her, but wanting to set me up with one of his friends was too much. Now she'd got our families involved.

"I told Ma I don't have time for this. Besides, your wedding is coming up. Aren't they busy with one child's nuptials?"

"Make time for it, Durga. This is your future. Ma and Baba are concerned, this is all they're talking about. My wedding has taken a backseat. They're worried you'll turn into an old maid. If this works out it would be ideal, wouldn't it? Surjo and Bikram have been friends for years, they're like brothers. We'll be like sisters-in-law. Also, doesn't Arjun's approval count for anything?"

"Tia, I *am* your sister. We are real-life sisters. We don't need to simulate it."

But she was right about Arjun. I considered my brother to be the most reasonable person in our family. I'd hung on his every word when we were children, and the fact that he was friends with Surjo too made me curious. I'd always wanted to be friends with Arjun's friends, and maybe I needed to see what else was out there. That might help stop this constant ache I was experiencing from losing Jacob.

"You know what I mean." Tia clicked her tongue. She was exasperated with me.

"Did you and Bikram make the honeymoon arrangements?"

"Don't try to change the subject." Tia switched the treadmill off, and I could picture her dabbing a towel over her face. "Fine, I'll tell you about the honeymoon plans, and then you can give me your word you'll meet this guy. Bikram wants to go to Switzerland, like everyone else does. It's so unimaginative. How many Indian women have lost their virginity in Interlaken and the surrounding areas? So, are you going to meet him?"

"Surjo Sengupta?"

"Who else, Durga? Ma is waiting for an answer, and she knows you'll kick up a fuss with her."

"She doesn't like it when I have an opinion."

I could talk about our mother this way only in her absence, because face-to-face I wouldn't dare to talk back. Her lips curled over her teeth if my siblings or I ever attempted to contradict her, but her bark was stronger than her bite. As much as she nagged and lectured us about being respectful, she'd never raised a hand to us.

I resented my parents for their traditional values, but still bowed to the sense of duty they'd instilled in me. It wasn't uncommon in my generation. Even though I was living abroad, I was still up-to-date with my friends' lives through social media. I could guarantee that their families were completely in the dark about their partying and drinking and casual sleeping around. Our parents had collectively raised a generation of masked rebels.

"You're going to be twenty-seven next year," Tia said.

"And you'll be twenty-nine. Your point?" My defensiveness made me snappy. I needed to find a way to stop this from snowballing out of control.

"Ma and Baba have never rushed me to marry Bikram. I've had time to work and save up money."

"And now you can retire and make babies."

Taking digs at my sister was my only recourse. I hoped she'd be too annoyed with me to continue this conversation.

"Durga! We're not doing this again."

"You've known Bikram all your life. I don't want to marry a stranger."

"Everyone is a stranger until you start sharing a home with them. Do you think I know if Bikram snores in his sleep? He might turn out to be the kind of person who forgets to flush. Imagine that." Tia's voice was echoing now, she was in the gym's changing room. "Nobody is expecting you to marry the first guy you meet, or marry him *now*. We're not in the Dark Ages anymore. You can take your time to get to know him. But I think you'll like this guy. Bikram only has good things to say about him, and so does Arjun."

I didn't want to tell her I had no faith in her fiancé's opinion. She already knew my reservations about him, that I thought he was a pompous show-off, that I'd heard rumors about him skirt-chasing while already engaged to Tia. And yet she was choosing to go through with it. She was willing to overlook all that for the sake of a verbal agreement made between our families many years ago, before any of us could have known what kind of man Bikram would grow up to be. There was no point bringing up my impression of Bikram again.

"I can't take any more time off to go meet him in London. I have two weeks set aside for your wedding this year. I have chores and admin things to catch up on over the weekends."

"He'll come to you. Bikram's mother said he can pop over for a quick lunch some weekend. What is it, an hour's flight to Cork? We'll set it up."

"No, Tia, I have a lot going on."

"Like what?"

I kneaded my forehead with a hand, the dull throb was getting louder in my ears. I wanted to tell her about Jacob, to explain why I didn't have the brain space to deal with this. I barely had the energy to fight her.

"Durga, just meet him. One lunch. How could that be so bad?"

"I don't . . ."

"What if you like him? What if he's the perfect man?" Tia said.

I'd had trouble with saying no in the past. When I was ten, my mother suggested painting lessons. My parents were worried because I didn't have a hobby. My brother, Arjun, had cricket. My sister Tia was training in classical dance. The youngest one, Parul, who was only three at the time, was already showing signs of being a child genius. Nobody had proactively taught her how to count, but she could do simple arithmetic with ease.

My parents were worried that my life would be less fulfilling if I didn't have an extracurricular activity to occupy my evenings.

I went to the painting lessons; big pad of blank sheets, an expensive set of watercolors, and graphic pencils in tow. After the third lesson, the teacher met my father at the door when he came to collect me.

"Durga has no potential."

"She is only just starting off," my father said.

"There is no hope for her."

The two men were speaking with me standing between them, my face was turned up to theirs.

"She's a quick study. Let's give her a few weeks," my father said.

The teacher looked down at me, with his brows raised. I slowly slid the sheet out from my folder, which I'd hoped would remain hidden from my family.

My father blinked at the two comical blue strokes that ran across the page. A darker blue had been used to make squiggles between them. One brown line sat vertically above, with green dots sprinkling the top of the page.

"They were painting a village scene today. That's a river, and that's a tree." The teacher pointed to the green bits.

My father sighed at me, and a look of worry washed over his face. I knew he was considering the bleak future awaiting me. All his other children would have to rally around this underperforming one, hold her head above water. I wished I could have told him *I told you so*. But I couldn't, because I hadn't refused the painting lessons, even though I knew I didn't have one artistic bone in my hands.

My father told the teacher he wanted his money back, and when we went home my mother said: "It doesn't matter. We don't need another artist in the family."

She was referring to her uncle, who was a celebrated local artist. He had made a small fortune painting theater sets and then graduated to designing sets for film productions.

"She's always had an ear for music, hasn't she? I'll call Nita. Her neighbor is a professional singer, maybe she'll take Durga on as a pupil," she added.

And that should have been an early lesson in the importance of following my gut feeling. However, I pretended to enjoy my musical education for five years until Miss Sarita politely dropped me, by claiming she was moving to the States. Nita mashi never mentioned her neighbor's sudden move, which made me believe that they'd discussed my incompetency, that Miss Sarita was still very much living where she'd always lived, that she'd decided not to waste her time on me. My parents remained in denial, and bragged to the extended family about how I was an accomplished artiste. While I, to this day, have refused to so much as hum a tune in the presence of another soul.

So really, I should have put a stop to the idea of Surjo now. Instead, I said: "Fine."

"Really?" Tia sucked in her breath.

"I'll have lunch with him, if that's what you all want from me."

She whooped with excitement. "You'll like him. He's very dashing; I've seen his photos. And he's not your run-of-the-mill engineer or doctor. He's a chef."

"Okay."

I was agreeing to this in part to shut Tia up, but I was intrigued to meet one of Arjun's friends. Also, I could use a distraction from Jacob.

"Promise me you'll be a little more enthusiastic when you meet him?"

"I'm not promising anything. And tell Ma to ring me herself, instead of getting you to do her dirty work."

"This is holy work, Durga." Tia was laughing.

"Go have a shower. You must stink."

I knew that would get rid of her. Tia couldn't stand smelling of anything other than Marc Jacobs's Daisy.

"I'll call you when everything's decided. Please answer the phone."

I threw my phone on the bed and sighed. I wished I knew the right thing to do. For someone to give me the right answers.

Chapter 10

NOT LIKE I WAS AN EXPERT AT SEX, BUT I HAD THE FEEL-ing that our generation had it worse when it came to bringing a man home for a casual night of unbridled passion.

Millennials, who live in shared spaces for half their lives, run the risk of their flatmate(s) listening in on their moments of abandon, learning very quickly what your average shower time is, if you're a snorer. Privacy is well and truly a thing of the past.

So there wasn't much I could keep from Joy. I'd been officially broken up from Jacob for three weeks. If I was going to have other dalliances, Joy would inevitably find out. I'd told her about Surjo Sengupta and she thought I should do it. Just to get my mind off her brother, and if for nothing else but to shut up my family and buy more time.

My inexperience with arbitrary sexual encounters also accounted for not knowing how to best drop hints so the stranger left at a respectable time the next morning—which was that sweet spot after your polite offering of a coffee but before the need for breakfast. There were many reasons why a one-night stand was something I should have carefully planned and prepared for.

Since the breakup, I'd spent many evenings attending art exhibitions after work, or dragging Joy to the cinema to watch films neither of us was interested in. I even deep-cleaned the bathroom and kitchen one night. Nothing worked. My every breath came with the urge to open that folder on the Cloud and look at my photos with Jacob. If I forgot him for a moment, maybe when I was crossing a street, or while on the phone with a difficult client, I savored it.

Last night, in the middle of brooding, I'd marched into Joy's bedroom and demanded that she take me to the party with her. She turned from her mirror, which she was leaning into so she could better see what she was doing with her eyeliner.

"I thought you don't like these house parties," she said.

I didn't know why I thought I'd be met with resistance. Joy invited me every time and I made up excuses not to go. I went so far as to sign up for a gym membership so I'd have a legitimate reason to skip her plans.

"I have nothing else to do. It's not like I'll go to the gym," I said.

Joy put down the eyeliner and turned to me. "I get it. Come."

I'd put on a short sparkly dress, high heels I knew I'd be uncomfortable in. I'd even watched a tutorial for a smoky eye and failed at it.

"Why am I doing this?" I dropped the eyeshadow palette in frustration and pulled out a wet wipe.

"It's just a casual thing, Durga. A couple of us chilling at Billy's place. We'll play Jenga, eat some nachos, and come home." She watched me rub off a full face of makeup.

"Are you saying I'm overdressed?"

Joy shrugged. She was in wide-leg jeans and a slinky crop top that showed off the muscular ridges of her slender brown arms. Yeah, I'd tried too hard.

"I look silly."

When I started taking off my shoes, Joy came toward me with her arms outstretched.

I allowed her a hug, then manically rifled through my wardrobe until I'd found a long gray stretchy dress with a slit on the side. I wore flat black pumps instead of the heels. I gave my hair a quick brush and didn't bother with another round of makeup.

Joy looked almost worried. "You're ready to go?"

"Why would I not be?"

She slid her arm through mine and led me to the door.

I wanted to go to this party because I wanted to see other people, talk to someone who wasn't a Cronin. At the office I'd spent three weeks avoiding Fiona and the others in the cafeteria because I thought I needed to be alone with my suffering, to sweat it out and purge myself of this illness. It had led nowhere. Every time I thought I could see Jacob from the corner of my eye, I got up and left the room. He seemed to be everywhere. At work, at home, every time I looked at Joy.

I yearned to fall back into the comfortable routine of having him around, of not having to navigate social life as a single woman in her twenties who wasn't partial to booze. I'd only ever attended Joy's parties out of curiosity before. I was able to flex a muscle here in Ireland that I couldn't when I lived at home, and I'd wanted to experience that. Last night I wanted to go to one as a woman on a mission. To live a little.

These house parties started off deceptively tame—with someone strumming a guitar and a few bottles of Peroni being passed around. Within the hour, joints would be rolled, the acoustic strumming would be replaced with the speakers thumping out music. A former couple would begin kissing, then dry humping on the couch.

Maeve had been drinking by the time we'd got there, and she was way more chirrupy now than she was in daylight. She'd decorated her face with stick-on gemstones, and had raided the nearest wardrobe to dress herself in feathery scarves. By the time Joy and I had found drinks, Maeve was gyrating on a coffee table, making everyone laugh.

Joy found Maeve charming for some reason. They had a long-winded romantic history between them. Navigating puberty, stolen kisses as teenagers, jealousy, dating other people. They'd never been a couple, not in the real sense, but none of their friends batted an eyelid when they started making out at one of these parties. Joy was smitten with Maeve, had been since they were kids, and Maeve gave her just enough to keep her coming back for more.

Joy was so headstrong about everything else in her life, other than about Maeve. I wished she'd cut her off. But I couldn't complain to Joy about it, because *she* wasn't complaining. If I ever brought it up, Joy brushed it off with a: "This is how we roll. Not every relationship has to involve baking cookies together."

I thought I was prepared for this party, ready for all the fun I was about to have. Despite my plans for a big night, where I'd at least get drunk, I found myself in a corner again. I was stuck to a wall, trying to avoid eye contact with Joy, who would inevitably try to get me to dance with her.

She'd downplayed the scale of this party. This was no cozy circle of friends playing board games. There were at least twenty people cramped inside Billy's small flat, which he shared with two other men. People were practically shouting at one another over the karaoke machine Maeve was using. There was a lot of weed, a lot of cans, and the only thing that was remotely edible were a few stale brownies in Billy's fridge. I didn't touch them because they looked homemade and I had some idea what he might have put in them.

I stood alone, biding my time, keeping an eye on the way Joy stared at Maeve singing out of tune to "Islands in the Stream." Joy looked at her like she was an undiscovered musical prodigy, an angel descended to Earth. Their fingers were entwined, their cheeks were flushed. I knew Joy loved her, as complicated as it was. No matter who else Joy kissed, nobody would compare to Maeve.

Joy had never dated anyone seriously. She'd had her fair share of one-night stands, had even been on multiple dates with this one woman called Lisa last year. She always came up with new reasons not to keep seeing them.

LISA AND JOY together had filled me with confidence at the time. Lisa was sweet, almost timid, and a slightly older, more mature woman. She had a short pixie cut and wore a lot of stripes. She spoke in a low whispery voice in person, but was confident and precise in the crochet tutorials she recorded for her vast number of followers online. On the morning of their fifth date, Joy woke up with a runny nose and a bad cough. She had to cancel that date for a legitimate reason.

"I caught that horrible flu from Lisa. Haven't you noticed how she's always sick and run-down? Poor constitution."

That was Joy's excuse for never responding to Lisa's texts again.

Maeve's green eyes glowed like a cat's. Her long golden hair was unkempt and her fringe was damp, like she'd been dancing all night. She wore white eyeliner and a short leather skirt and thigh-high boots, with a leopard-print strappy top. Maeve had the same appeal as Shania Twain from the nineties. All thin wrists and liquid hips.

Joy was smart in so many other ways, but when it came to Maeve, she was a doddering fool. No better than me, really, in my inability to get over Jacob, I thought as I saw Maeve lead Joy away to a different room.

Someone came to stand beside me and I gave him a cursory look. His was a familiar face, was an old-time member of Joy's friend group. He reintroduced himself to me. Luke. I'd met him at a previous party, but he was the kind of man who didn't expect anyone to remember him.

"I'm friends with Maeve . . . and Joy, of course. We were in secondary school together," he supplied.

I knew all this already, but I allowed him to continue, having something to fix my gaze upon.

He had a nice face, soft and warm, and I thought of freshly baked bread. His smile had the same effect on me as walking into a bakery first thing in the morning, and being greeted by the mouthwatering aroma of gluten. His hair was so blond and buzzed so short, for a minute I'd thought he was bald. When I looked closely it seemed to be gold velvet.

We fell into silence briefly and I noticed how comfortable this was. Like he didn't expect anything from me.

Eventually, Luke turned to me and asked the usual questions about my work, which I mechanically responded to. He mentioned he had worked at the Guinness Storehouse in Dublin as a tour guide. He did most of the talking, not necessitating much input from me. He'd either sensed I wanted a quiet night, or thought I was too drunk to string a sentence together. But I was enjoying his company and the attention.

He brought up his interest in indoor plants and how he had a flat full of them. Forty-two at last count.

"Peace lilies are drama queens. They play dead, all droopy and turning brown, until you water them. Then they spring to life almost instantly, like it was all for show," he said.

I smiled at that and it encouraged him to tell me about how he watered his plants in the bath, arranging them neatly under the shower so they got the full "rainforest experience."

"What's your thing? Do you have a thing?"

He spoke in that sweet West Cork accent, more melodic than Joy's city one.

Houseplants were clearly his thing, and it was a legitimate question. I didn't know if I had a thing. Before Ireland, before Jacob, I was one of many in a bustling household. Tia had dance, Arjun had cricket, Parul had math. I had my cat and my books, and my cat was gone now.

I took a sip of my beer just to delay answering the question. Then I spluttered because it was bitter and acidic.

"You all right there?" Luke said.

He had a thin mouth but a pout for a bottom lip. There was a permanent cleft between his brows, like he'd done a lot of thinking in his lifetime.

"Yeah, I'm fine. I don't drink much," I said, and wiped a hand over my mouth.

Luke looked at the can in his hand. "Yeah, me neither, but don't tell my friends." He laughed nervously and looked around the room.

The group had significantly thinned by now, it was nearly two A.M. Most of the others had made use of the old Irish tradition of leaving without drawing attention. Pretending to need the toilet and then exiting the house.

"Have you two hit it off?" Maeve said.

She and Joy had appeared out of nowhere. Maeve always looked unkempt, which was her general vibe, but Joy's pale pink lipstick was smudged too. Her pupils were dilated, from the weed and the booze, but there was another kind of dazed look about her. They'd gone to some room to make out, that much I could deduce. Why didn't she ask more of Maeve, if this was how she made her feel? Why didn't they want to wake up together every day? I was envious of Maeve, of them—that they could have this good thing going and refuse to ruin it with legitimacy.

"If you're planning on taking him home, you should know, this one is so unattached he might drift off into space," Maeve continued. She was oblivious to the way Joy was looking at her, or how uncomfortable she was making me. "We're cut from the same cloth, aren't we, Luke?" She laughed boisterously, slapping Luke's back.

He gave me a look like he knew that Maeve was brash when she'd been drinking. I considered Luke, what Maeve had just said about him. Maybe I needed to try someone like that, something like what Joy had with Maeve. Someone so free-spirited that you had no hope of tying them down, so you simply didn't bother.

"Chill the fuck out, Maeve. We were just talking," Luke said, and shifted his shoulder out of her grasp.

Joy was swaying to the music, taking this all too casually.

"I was going to head home. Nightcap at mine?" I spoke directly to Luke, looking past Maeve. I wanted to knock out two of Maeve's birds with one stone: that Luke wasn't interested in me, and that I was too uptight to invite a man home. Then I turned to Joy. "Unless you're coming back with me now?"

Joy shook her head, glancing lightly at Maeve. "I think I'll stick around here a bit longer. Don't drink all my tequila."

Joy appeared surprisingly unaffected by me taking another man home who wasn't her brother. Another man who was also one of her friends. Maybe she just wanted to get rid of me, maybe she was riding the high of being with Maeve and nothing else mattered. It had been three weeks since I'd last seen Jacob; she and I both knew he wasn't changing his mind.

I'd already clocked the way Luke had looked at the slit in my dress; the little peep show my thigh put out every time I moved. He was too much of a gentleman to stare, and had been embarrassed every time his eyes were drawn to it.

Before Jacob, just the thought of this would have left me mortified. I hadn't had any sexual partners before Jacob, and meeting a stranger and inviting him home would have been out of the question. The pictures of my friends in India I saw on social media presented an entirely different image of what was happening back home. They were more sexually free and fluid than I was, despite me being the one living away. I had moved abroad, didn't live with family anymore, had the means and freedom to sleep around, but I hadn't wanted to. I'd found myself a nice man almost as soon as I landed here and become comfortable.

Jacob was gone; he'd told me he wanted me to go out and live my life; my family was trying to arrange my marriage. If I couldn't be brash for a night, then what was I even doing here?

Luke was smiling. "A nightcap sounds good."

He even put a hand on my hip as I led him away. At the door I turned to look and saw Maeve and Joy kissing.

It wasn't a sloppy snog, but a fully realized emotional kiss after years of navigating sexual identity and each other's trespasses.

It was chilly outside and Luke offered me his hoodie. This reminded me of Niall from the park, and how he'd offered me a piece of his clothing too. There was a chance I was going home with Luke because I regretted what happened that day. Ditching Niall, going to the restaurant with Jacob. Because I'd made a mess of everything, and wanted to regain some semblance of control. Taking Luke home was a conscious decision I was making all on my own.

"I thought you don't drink much," Luke said, as we stood outside the house.

"I wasn't planning to," I said, feeling suddenly brave.

He watched me with a smile while I slipped into his hoodie. It smelled like a stranger; freshly washed linen and beer that he'd dribbled that night. It made me starkly aware of how little I knew him. I caught myself wondering how often he laundered his clothes. If he'd picked this hoodie because it was the only clean piece of clothing in his wardrobe. Did he even have a wardrobe? Or just a pile of clothes in a corner of his room?

He reached for my hand as soon as I'd pulled the hoodie down over my hips.

"I just realized I've never been to Joy's new place," he said, like touching me was the most natural thing in the world.

His hand was new too. Not soft, but big and rugged. When he laced his fingers with mine, he seemed to engulf my hand whole. I felt dazed, and for a moment I thought I didn't know the way back to our flat. I stared down at our hands joined together, and all courage had left me.

"Durga?"

I met his eyes, an unfamiliar face. This would have started to feel like a bad idea if he hadn't smiled at me in that moment. It was a warm smile, like he knew what he was doing. He was taking charge, the burden of responsibility was on his shoulders.

"I wasn't planning on staying for more than one drink tonight, and then I met you," he said.

"Me neither. Come on, it's this way."

I tugged at his hand and we walked together to the flat.

Chapter 11

THE SEX WAS SURPRISINGLY VERY GOOD. NEITHER OF us were drunk, every move was a fully conscious decision. I could identify what I was feeling—a physical response to Luke touching my body, taking my breasts in his hands, the tip of his tongue on the base of my neck.

But I woke up today with a feeling of emptiness, like I'd fulfilled nothing. Last night had felt good and I hadn't thought about Jacob once, but now I looked over and saw the man lying beside me wasn't him.

I'd thought I could be like Joy and Maeve, like my own friends back home. Spontaneous and free. But I didn't feel free. I was still tied to my loss.

Luke was on his belly in the morning, spread-eagled and taking up most of my bed. His back muscles were rigid as he hugged the giant cat stuffy that lived on my bed. I left him there, brushed my teeth, and went to the kitchen for coffee.

I was surprised to find Joy on a barstool, a bowl of soggy cereal in front of her and a cup of rooibos tea going cold. She was in her previous night's clothes. Her glitter eyeshadow was spread all over her face, so she looked less human and more shiny disco ball. Her hair was matted and dried out, having been slept in without a bonnet.

"Oh! Hi. You're here early," I said, trying to pretend like nothing was out of the ordinary.

"I spent the night at Maeve's place."

I inserted a capsule in the coffee machine and placed a mug under the nozzle. It started up with a gurgling sound.

"How'd it go?"

"Good. Fine. Great. How was your night with Luke?"

She lifted up the cereal bowl and banged it on the table, making some of the milk spill out.

"It was fine."

"Are you two a thing now?" she snapped.

I poured a heaping spoon of sugar into my coffee. Joy stuck her hands between her thighs and sat with her shoulders hunched.

"I thought you were okay with me bringing Luke back here," I said. "You should have said something last night if you weren't."

She interrupted me by slurping some milk from the spoon. "I should be pissed you're banging my friend, right after you stopped banging my brother."

"So you are?"

"I'm not. You have the right to move on with your life. I just don't think Jacob has."

She hadn't mentioned her brother in weeks, and even then, it was only in passing—like something funny he'd said at their family's Sunday lunch. She always apologized when she let his name slip into conversation. But knowing Luke was asleep in my bedroom had brought her suppressed rage to the surface. I'd been wondering when she'd finally tell me how she truly felt about the breakup.

"What do you mean he hasn't moved on?" I asked.

"I mean he's not seeing someone, he's not sleeping around."

"Joy, he wouldn't tell you if he was. He knows how close we are."

I was both filled with relief at the idea that Jacob wasn't seeing anyone, and guilt at what I'd done last night. As always, Jacob was the bigger person.

"He would be here, having breakfast with us now, but instead you have another guy in your bed."

I sat down slowly in the chair beside her. "I wish I could change things."

"You didn't want to introduce him to your family. And I would have to be a part of that lie, Durga." She was talking loudly now, almost like she wanted Luke to hear. "I've been thinking about it more, and it's really messed up."

"I know. I'm an idiot."

Joy rubbed a hand over her face and her eyes softened.

"I'm sorry. I shouldn't have slept with your friend," I said.

"Luke is not the problem here. I just miss having my brother here and I wish everything wasn't so complicated." She sat with her eyes closed, concentrating on her breathing.

"Is everything okay with you and Maeve?" I knew it wasn't the right time, but it had to be asked.

"Why would something be wrong? Anyway, I need sleep," Joy said.

She barely even looked at me before leaving the room. We'd left too much unsaid but I didn't want to keep her, to continue this conversation with Luke still in the flat. Who knew when Joy would be prepared to talk about her brother again.

Last night was a mistake, I could see that now. I shouldn't have gone to that party, tried to fit in.

I left the kitchen and was about to go into my bedroom until I remembered Luke was in there. He was pleasant, handsome, and hadn't once asked me where I was from. But there was nothing more I had to say to him. So I went to our living room instead and switched on the TV.

I kept expecting Joy to join me, and I turned the volume up louder, hoping she'd get out of bed and come sit with me.

It was Luke who came in eventually, to take his leave.

"*Arrested Development*? Nice," he remarked, coming to stand beside me and stare at the screen.

With his hair so short, he didn't look like he'd just got out of bed. I felt strangely comfortable in his presence, even though he had seen me naked the previous night. Like it was completely natural to be back to being clothed again. I suddenly recalled our dirty talk from last night. Something about what a good girl I was, if he'd fit inside me. That got the blushes going.

"Would you like a cup of coffee? Tea?" I could barely get the words out.

Luke shook his head. He looked at the door, blatantly revealing an itch to get away. "Better go. Before Joy kicks me out."

Maeve had been right about him, and he'd been just what I needed. "You probably should."

He leaned over and kissed me. It lasted so long I thought he was going to take my clothes off again. He tasted of my toothpaste.

"Have a good life," I said, as he made to leave. It was my awkward attempt at making clear that I didn't think I'd be seeing him again.

Luke stopped in his tracks and turned with a laugh. "I was about to say have a good day, but sure, best of luck with your life too."

Chapter 12

SURJO SENGUPTA HAD A TINY TURNIP TATTOOED ON HIS middle finger. He was skinny with a stubble, and had a receding hairline.

My date with Surjo was set for the afternoon, only a handful of hours after Luke left our flat. I was certain Joy didn't remember, and I didn't want to remind her either, not after the conversation we had that morning. When I'd told her earlier that my family was setting up this date with Surjo, she'd pretended to not care. I'd insisted I was only doing it to appease my mother and Joy had even supported me in my decision then, claiming that meeting this man would be the distraction I needed from Jacob. But I wasn't sure anymore if that was how she truly felt. If she wasn't just putting on a brave face to avoid a conflict with me. Maybe she thought the same as Jacob did— that I was too spineless to stand up to my family.

Joy had been asleep on the couch in front of the TV when I left and I didn't wake her.

"Does garam masala have a shelf life?" I asked, after we'd ordered food at the restaurant.

"I don't know. I'll have to ask Ma," he said.

"Aren't you a chef?"

We both laughed. It had become a running joke in the short time we'd known each other: No matter how independent we thought we were, we'd never outgrow the crippling dependency on our Bengali mothers.

Surjo had surprised me. I was fully prepared to detest him, given his choice of friends. I was expecting more of a sleazeball. Bikram's friends circle consisted of rich doctors, lawyers, and politicians' sons. The offspring of fathers who'd minted money off building hospitals and taking commissions from big construction jobs in Calcutta. They had that particular swagger of inherited wealth about them. I'd observed them from a distance of course, never having been a part of the circle. They lived in sprawling mansions, shutting out the homeless people who pitched tents on the streets outside.

But Surjo seemed different, more down-to-earth, like he recognized his privilege and didn't take it for granted. My trust in Arjun's judgment grew.

Surjo told me he left India not because he wanted to live abroad, but because he couldn't stand the injustice of the class divide. I wanted to hug him, to shout, *Yes, exactly*.

The restaurant was gorgeous, located in a pretty corner of a garden center. We were seated inside a glass conservatory, with a mature lemon tree in a gigantic pot at our side. A carefully preserved terrarium was on the table between us. A pot overflowing with string-of-pearls hung above Surjo, gently grazing the top of his head.

My curiosity in him had developed into beguilement. I was enjoying our conversation, our shared observations of living abroad. I felt starved of familiarity, and he was satiating that particular craving I had for home.

"Does your ma call you five times a week?" he said.

"And never replies to my texts."

"I work in a kitchen, and she worries I don't eat enough."

"What will she do when you're married?"

"Make my wife's life hell. Calling incessantly to check if I've been gargling with salt water every time I sniffle on the phone."

Surjo loved his mother, every Bengali man did. My own brother's first word every morning when he woke up was still *Ma*, which he shouted from his bed. Then my mother came rushing in with his first cup of tea. She sat on the edge of his bed, giving him a rundown of what her morning had consisted of thus far, and he listened silently.

They were still little boys around their mothers.

The food arrived and Surjo looked pleased. "We have two very proud mothers today. We are such dutiful children," he said, dribbling aioli over his salad.

I watched the way he ate. Wolfing down a big forkful without any airs of being a professional or purporting to know the best way to eat a salad. He clearly enjoyed food, in all its forms, and he ate without inhibition. He even made little satisfied grunts between bites and I was filled with pride at having made an excellent restaurant choice.

"I should come down to Ireland more often. They've started to really experiment with food. I never thought of tandoori chicken in a Caesar salad." He spoke through a mouthful of food, and I didn't mind. Already, there was no formality between us.

"You should. I mean, you could, if you like."

I did want to talk more about what it felt like to be a Bengali living abroad, to feel a bit more connected to home. I wished I had more control over my inadvertent facial reactions. I was signing forms at the Immigration office once and couldn't stop my face from reacting with disgust at the officer's fungal fingernail. I was sure she'd reject my work visa. I knew Surjo could see how eager I was to see him again. To continue this conversation about our families.

He drank from his glass of pomegranate juice, then cleared his throat.

"On the list of things we do to please our mothers, this has been the least unpleasant," he said.

I agreed. He'd been pleasant company, and I hated admitting that my family had perhaps made a good choice.

"But you should know, I have a girlfriend," he said.

* * *

I'D CALLED TIA from the bus, on my way back from meeting Surjo.

"So . . . how did it go?" Tia asked excitedly when she answered the phone.

Clearly, the photographs circulated between the families had been of a younger Surjo. Tia wouldn't have thought him attractive if she knew he was losing hair. I didn't mind it so much. It told me he was comfortable in his skin.

"So Bikram set this up, did he?" I hissed into the phone.

"What? Yeah, he's Bikram's friend. His mother connected us to them. Why? Durga, you sound angry about something."

"I've met this guy like Ma wanted me to. Now I've done my duty. Don't you dare make me do this again."

I'd been nervous about this date, convinced my family was setting me up for disaster, but I'd been surprised by Surjo. If I was being practical, thinking of a steady comfortable future, he was a good match. It had started so well.

"Don't talk to me about duty from a million miles away, ha? I'm the one sitting here washing rice for Ma and learning to make round rotis."

"I've never seen you wash anything other than your face."

"Kobita had to go to her village to visit her nieces last week. I helped Ma in the kitchen, I'll have you know. She said I need to practice for when I'm a married woman. Anyway, what did you eat? Surjo must have high standards since he's a chef?" Tia said.

I leaned on the tall window beside me and closed my eyes. "Tia, he has a girlfriend. Bikram had to have known."

There was an old woman sitting beside me on the bus who had nodded off and was using my shoulder as a pillow. I readjusted my-self so she'd be more comfortable. I could feel her warm rhythmic breath on my blouse and for a moment I imagined she was my grandmother, having fallen asleep in the middle of telling me a story like she used to do.

"Excuse me?"

"She's French. Also a chef. He's waiting for the right time to introduce her to the family. Apparently she cooks him daal."

"So he came all that way to meet you for absolutely no reason?"

Tia was furious. I could picture her pacing around her room, clutching the phone to her ear, torn between itching to fling it at the wall and wanting to hear the rest of the story.

"Maybe like me, he's tired of being badgered by his mother."

"Your mother wants to see you happily settled with a nice man."

"Maybe that's what will make *you* happily settled."

"You don't want a nice man?"

"I don't want one forced on me, no."

Tia sighed. She'd stopped pacing. I could sense she'd sat down somewhere, probably on her bed, pressing her nail into the fleshy pad of her thumb. It was how she kept herself from erupting.

"You'll want some stability in your life, Durga. A family of your own someday. You need to lock it down before it's too late."

"Have you given this speech to Arjun and Parul too?"

"I don't concern myself with them. I care only about you."

She was lying, I knew. Tia was the only one crying when Parul was admitted in hospital to have her appendix removed. She told Arjun everything, because she knew he didn't judge her for her girlish dreams.

My bus had arrived at the stop and I slowly moved my shoulder so the woman could continue sleeping undisturbed. But her head bobbed with a jerk when the bus halted and she looked up at me with red sleepy eyes, offended at being woken so rudely. I apologized to her and slipped past her frail knees.

"It doesn't matter why Surjo came to see me. I was duped into meeting him, by your fiancé, that is what's important here."

"Bikram couldn't have known. He would have told me."

"They are close childhood friends, Tia. Of course Bikram knows about the girlfriend. I don't get why he thinks I would want to marry a man who is in love with someone else."

I wanted to plant this seed of doubt in my sister's brain. Make her question what else Bikram was capable of. Another woman on the side?

It was drizzling when I stepped off the bus. I hated the sensation of wet clothes, and yet people around me were walking around unhurriedly in damp sweatshirts.

"Don't be silly. Maybe you are the first person Surjo is telling about this girl. Bikram would never do that to my sister."

I jogged to the house and took the stairs up to our flat. I couldn't tell Tia this, but despite the fact that Surjo was a dead end, today had made me hopeful for the future. There were other good men out there. If I kept looking, I might eventually find someone who matched up to Jacob.

"Whatever, Tia. I'm home now, I have to go."

I ended the call while Tia was still speaking.

I OPENED THE door and found the flat in a mess. Joy usually cleaned up on Sundays, either before I woke up or when I went out without her. But today there were crisp packets in the hallway, our ficus had shed some dry yellow leaves I hadn't noticed before, and they hadn't been swept away. Just one light was on, in the living room. There was no music playing, the TV wasn't on either. A sense of doom filled me instantly.

I ran to the living room to find Joy slumped on the couch. Her eyes were closed, her arm had fallen limp over the side. A glass of water had been knocked over and there was a damp patch on the dove gray carpet.

I screamed.

Joy opened her eyes. Red swollen eyes. She'd changed into pajamas but glitter still streaked her face from the night before.

"Joy. God! I thought . . . I don't know what I thought."

I crouched on the floor beside her, took one cold hand in mine. I knew she didn't have a migraine because it made her sensitive to light and she would have turned them all off. She blinked her eyes slowly, dried tears tracked down her cheeks. I was afraid she'd taken something. My mind struggled to find a reason why. Had I missed all the signs? For self-harm or depression? I was the worst friend. I needed to call an ambulance, I thought, her movements were so slow.

"Durga. Jacob is dead," she said.

Chapter 13

I RECEIVED THE INFORMATION ABOUT JACOB'S DEATH IN one quick burst. Joy shouted it all at me, screaming through tears.

He had died of a brain aneurysm.

Jacob had driven to a friend's house directly from a Sunday sales pitch, which he'd closed over a game of golf.

A friend offered him a high five but Jacob had darted to the toilet to throw up viciously. Someone made a joke about how Jacob was the only guy who could close a deal whilst hungover. He emerged from the toilet with his head in his hands, doing a sort of drunken dance. The others were still laughing. A suggestion was thrown around to go to the pub, and that some hair of the dog would do him a world of good. Jacob, unsteady on his feet, deposited himself on the nearest chair and complained that he had a splitting headache. He'd said he could barely see through the blur. Another friend clapped him on the back and Jacob hurled the remainder of the contents of his stomach on the floor. Then he collapsed.

"Just like that. He was gone before the ambulance arrived."

Joy went from being comatose on the couch to bouncing off the walls within minutes. I couldn't believe it. None of the words coming at me sounded logical, and I was waiting for the punch line.

"But you saw him yesterday," I said, when there was a lull in her roaring.

As though, somehow, evidence of his presence in our lives until yesterday negated the fact that he was dead now.

"My parents are with him. I can't go. I refuse to look at him. I won't see him this way."

Joy was talking to herself. I might as well have been a light fixture on the wall.

I hadn't said goodbye to him, not in a forever kind of way. Everything bad that had happened between us seemed trivial now. I'd hoped for an eventual reconciliation, even if it meant having to wait many years. At the back of my mind, while I slept with Luke, had lunch with Surjo, I believed this was temporary. That one day, in the distant future, after we were done trying to live our lives apart, Jacob and I would be together again.

I approached Joy slowly, with my arms wrapped around myself and my wet raincoat. "This is real? Jacob is gone?"

She lifted the TV remote off the mantel and flung it at the wall. It didn't seem to damage the remote, but lifted some paint.

"Let's find other things to throw," she said.

I ran to the kitchen to pull out all the mugs and glasses and went back to the living room. I was nervous at first, but Joy took a glass out of my hand and dropped it on the floor, where it cracked beside her feet. I took her cue and broke the others in the same way, breathless. She took off the cushion covers and ripped them easily. I attempted ripping the throw on the couch but it was too heavy and left a red blotch on my hand. She took the dried flowers out of the whisky bottle we used as a vase and handed it to me. I smashed that on the floor too. There were some framed art prints on the wall, which the landlord had bought cheaply from a charity shop, and Joy took them down. Neither of us cared that I was losing my deposit. She threw one frame across the room and it smashed on the wall, and I threw the other one.

Joy went over and kicked them with her Birkenstock sandal. Then she stood over them with her shoulders heaving. I hadn't given myself a moment to think it over, for the news to truly sink in. It was impossible that I'd never see Jacob again. I'd prepared myself for a lifetime of him.

"He was so good. He was a good man. A good bloody brother. Mum's favorite." Joy was crying.

"Yes, he was."

"He didn't deserve to die. All these other people, blaring their horns at learner drivers and running puppy farms, they deserve to die. Not my brother. He would set all those puppies free."

She was right, I knew he would. Jacob didn't have a mean streak. I wanted to say he was too young to die, but that wasn't right. This was how I'd have felt no matter *when* he died. My feet sinking in quicksand, lost and unsupported.

This couldn't have happened to him, to me, to us. It was so ridiculous an idea that I almost laughed. I covered my mouth with a hand, not wanting to appear insensitive. Joy strode around the room, stepping over the mess we'd made with a crazed expression on her face. The color had drained from her. In the low light of the living room, with old makeup still on her face in blotches, she looked like a pale ghost.

I shivered in the wet raincoat and hunched down on the floor. My face was in my hands. The bubbling laughter had turned to sobs.

I took my phone out, to scroll through our messages, for some sign of him. I shook my head, refusing to allow this to become my new reality. A world where I wouldn't be able to send him an ill-conceived text. Where there was absolutely no hope for reconciliation. The only way I was even able to get out of bed each morning was knowing Jacob was here, somewhere in the city, living and breathing.

"Do you want to look at pictures?" I offered.

I clicked quickly into the Cloud folder I'd avoided for so long. I needed evidence he had truly been a part of my life.

Joy sat down beside me on the carpet while I swiped through pictures. Quickly at first, with shaking fingers, wanting to lap up as much of him as I could. Sometimes Joy smiled, mostly she cried. I slowed down eventually, drinking in the sight of him on my phone screen.

Jacob lying on my bed, propped up by pillows, his long legs stretched out and ankles crossed. Reading a book. Jacob standing at the very edge of a cliff, the wind nearly ridding him of his coat. A blurry selfie of us in his car. A selfie of all three of us at a petting farm, with an alpaca in the background. It had a pink tongue sticking out and a cute overgrown mullet.

"He'd be surprised to see me cry. I think I went through my whole childhood without shedding a single tear. Jacob was the crier in the family. Him and Daddy," Joy said.

We'd calmed a little now. I was self-conscious of saying the wrong thing, to make this loss about me when she'd known him longer, when they'd shared a childhood.

"I'm going to miss him. I'll spend my whole life missing him," she said.

"Me too."

My stomach cramped from the ache of this loss, from the missed potential of a life well lived. As much as I tried not to, my brain went there—the impulse to text him. To tell him about this death that would alter me forever. He had to know what was happening to me.

"How could this happen?" I whispered.

"I just want to sleep," Joy said.

"Are you sure?"

"I just want to be left alone."

We stood up and slowly left the room. I followed her to her door and watched as she threw herself backward on the bed like a heavy sack. She didn't bother with the duvet, didn't arrange the pillows or make herself comfortable. She just continued lying there with her eyes open, staring at the crack that ran across the ceiling.

"Text me if you need anything, please?"

I shut the door and stood outside her room for several minutes. I checked my phone and saw a message from Naledi, asking if Joy was okay. She hadn't been answering their calls.

Our previous texts had been casual greetings, birthday and Christmas wishes exchanged, Naledi asking me to tell Joy to answer her phone. Today, I told her Joy was heartbroken but trying to cope.

I took a shower, drank a glass of Coke, changed my bedsheets, hoovered the floors, loaded the dishwasher, and watered the plant. Our one ficus that still lived, by the TV, was in full view of the sun. I was determined to keep it alive even though it had started to lose leaves in the past weeks.

I tried to find anything to keep me going, to continue being able to live. It was a selfish preoccupation, I realized, the act of grieving.

At midnight I checked on Joy. She was asleep and there was a wet patch on the sheet where her face was. I left a bottle of water on the bedside table, and a few biscuits on a plate.

I turned on the music in my room and slid into bed, with no hopes of falling asleep. I knew I would stay awake all night, painfully reliving every moment I had spent with him. It was a coward's exercise, to dream about those memories from a safe distance. Those days that were short-lived, not treasured enough. I'd thrown it all away, not knowing what lay in the future. If I'd known I'd lose him so soon, so permanently, I would've done anything to have more time with him. I would've proposed, taken him to India, told everyone about him. I would have celebrated him every day.

WHEN JOY, JACOB, and I lived in the exquisite glow of our contentment, she told me the story about the birdhouse.

Their father had bought it for Joy one summer. She was still a child and her brother already a teenager.

Joy had spent some days painting and decorating it with seashells and shiny streamers, then employed Jacob's help to nail it to a tree in the garden. It was on a branch that was easily visible from her bedroom window. She kept a close eye on it, delighting in finding two coal tits regularly bringing straw and worms to the house she'd propped so invitingly for them.

At the time, they had a cat in the house, whose name Joy never mentioned to me. Joy used to be a cat person as a child, and she used to spend all her evenings with this one, even sitting at the dining table with him curled in her lap and feeding him scraps. The cat was so attached to her that he would wake her every morning by chewing on her hair. Joy took it to mean the cat was trying to groom her.

Then one night, while she was asleep, she heard the birds chirruping in the garden. She awoke with a start, dazed, thinking it was dawn. Even as a child, she'd made the connection that something was wrong, because the birds were never awake or active at this time of night.

She looked out of the window to find the cat pawing at one of the birds, rolling playfully in the grass while the bird screeched with fright. The cat had set off the motion sensor for the garden lights, and the grotesque scene was lit up for Joy's clear viewing.

Joy screamed and Jacob rushed into her room. She left her parents out of the events of this night, and I deduced they were either out late at the pub or in deep slumber.

Jacob rescued the bird from the cat's playful claws. It was thankfully still alive but now had a broken leg.

Joy was too young and conflicted by her love for the cat. In her eyes, he had now proven himself to be a monster by bringing her an affectionate gift of a bird he had tried to kill.

Jacob used tongs from the kitchen to place the bird in a cardboard box and Joy followed him to the shed. All the while, the cat purred and rubbed himself on her leg. She had cried for the rest of the night because she couldn't bear to look at the cat anymore.

Jacob fashioned a splint for the bird's leg using a Q-tip and masking tape. Over the next few days, while he checked on the recovering bird in the shed, sprinkling chia seeds in the box for it to eat, Joy developed a loathing for the cat. She didn't pet it even when he came to sit in her lap.

Jacob tried explaining to her that it was the way of the natural world, the order of the food chain, that the cat had probably killed hundreds of other birds unbeknownst to them. Joy would never look at another cat with tenderness again.

Twelve days later, when Jacob opened the shed door, the bird hurtled out, whacked its head on a wall, disoriented, then flew into the sky. Jacob had already removed the birdhouse from the tree. With the cat around, it was like setting a death trap.

Joy never forgave the cat, and she refused to let him in the house again. Jacob still fed him when he came around, meowing and trying to get Joy's attention.

When she told me the story she said she maybe understood it better now, as an adult. That everything had a place in the world. That evil was only perspective. Even a teenage Jacob was wiser than we were as grown adults.

Chapter 14

I WENT TO THE FUNERAL THREE DAYS LATER. IT WAS HELD
in a village in West Cork where Jacob's father, Eric, originally came
from. None of them had ever lived there.

Eric moved to South Africa with his parents when he was an in-
fant. It was in the years when Irish people were emigrating in droves,
in search of a different life. Eric's father had found a teaching position in Cape Town and they'd hoped for more money, better weather.

Joy went to the village with her parents the day before the funeral.
So I had no choice but to accept Lorna's offer of a lift in her car. I
didn't want to spend time with her, but more so didn't want to take
the bus with strangers.

But Lorna cried bitterly as she drove, "I just can't believe he's gone,
you know?"

This had to be the twentieth time she'd said it. She was echoing
how I was feeling, still utterly bewildered to allow the full shock of it
to hit me. But I was keeping it to myself. With Jacob gone and Joy
barely speaking to anyone anymore, I had nothing much to say.

Since Jacob's death, I'd developed a phantom pain in my right
wrist. I could feel the pulse throbbing, hear it even. I rotated it gently
as I sat quietly in the car, trying to exercise the muscle, gauge the
damage. I winced from the pain. There was no explanation for it in

my memory. I hadn't banged it, crushed it, even so much as scratched it. It was as though my body was slowly falling apart.

"Can you believe it? That Jacob is gone?" Lorna persisted.

"No," I finally said. "I'll never believe it."

JACOB WAS BURIED on the grounds of the little church that his ancestors had visited every Sunday for Mass. Joy was angry for many reasons, but this particular fact was what she clung to right now.

"He wanted to be cremated and planted with a seed, so he'd grow into a tree. He saw a company advertise it online and talked about it all the time."

Joy and I were sitting in her great-grandfather's garden, on damp summer deck chairs where the weeks of rain had soaked into the cushions and nobody had covered them. A whole host of people were inside, including Lorna, who refused to leave Naledi's side.

Jacob had talked about bringing me here before, and the mixed feelings he harbored toward the village. Unlike Jacob, Joy used to like coming here. She had fond childhood memories of the village. Her granny, Eric's mother, had moved back here from South Africa, shortly after Joy was born.

Joy had spent many an Easter break sitting on these chairs in this garden. A soft stream ran through the woods at the back of the house, where her granny would take them for picnics on warm days. It was also where their neighbor, an old bachelor, left his butter in plastic bags tied to rocks so it would stay "fresh and cool." Just across the road from the family cottage was the village graveyard, which Joy had looked at through the kitchen window when she visited. Her brother was buried there now, as though it had been waiting all these years to devour him.

"Did you tell your parents he wanted to be cremated?" I asked.

Joy scoffed and took a drag of her cigarette. She hadn't been smoking much recently, but in the last few days she'd consistently had a fresh one tucked behind her ear.

"You're staying tonight?" she asked.

"Lorna's offered to give me a lift back, but I think I'll stay and go back with you tomorrow?"

"If you don't mind sharing the couch with me. We have a full house."

"I could check if the B&B has a room."

"Can I stay with you if you're booking it?" she asked.

"Of course. Your family won't mind?"

"I'm the last person any of them are thinking about."

"Joy, your family cares about you. Naledi asked me if you've been eating."

She ground the cigarette under her shoe, then picked it up and threw it over the fence. It landed in the adjoining field.

"I'll talk to her. Daddy said she hasn't eaten anything other than a few digestives since Jacob died. She's projecting on me."

Joy had an old hoodie on, with her favorite ripped blue jeans and red canvas shoes. This was one of the only times she'd left the house without eyeliner on.

"Anyway, Tia's wedding will be the perfect distraction for you," she said.

Joy was mean when she was sad. Since her brother's death, like my inexplicable wrist pain, Joy's nasty side was showing.

"No, Joy, it won't. How could I possibly be distracted from Jacob's death?"

"But you're still going."

"I have to."

She nodded and looked away.

"You can still come, can't you?" I said.

"I'm not going to a wedding celebration when my brother's just died."

"Of course, I'm sorry."

I was going to be Joy's punching bag for the night. I'd already prepared myself for it.

Joy made a hateful face at me, then got up and went inside, leaving me to sit in the drizzle. I reminded myself to be patient with her.

I wished Jacob were here, giving me a history lesson on the local family feuds. Each person in this house had known him longer than I had, but I'd known him deeply. We spent entire nights talking about his parents. If I closed my eyes, I could taste the exact ingredients of the biltong Naledi ate every day in her other life in South Africa. He'd described the smell of worn tangy leather he associated with his father, because of the old wallet he carried around.

Eric Cronin stepped outside, with a glass of whisky in one hand and a half-burnt cigarette in the other. Naledi must have caught him smoking and commanded him to take it outside. We'd never spoken in the absence of Joy and Jacob, so we gave each other a nod of acknowledgment and said nothing.

Jacob and his father butted heads when he was growing up, but there was affection, in the only way Eric knew how to show it. Eric wanted Jacob to be more like the Irish lads, to get involved with GAA. He wanted his son to fit in, to make it so that the people around them didn't notice Jacob's less than white complexion. And he was grieving now. He'd lost his son. How many regrets did *he* harbor?

Eric finished smoking then went back in. He'd been struck into silence since his son's death, and had made animalistic grunting sounds at church during the service. We'd all turned to him, expecting to find him crying, but his eyes were wide and dry, like he was watching a horror film.

An uncle and a distant cousin came out after he left, seemingly to have a private conversation. They drifted around to the front of the house when they noticed me.

Then Naledi appeared, with Lorna close behind.

She gave me a forlorn look, with a cream cracker in her hand. Lorna leaned in to whisper something in her ear but Naledi waved her away and handed her the cracker.

"Thank you for coming, darling."

She came to sit in Joy's chair. Nobody, other than I, appeared to mind the furniture being damp. She smoothened her dress over her knees and crossed her legs.

She was full of grace and beauty, Naledi. Not a woman who experimented with makeup much. I'd only ever seen her wearing a faint red lip stain and some mascara. Her clothes, however, were carefully planned out. To her son's funeral she wore a green-and-black-check pencil dress that clung to her shape, pumps with manageable heels, and a black hat with a feathery fascinator which she'd taken off now. Nobody wore black to funerals anymore, but Naledi stood out nevertheless.

Jacob had once told me that he believed the way one presented themselves to the world was a subconscious way of declaring how they wanted to be treated. He'd learned it from years of watching his mother.

"I'm so sorry for your loss, Naledi. I am heartbroken for you all," I said.

Lorna was standing behind her, with her face turned down and the cracker still in her hand.

Naledi reached for my hand, hers was clammy and cold. "He drank too much. At least that's what I'm telling myself, to make sense of this."

She'd been crying and her long eyelashes were wet. If Joy were here she would remind her mother *why* Jacob drank. He'd grown up watching his parents drink at every meal, go to the pub several nights a week.

"He was too young," Lorna said. She placed a hand on Naledi's shoulder, who patted it.

"How are you doing, darling? This can't be easy for you either. He loved you very much," she said.

The tears came then, just from this acknowledgment that we'd had something, that I'd been something to him. They had an entire lifetime's worth of memories with him, and I'd had him a few nights and days in comparison.

Naledi leaned in to hug me when she saw me crying. "I don't know what happened between you, but I know he was very sad to lose you. I want you to always remember that."

I blubbered like a child on her shoulder.

"Would you like me to stay the night, Naledi? If you need help with anything," Lorna interrupted.

"No, darling, you go on back home. There's nothing left to do. We all have to carry on now, the best we can." Naledi gave me a weak smile as we pulled apart, and Lorna stormed off. "You will mind Joy for me, won't you? I know she's miserable and she blames me. As if I had any control over Jacob's life."

"She doesn't blame you, Naledi. She's just angry and frustrated, but she loves you."

She leaned into me again, throwing her arms around my neck and holding me close, sobbing into my hair. I shook with her every shudder, and we sat like that, getting soaked in the drizzle, which turned into rain.

We all had complicated relationships with our mothers, my generation. Our mothers hadn't known how best to rear us, to give us our independence, to treat us as equals to their sons, and to keep us safe. We, in turn, blamed them for everything.

I looked at the kitchen window, where Joy was standing with a bottle of beer in her hand. I willed her not to, but she took a big defiant chug.

JOY WAS WASTED by the time we checked into the B&B.

Despite my insistence, we were not being charged for the room because everyone in the village knew the Cronins were in mourning.

Joy was snoring again, the way she used to when she was drinking more regularly. I hoped she'd regret this tomorrow, instead of trying to numb the effects of the hangover with more alcohol.

With Joy breathing through her mouth beside me, I logged in to the folder with all the photos again. Pathetically, I could do nothing more than repeatedly revisit the past. I looked in the folder marked "Private," the ones I hadn't shown Joy the other day. My wrist ached again as I scrolled.

We didn't have many pictures together because Jacob got uncomfortable when asked to pose. If he knew a camera was pointed at him, he didn't know how to hold himself.

Instead, I had pictures of him cooking me breakfast with his back turned to the camera. His stack of books on my bedside table, which I kept as reference so I could buy him a book he didn't already own. There was a picture of just his hands, while he cut a slice of Wagyu beef at a restaurant. I'd taken it on the pretext of being blown away by the perfect plating of the meat inside a necklace of roasted Brussels sprouts. But really, I was admiring his large hands, the sexiest part of his body.

I had pictures of his spectacles in my bathroom, of my feet on his bed with an out-of-focus version of his naked body in the background, his mud-splattered boots after we'd returned from a walk and before he carefully wiped them clean. Of the places we'd been together—Blackrock Observatory, Blarney Castle, Old Head of Kinsale. A shot of Jacob feeding a carrot to a deer through the fence at Farran Woods.

I'd starved myself of them, and now I wanted to fill up with him again. Since he died, I looked at these photographs several times a day. Longing for him, knowing he'd been taken from me, from Joy, never to be touched again. He would be cold and alone in the ground forever, with not one book to read.

I'd wanted to shout when they were lowering the coffin into the ground, my inner Kali bursting forth. She was outraged by the unfairness. That this could happen to Jacob, to me, was wrong. Kali wanted to tear down everything. She wanted these people to know, the ones with tears in their eyes now, that Jacob had secretly wished he had a childhood in South Africa. That he had obsessively researched his people's history on the internet to feel closer to them. She wanted to shatter and smash. The coffin. The flowers. Dismantle the coffin. Wreck the place.

Kali would bring him back, breathe life into him with her own mouth, but I couldn't.

Chapter 15

JOY AND I TOOK THE BUS BACK TO THE CITY THE NEXT day. There was only one route and a bus was scheduled for once every hour, or thereabouts. I understood, after an hour and thirty-five minutes of waiting at the bus stop, that this was a fairly ballpark estimation.

The bus did eventually arrive. Joy and I had our pick of seats since it was almost empty. We sat apart, in separate seats, because I'd made the mistake of asking her how she was feeling when she woke up. Joy had taken that as an affront, as an attack on her alcohol consumption the previous night.

She was irrational in her grief, and I was too spent to fight her.

The three-hour bus ride, which would have taken us half that time by car, ended with Joy storming off when we reached our stop in the city. I went after her, as much as I wanted to let her walk it off. Her brother had just died and I didn't want her making foolish emotional choices.

She walked into a sportswear shop, even though I knew how much she despised yoga pants and sweat-proof tank tops. This was another sign she wasn't thinking straight.

I caught up with her while she was browsing through a rack of discounted sports bras.

"Joy, what are you doing?"

She glared at me with her chapped, bitten lips hanging open. "Are you following me?"

"I traveled back with you, on the same bus, in case you didn't notice. Can we please talk? I don't want us to fight, not at a time like this."

"What? When my brother is dead and my best friend could care less by flying off to India for a wedding?"

I should've become accustomed to people eavesdropping on our public conversations, because even on a non-calamitous day, Joy's voice invited everyone to listen in.

"We should go home and unpack how you're feeling."

"That's right, a bubble bath and a charcuterie board will fix this," she said.

She pulled out the bottom of a tracksuit and held it to her waist with shaking hands. The old Joy would've made an ick-face at it.

A child had broken away from his father and was standing near us, watching Joy combusting into flames. The last thing we needed was someone recording this and posting it on the internet. So I reached for her elbow and tried to steer her out of the shop, but Joy put up a struggle.

"Go home. Can you please leave me alone?" she said.

"I don't want you to be alone."

"*You* don't want to be alone, Durga. I'm fine."

She knew all the ways she could hurt me. My hand dropped from her arm and I took a step back.

"I wish I could stay, Joy, I don't want to go to a wedding either. But it's my sister. She'll never forgive me if I miss it."

"Or maybe you *still* don't want to tell them about Jacob. That you were together for two years. That *you're* grieving him too. Maybe, subconsciously, you like this way better, so you'd never have to bring him home to your family."

"Joy, stop, you're hurting me. I know you're devastated by his death, as am I. But it's not my fault he died."

She made a face with her eyebrows raised, as though questioning the possibility that it was. All my fault. I had to leave her there, determined to show her I was capable of being alone.

IT WAS UNSETTLING having nobody but myself. Even with music in my ears, with Florence Welch reminding me she was no mother or bride but a king, memories of recent distressing encounters trickled in. I was suddenly alone, with the aftereffects of Joy's words, and I was punishing myself because she was right about me. I was selfish, and a coward.

I walked around shops in the city now, fixating on other times I'd felt like a low-grade human being. Like the time when I said "thank you" to my boss after I held the door open for him, or when a tiny speck of spittle had flown out of my mouth and landed on a cashier's eyebrow while I was making small talk at the till. I'd continued speaking, hoping he hadn't noticed, but he'd lifted a middle finger and wiped his brow.

I was descending into a looping reel of madness. It didn't feel like it was even about Jacob anymore. It was purely selfish. All about me. All about how I didn't deserve to be happy because I didn't know how to live as a self-sustaining and fully functional adult.

After I'd cleaned the flat to the best of my abilities, watered the ficus again, and sunk low enough to pull out Jacob's box of belongings, I'd had enough. Luke and I had exchanged numbers at the party, before I'd invited him home, and I hadn't thought about it until today. I texted him now, to ask if he'd like to come over. I wanted to feel anything other than this. The rain outside sounded like a thumping drum in my head.

LUKE ARRIVED IN thirty minutes with a bag of lightly salted crisps. This was his second time coming to the flat and it was awkward at the door. I knew him intimately in some ways, but fundamentally, we were still strangers.

"Howya," he said.

He stooped to hug me. I was shorter than everyone in Ireland.

Luke held a neutral expression at all times, as though he didn't form opinions on anything ever. But his soft baby face made him nonthreatening. The sportswear shop Joy had walked into earlier was probably where he got all his clothes. His hair hadn't grown at all since I last saw him. It was so closely cropped I could see his scalp.

I'd texted him because I was feeling sorry for myself, and required the company of a man who could throw me over his shoulder. But the last time I saw him, Jacob was still alive. That time I wanted to get over my ex. This time was going to be different. I wondered if Luke detected my sadness.

He made himself comfortable on the couch, positioning his legs apart and dropping a hand between them, as though he needed to ensure the whereabouts of his crotch. An image flashed through my mind—of Jacob, poised and proper, in the same room as Luke, looking at him with judgment.

They had both sat on this couch. Jacob too had looked up at me, smiling like this.

I knew this was an ugly thing I was doing, and I lauded myself for being as despicable as Joy thought I was.

Joy and I hadn't talked about Luke since that morning. Jacob had died that very day. If she walked through the door now and saw Luke in our home, splitting open a bag of crisps and strewing crumbs everywhere, she would slap me across the face.

"Drink?" I said.

"I'm grand. Not thirsty."

As though having a drink was a matter of being parched, and not part of our everyday social construct, a way to keep our hands occupied.

If he knew I'd been in a serious relationship with Joy's brother, he didn't mention it. Joy and Jacob had some mutual friends, but they mostly moved in different social circles. Nonetheless, Luke had to have heard about Jacob.

Luke's eyes drifted to our plant next to the TV, and I was embarrassed by the handful of yellow leaves clinging to its drooping branches, knowing he was a homegrown expert at these things.

"You're watering it too much. Probably has root rot," Luke said.

I nearly offered it to him.

"Shall we go to my room?" I said, suddenly remembering that Joy could potentially walk in at any moment.

Luke shrugged and stood up, then started taking off his sweatshirt as he followed me.

AFTER WE HAD SEX, Luke and I lay in bed, in the semi-dark. He wasn't quite the teenage fantasy I'd had, of tenderness and gentle missionary, which was more what I'd had with Jacob. Luke was the anti-fantasy. He offered what I, no longer a teenager, didn't know I needed.

I was grateful for Luke today. He'd given me a safe way to numb my feelings.

He'd fallen asleep while I was on my phone and I woke him with a gentle tap on the shoulder.

He rubbed the sleep out of his eyes and wrapped an arm around my shoulder, gifting me the creamy scent of his deodorant. I'd already put some clothes on and my mood had changed, so I pulled away from him.

He wasn't offended, and sat up to fluff the pillow so he could rest against the headboard.

His front tooth was chipped and I didn't ask him how it happened. A fall, a brawl. Some bit of his life I didn't need to know about. It was the same as him not asking about the unmissable scar on my left knee.

My brother, Arjun, accidentally knocked me off a bicycle when I was four, and I fell on a bed of gravel. My memory from that age was patchy, but I could recall the searing sensation of my skin splitting open, and the confusion of looking down to see blood from my leg dripping on the ground. Arjun started howling before I did, so my father had rushed to him, assuming he was the one hurt.

"Joy's brother died. You heard?" I said to Luke.

I was thinking about brothers and now it had spilled out of me. I'd broken the spell and he stopped fluffing the pillow to look at me.

"Yes. Fuck. I texted her but she never replied. How's she doing?"

"He was also my ex. We were together for two years."

Luke considered this information, playing it over in his mind in silence. He rubbed the back of his neck. His nerves were jangled, and I regretted inviting him into this space.

"Maeve told me you went on a few dates."

"Maeve lied," I snapped.

"Okay, yeah. I wouldn't have come today if I knew."

Luke wasn't as relaxed anymore, but was sitting up with a straight back. He moved to cover his nakedness with the duvet, assumably out of respect.

"Sorry for dumping this on you. I asked you to come, I shouldn't have."

"Durga, stop. You're sad. It makes us do weird things. When my mam died I walked out of the hospital and took a bus straight to the airport. I went backpacking for a year and missed her funeral."

Luke was the one uncomplicated thing in my life right now, and I wished I'd kept it that way. I reached for his leg with my toes under the duvet, and stroked the soft hairs on his calf. It should have been enough to set him off but he moved away gently, giving me a sad little smile.

"Do you want to stay for dinner? I could make some pasta?" I knew it was a losing battle, even as I said it.

He bent sideways to get his clothes off the floor, and began dressing himself.

"I'm going to head out, actually. I have to do this thing."

I sank back in the bed, defeated, sensing the prick of tears in my eyes. The gentleman that he was, Luke still came to me for our parting kiss. I dug my fingers into the back of his head, relishing the grainy texture of his stubble, and the salty taste of crisps on his tongue.

It was obvious he wasn't going to become a permanent fixture, and it wasn't like he intended to. I'd got exactly what I wanted—a male version of Maeve. Detached, aloof, and who left me with no sticky feelings. I knew what I was using him for, and I didn't want to know what he was numbing with me. And if we ever bumped into each other, ten years from now, we'd avoid eye contact in order to avoid explaining this history to our respective partners.

Luke left without much festivity. I heard the front door shut and then a few minutes later it opened again.

There was familiarity in Joy's motions outside my room. I heard the thud of her shoes where she flung them down the hall. The *smooch* of the fridge door being pulled open and then shut almost immediately after. The plodding gait to her bedroom and then returning to knock on my door.

"Are you awake, Durga?"

She knew I was because there was no music playing in my room yet.

"Are you okay?" I asked, when she came in.

She walked over to the end of my bed and sat down where my feet were under the duvet.

"I just want Jacob," she said.

Joy dropped her face into her hands, but she wasn't crying. I could barely see her in the dark, and it was easier this way. We didn't need to look at each other.

"Do you want to sleep here tonight?" I asked.

She got in beside me and took her jeans off. I got up to turn the music on and brought a bottle of water to the room. Joy had her eyes closed but she whispered a thank-you, and then we both went to sleep.

As much as I wanted to be here for Joy, I was glad I was going home soon. We couldn't continue this hot and cold relationship forever, and some distance apart might help us decide. Just the way Jacob said it would.

Chapter 16

WE SPOKE LITTLE ON THE DAYS FOLLOWING JACOB'S funeral, which was probably for the best because I couldn't predict what would come out of Joy's mouth when we did. I knew she hated that I was still going to India, but I had no choice. Moreover, I was feeling terribly guilty for having invited Luke over and keeping it a secret.

Joy started leaving for work earlier than usual.

She worked as an engineer for a company that manufactured parts for medical equipment. She was responsible for overseeing the design and manufacture, and downplayed her role as being a small cog in the wheels that kept the medical industry turning. When she was drunk she made self-deprecating jokes about how she was as good as a drug mule, which made no sense at all.

I went to work and every day I was repeatedly pulled into melancholy, no matter how far I'd managed to crawl out of it the previous night. Even though Jacob and I hadn't interacted much at work, I experienced an absence now that overwhelmed me.

One of those days in particular, I had trouble entering the building, and I stood clutching my backpack, worrying the straps on my shoulders. I was going to be late for a team meeting, and nobody at that table would know about my loss, or why my resting bitch face looked more grim than usual. I hadn't told anybody that Jacob's sister was my flatmate, that our lives encircled each other's in endless ways.

Once inside the building, I purposely walked past the corner cubicle where Jacob had sat, to further punish myself.

When we were together he'd gaze at me over his shoulder, passing me a smile if nobody was around, or secretly brushing my coat or bag if I happened to be close enough. I always had a text from him by the time I sat in my chair. Wishing me a good day, or complimenting my hair or reprimanding me for wearing the perfume that would make it impossible for him to focus on work.

After we broke up, I avoided going near his desk if I could, weaving my way around the longer route instead. Even though we made no eye contact and my heart broke a little every time I overheard him laughing with a colleague, I hadn't experienced *this* feeling before. Of knowing I'd never see him again. Even if it was only a cold stare I could hope for.

I realized I'd been standing at his desk when I caught Dennis's reflection in the blank computer screen. He was beside me, joining me in an eerily companionable silence, each of us preoccupied by the memory of our own version of Jacob.

Being Jacob's closest friend since childhood, Dennis was the only person at work who knew about us.

"Fuck," he said.

We'd seen each other at the funeral, but hadn't spoken. I'd always got the feeling Dennis wasn't my biggest fan. I once arrived at Jacob's house while the two of them were rewatching *The Walking Dead*, sharing a big bowl of popcorn like a happy couple. Jacob had promptly kicked him out of their house and Dennis had given me one of those parting looks that was more a threat than a goodbye. Unlike Joy, Dennis must've been thrilled when we broke up. He was never part of our closely guarded trio.

"I don't want to hear people talk about him, I don't think I can stand it anymore," I said.

Jacob's desk was antiseptically clean, with almost no personality that set it apart as belonging to him. The only thing to look at was the multipack carton of protein bars next to the keyboard, which was one of the few packaged snacks Jacob indulged in.

"The one thing these geeks are not is gossips. They won't know how to begin to talk about an emotionally tricky subject such as the death of a colleague," Dennis said.

"The women talk about him. I have to listen to it every day, about how shocked they are, how handsome he was, how young and polite. Fiona even broke into tears when that email announcement went around."

Dennis patted my shoulder, then he reached for two of Jacob's protein bars and offered me one. We stood there and ate in silence until I couldn't ignore the fact that I was now fifteen minutes late for my meeting.

After the meeting, I went to my desk and texted Luke to come over later.

He messaged back to say there was a rugby match on and he was watching it with his friends at the pub. A few minutes later he asked if I'd like to join them. He made it sound like it wouldn't affect him either way—like he wouldn't mind having me there, but wouldn't miss me if I didn't show up.

When I replied saying I wouldn't make an enjoyable rugby-watching companion, he sent me a laughing face emoji and then a thumbs-up.

I wished for the will to block him. To put an end to this relationship now before I had to face another stern-faced rejection. I didn't even know if Luke had siblings, or where he'd gone to college. *If* he'd gone to college.

He did find my clitoris quickly, and so far that was all I needed to know about him, but Jacob's death had left me feeling needy. Luke hadn't signed up for being my therapy booty call, and I didn't want to use him as one.

* * *

THE EVENING BEFORE I was leaving for India, Joy came home with a bag of takeaway food. I'd just boiled water to cook pot noodles.

She sat the big plastic bag on the table and began unpacking it. There were two curries, a large portion of rice, chips, chicken balls, and a box of cream-filled buns.

"I didn't know what you were in the mood for," she said.

"Wow. Thanks. I could eat all of it, I'm starving."

We got plates and napkins, then sat on the barstools to eat. This was something we hadn't done in days because we'd been eating our meals separately. Both of us were quiet around the house lately, and I noticed she'd been working late. Since Jacob died, I'd already been in bed when she returned every night.

"All set?" she asked.

She knew I hadn't packed yet, that I'd leave it till the last moment and forget to take my hairdryer or the shoes I'd bought for the wedding day.

"I'm sad you're not coming. Everyone wants to meet you," I said.

"I'll go with you next time. I'm sorry about what I said that day. I wish I could have gone with you but now isn't a good time. I'll just be thinking about Jacob."

I wanted to hug her, kiss her, and thank her for this. For recognizing the need to talk before I left. But any jerky displays of affection would've spooked her and I wanted her to remain in the room with me. She was like an injured kitten, the slightest sharp movement could scare her away.

"Of course. I understand. I know you don't want me asking, but will you be okay?"

"Durga, don't worry about me. I'm a bit mopey, but I have to get used to this not-having-Jacob-around thing. I'll text you."

"I wish we'd been talking more, but I'm glad we're talking now."

"I'm not going to magically bounce back. I've never known a life without my brother."

She'd pierced through a fried chicken ball with a fork and now there was grease coating her mouth. "These are shit," she said. "Hope you enjoy the food in India."

Then she went to her room, and I didn't see her for the rest of the night.

Chapter 17

IT WAS HARD TO GET EXCITED ABOUT MY TRIP.

I was left alone for the night. There were no sounds coming from Joy's room, and I assumed she'd already gone to bed. There was nothing to do but to finally pack my bags.

Most of the wedding outfits were being arranged for me in India. Ma and Tia sent me photos of saris, blouse designs, and jewelry, and they made the final selections. Pink wasn't my color but I had to concede to Tia because this was all about her and she was used to getting her way. When we were kids, I'd let Tia pick out the wall paint for our shared bedroom every time Ma thought we needed a refresher. She got to choose her side of the bed every other year when she decided she needed a change in life, the posters on the walls were hers, and I didn't complain about her loud phone calls with friends. That way, when it came to keeping the lights on late at night so I could read in bed, I had a few things to hang over her. Small wins.

I tried to pack my bags as diligently as I could, but my mind drifted. I didn't have Joy to remind me to take all the chargers for the various gadgets I owned. I checked three times if I'd packed my fitness watch's cable.

As I gathered my things, I found small forgotten fragments of

Jacob in my room. The white resin Montblanc logo had fallen off his wallet several months ago. It was a gift from Naledi when he graduated college and he'd looked for that piece of hardware everywhere. Eventually he'd bought a replacement off eBay. I found it under my bed when I went looking for a shoebox for my sandals now. I held the tiny circular logo in my hand, pressing it into my palm, fighting my tears. There was no hope of throwing it away.

In the bathroom, under my bottle of moisturizer, there was a ring of brown soggy dirt. When I went to wipe it up, I noticed tiny clippings of dark hair. Jacob shaved there, standing over the basin, with his back to me while I lay in bed in the mornings.

When I'd finished packing, it felt like I was leaving for good. My room looked empty, neat, and wiped of all signs of the life I had here. I fantasized about never coming back. Going to India and simply staying there. I didn't want to do that to Joy, but it would be an easy way out for me. To simply close the Ireland Chapter and pretend it never happened.

My life in India was so different. Nobody knew about Jacob. There would be no reminders of him. It could be a peaceful transition to my old life, an unceremonious slipping into a comfortable garb. But perhaps that outfit didn't fit me anymore.

I ARRIVED IN CALCUTTA after a seventeen-hour journey with two stops along the way. I'd slept through most of it, and only awoke when the wheels bumped and skidded on the runway.

I exited the airport gates with two bags. Dazed from all that sleep, I experienced a sensation like being newly born into a strange, warm, noisy world.

I'd spent the first twenty-four years of my life in this country, but the year since my last visit was long enough to induce a sensory overload.

A large crowd of porters, taxi drivers, and other unidentifiable parties were hanging over the low metal barrier separating them from the airline travelers. They were shouting and beckoning us, and my skin prickled. This was probably how celebrities felt when leaving a restaurant after a dinner with a date, suddenly confronted with the honking calls of paparazzi and flashing lights. *I'm just trying to live my life,* I wanted to shout back.

I knew I would never hear my family over the din, so I went on my tiptoes to try and spot them.

Arjun was waving his arms wildly over the heads of others. It was the only way he'd managed to disappoint our parents—by being short, not having grown to be as tall and stocky as our father. Arjun and I stopped growing when we reached the exact height of five feet and four inches each. I'd heard Ma whispering to Baba that the reason Arjun refused to marry was because he didn't want to face the prospect of being repeatedly rejected.

"I understand his fear. What if someday his wife wants him to fetch a box from the top of the almirah, and he has to go bring a chair and a few cushions to reach it. He'd be ashamed." Ma had wiped a tear from her eye.

In reality, Arjun didn't want to get married so he could watch cricket after work in peace, without a wife demanding his attention. And frankly, I supported this choice. No woman deserved to be second priority to cricket.

I stepped around the crowd toward him and only when I drew closer did I notice Parul standing beside him. She was at that age where she looked different every time I saw her. This time, her hair was cut in a bob that grazed her shoulders, with a red silk scarf tied like a headband. She was looking the other way when I headed toward them and no recognition crossed her face when she did spot me.

"Durga! Parul, she's here."

Arjun pulled me in for a hug and I nearly cried when I rested my face on his chest.

A full force of familiar scents had hit me when I came out of the airport gates: a heady combination of diesel, warm rotting rubbish, and human bodies. However, leaning on Arjun grounded me in the familiar bouquet of home. The detergent Kobita had been using for years to hand-wash our clothes, the mustard oil Ma must have cooked Arjun's lunch with, his Brut aftershave.

I was smiling when I reached for Parul next, to breathe in the scents she'd brought with her, but she was looking at my clothes with some judgment.

I pinched my crumpled white shirt, which had been underneath the jumper I was no longer wearing. I held it away from my body in an attempt to get some air on my sticky skin.

"Can't wait to get out of these."

I'd said it for Parul's benefit, hoping to imply that I had better dress sense when I wasn't traveling.

She was in an oversized pair of cotton dungarees. Baby blue with white pinstripes. A white sleeveless top underneath, and comfy leather sandals. Parul was the picture of cool and comfortable, like a nineteen-year-old who had it all figured out.

I felt an impulse to show her a picture of Joy, to prove to her that I had friends now. Tell her I went drinking in pubs. Parul didn't think I was cool enough for her and her friends. I wanted her to know I wasn't the same sister she'd grown up with.

This reminded me that Joy had barely said goodbye when she was leaving for work, knowing I would be on a flight to India by the time she returned home. I lost the will to fight for Parul's approval.

"You've put on some weight, Ma will be pleased," she said.

Arjun was bent over, reaching for my bags, but he froze and looked up at our faces with concern. He'd grown up in a household of five squabbling females, and was hyperaware of the delicate shifts that could set off an avalanche.

Parul slipped her hands into the relaxed pockets of her dungarees, and was looking down at Arjun with a warm smile.

"What? What did I say? Doesn't Ma worry that Durga isn't eating enough in Ireland because the food is bland?"

Arjun straightened up, throwing my backpack over his shoulder.

"You look great, Durga. Parul, lead the way to the car."

She turned on her heel and walked quickly away from us. When I sighed deeply, my brother wrapped an arm around me.

"Truth bombs. That's what she calls them. Yesterday, she told Tia that her wedding sari has too much gold embroidery, and since Tia's complexion is cool, with undertones of blue, she should have gone for silver."

We laughed at that. Tia had to be hoarse from all the shouting she did yesterday.

In the car, I was confronted by Calcutta in full force. We were stuck in traffic every few minutes. Arjun turned the AC on because I was pumping sweat and Parul didn't want to roll the window down. She was right not to, the pollution would've brought on a coughing fit.

Arjun wasn't the type for road rage. He had endless patience, and didn't seem to notice when other cars cut him off.

I remembered the familiar slow pace again, how nothing seemed rushed here. Not the traffic, the people walking languidly on the footpaths, not even the dogs and crows that wandered into the middle of roads looking for scraps were in a hurry. I was already forgetting what it was like in Ireland. What it felt like to be sitting in a car going 80. The miles and miles of green fields, the sheep chewing grass, the gray clouds and sudden showers.

The Bangla I only spoke on the phone intermittently came naturally to me now. Phrases I hadn't used in months. I even laughed louder here.

Ireland felt like another life lived by another person.

Chapter 18

I T WAS OUR GRANDMOTHER DIDU, WHO CAME TO GREET me at the door. Unlike Parul, Didu looked exactly as she had since my first memory of her.

I must have been five. We were at the dining table, sitting around it for our Sunday family meal. I was between Tia and Didu, and our plates were heaped with identical servings of rice, batter-fried aubergine, a bowl of daal, and a piece of fragrant mustard fish.

Our parents were discussing hiring someone to paint our home's façade, and they couldn't decide which color to choose. Ma wanted to repaint it entirely in peach, while Baba hoped to simply add another coat of the old yellow. I looked over at Didu and she was busy swapping one of her aubergine fries for the fish skin off my plate, which she knew I abhorred. We smiled at each other, and I must have noticed the deep lines on her face for the first time that day because I would always associate wrinkles with that memory of her. Because of her, I didn't fear aging lines the way other women I knew did.

Today Didu was in one of her white khadi saris, which had dominated her wardrobe ever since her husband died several decades ago. She was a small, bony woman, having given up eating meat since her husband's death. Something to do with relinquishing earthly delights, she'd explained once. But she did make an allowance for dessert—the one earthly delight she couldn't give up.

I reached for her feet, touching them, as she stroked the top of my head to pass me her blessings. We embraced, and I remembered how it was only Didu who made me feel big and tall. She pinched my chin, looking me up and down with far more warmth than Parul had.

My siblings had already scattered. Arjun to go put my bags in the bedroom, and Parul to a private corner—where she could make more cutting observations, no doubt. Just in her head, I hoped.

"You are looking even more beautiful. Your cheeks are pink and your hair is so soft."

Didu spoke in Bangla, weaving her fingers through my hair and lifting a bunch to feel it on her cheek.

Behind her, Kobita was hiding with a shy smile and a broom in one hand.

"Hasn't she, Kobita? Look at her. A beauty." Didu turned to the maid but didn't take her eyes off me.

"How are you, Kobita?" I asked.

I longed to hold her hands, this woman who helped raise me, who walked me to school when I was little and told me stories about her childhood in the village she rarely returned to. But I knew Kobita would flinch if I touched her.

In her mind, now that I wasn't a child, I no longer had any need for affection. Kobita's role in our household hadn't bothered me before, but now that I'd been living away from home, I couldn't help but scrutinize this—my family's decision to employ a woman for life. I knew there were millions of women in India, in worse positions than Kobita, who struggled to feed their children or keep themselves safe from abusive husbands. But I cared about *this* woman, who'd been handed a raw deal. I looked at her profile, studying her wispy sideburns, and wondered what she may have achieved if she'd gone to school, if her parents had had money, if she'd been born into my family.

"We are well, the usual, you know. You look so grown-up." Kobita giggled and Didu was pleased.

"I brought something for you," I said.

I rooted around in my handbag and brought out the little ziplock pouch containing hair clips, scrunchies, and glittery claws. If there was one thing Kobita was proud of, it was her long hair, which fell in a thick swoop down past her hips when she brushed it out before bed. It was soaked in coconut oil and tightly plaited now.

"Now look, isn't Durga so thoughtful?"

Didu was eyeing the pouch as I passed it to Kobita. I would later catch them poring over the contents like they'd found treasure. Kobita was the only one who never threw away gifts.

I handed Didu a box of chocolate truffles and a tin of biscuits. I waited for her reaction while she peeked in the bag. The way she pressed her lips tightly together told me all I needed to know—I had chosen well.

She handed them to Kobita and whispered to her to put them in her room, which meant Didu didn't want to share. Kobita would get a taste though, the same way I would later spot one of the silky scrunchies I gave Kobita holding Didu's bun in place.

"Your mother is in the kitchen. She's been cooking for you all day. She's been so busy with the wedding arrangements, but having you home fills us all with so much joy." Didu stroked my cheek.

I had barely passed the threshold but I was already bursting with the sorrow of having to leave in fourteen days. The TV was turned on in a different room. Outside, a man was banging on the wall of the house, putting up lights for the wedding celebrations. I heard Ma calling for Kobita.

"I've missed you, Didu, everyone."

We were holding each other as we took the stairs up to the balcony, where she wanted me to sit with her like our afternoons of old. Ma would bring us lunch and we'd watch people walking past the house, while Didu kept an ear on the reruns of her soap playing inside.

But she stopped me just as we were about to enter the balcony. "Durga, I have something for you too, a little present."

I followed her gaze to the tiny white kitten sleeping in a shard of sunshine. The wrought-iron railings made dark stripes on her spotless fur. She was curled up in a ball on the mat by Didu's rocking chair.

"I thought you would miss Kaju," Didu said. Since this was India, there was no doubt in my mind where the kitten had come from. Not from a dedicated animal rescue, but either found by Kobita on the side of the road during one of her strolls to buy groceries, or from one of our neighbors whose cat had delivered a large litter.

I was moved to tears. I was thinking of the cat I had lost, whom I hadn't had a chance to say goodbye to. The best friend I had to leave behind when I left home. I'd decided I wouldn't speak of Kaju during this visit because it would upset Tia right before her wedding. But now I was crying. Red cheeks, red eyes, body shaking. Projecting Jacob's loss on my cat who had died. I was using this kitten as the only means to display my true emotions.

"She is very sweet, very friendly. Come, Durga, you can give her a name."

I followed Didu, who sat down in her chair, and I kneeled in front of the cat. She woke up, yawning, looking at me with her glossy amber eyes. I fell hurtling into love.

MA RUSHED ONTO the balcony to greet me soon after my arrival from Ireland. She had a cardboard box of sweets which she opened in front of my face, forcing me to pick one.

She found it impossible to meet someone empty-handed. She arrived at people's homes with stainless steel containers filled with sweets or snacks she'd fried. On the odd days she'd collected me from school instead of Kobita, she thrust bags of roasted peanuts or lollipops in my hands.

She bumped into an old friend once at the wet market she bought her fish and meat from. It was my turn to accompany her that day, and apart from the slippery pathways and the lack of light, I found it to be an interesting place.

Ma chatted with her friend for ages and when it was time to part ways, she held out the chopped pieces of fresh poultry she'd purchased. Her friend didn't want it, and I was distressed by my mother's panic. Ma insisted that the gift be accepted, because she had nothing else to give her friend that day. The woman eventually walked away, reluctantly, with the bag of chicken, and we returned to the butcher to buy some more.

Today on the balcony, Kobita was hot on Ma's heels with a tray of cups of tea and bowls of samosas.

I couldn't hug her straightaway because she was carrying the sweets in one hand and a big bowl of khichudi in the other. It was for the best, because a hug might have brought on another bout of tears from us both. This way, while she and Kobita set up the food and pulled in a table and some chairs, it gave us time to settle into a feeling of euphoria.

"My sweet little Durga. Let me see that face of yours."

Once Ma had wiped her cooking hands on the loose end of her sari, she seemed better prepared to face me.

We hugged, I kissed her cheek, she laughed and fixed my hair.

"Your plants are looking well, Ma," I said.

Curiously, none of the potted plants that adorned the balcony had grown or changed shape since the last time I saw them.

"Oh yes, they're well looked after. Sit down. Eat. Arjun? Where are you, Arjun? Bring Parul. The food will go cold. Arjun! Kobita, go fetch the children."

Didu sat rocking in her chair and I positioned myself cross-legged on the cat's mat. She was happy to snuggle in my lap, and Ma smiled when she saw this. She must have had an old memory cross her mind, the way it did mine. An image of me on the floor with Kaju in my lap, Didu rocking above me.

"She's lost her tan, hasn't she, Meenu?" Didu spoke to Ma like I wasn't there.

"Yes, skin is glowing. You've put on some weight. Good. Are you eating?" Ma said.

"I don't get to drink proper tea in Ireland. This is going to be heaven," I said, reaching for a cup of freshly brewed cha.

Kobita returned with Arjun and Parul.

"I ate before I left for the airport, Ma," Arjun said.

It was typical how quickly he reverted to the role of a whiny teenager in the presence of our mother.

"It doesn't matter. That was hours ago. Eat with your sister. Parul, serve Durga, will you? Put away that phone."

Parul rolled her eyes, and I could empathize. When I was her age, when Parul was too small, I'd been bossed around by the elders to satisfy Arjun's and Tia's every whim, or any visitors' who came to our home. The baton had now been passed to the youngest.

I served a big helping of khichudi in a bowl for myself. Every family had their own unique variation of cooking khichudi. A recipe that smelled particularly of their home. Ma made ours with yellow mung beans and rice, fried potatoes, cauliflower, peas, and a variety of spices; all slow cooked in one pot for a fragrant melt-in-the-mouth wonder that had filled my childhood afternoons with comfort. I was grateful to find that this reverie had remained untarnished by my newfound independence.

Arjun and Parul took adjacent chairs, not as enthusiastic about the khichudi because they were still eating it several times a week. The kitten tried licking my plate and I made a tiny mound of khichudi for her on the floor. Kobita, who was also eating nearby, kept an eye on the kitten and would be quick to mop the offending spot as soon as we left the balcony.

Kobita was someone who would've appreciated Jacob's high standards of cleanliness. I had managed to spend hours without thinking of him, and now he was back.

In my alternate universe I spent a lot of my time alone. I had a ready-made life here, and I'd given it up. For what?

"How's Ireland? So sad your friend couldn't come. So sad about her brother," Ma said.

"Yes. Sad." I could feel my face flushing and I hid my eyes. I wished they hadn't mentioned Joy or Jacob at all. I wished I could continue to hide my feelings.

NOBODY HERE KNEW what Jacob had meant to me. They knew Joy's brother had died, which was why she'd canceled her visit to India. Other than a few questions about the circumstances of the death, they hadn't given him a passing thought.

My place in Cork was my very own, made up of things I had the luxury of selecting for myself for the first time. The bed linen didn't belong to my family. They weren't in the garish floral prints Ma had chosen for the home when she was a young bride. I slept with music playing and a bedside lamp on, without having to hear Baba remark on the rising cost of electricity. I skipped the meals I wasn't inter-ested in, and ate pizza on the couch if I wanted to. I had more than one side of a wardrobe allocated to my clothes, didn't have to wear out Tia's hand-me-downs. I had sex.

However, this was home too, no matter how many privileges of privacy I had to give up. Despite the discomfort of Kobita's employ-ment, my mother's fussing and nagging to eat more. Even though I had now begun to question the way of life that I'd taken for granted when I lived here, there was still a part of me that thrilled in the nostalgia of the innocent and easy days of my childhood.

IT WAS EASIER to forget Jacob here too. I wanted to keep it that way and changed the subject.

"Where's Tia? Is Baba at work?" I asked.

"Yes, Baba is at work. He said he'll be home early today," Ma re-plied.

"Tia is at the gym. She's been going every day, twice a day some-times." Parul sniggered as she spoke.

"Do you remember the last time she became obsessed with going to the gym?" Arjun said, followed by Didu tutting.

"When she failed the AILET, again," Parul said, then burst out laughing.

Tia had wanted to study law before she followed in our father's footsteps into accountancy. She sat for the national entrance test for law twice and failed both times.

"Don't you laugh at your sister. Nobody passes those accountancy exams at first try, and she passed all of them no problem." Ma glared at Parul but my younger sister had to put her bowl down, she was laughing so hard.

"Do you remember? Right after the second AILET results, she went to KFC and ate an entire bucket of fried chicken, then rushed to the gym to burn it off. Then she called Durga, crying on the phone, because she'd farted very loudly on the elliptical and every-one heard."

Some grains of rice flew out of Parul's mouth as she tried to sup-press her cackling.

Ma scolded her and tried to shut her up, but even Arjun was laughing now.

"Wait, so are you saying she's nervous about the wedding?" I asked.

Everyone fell silent, as though I'd raised the curtain too early be-fore the show, and they'd been caught in the act of getting dressed and moving the set around.

"Her favorite movie is *Runaway Bride*," Parul said with a shrug.

Chapter 19

I HAD TO WAIT TWO MORE HOURS BEFORE I SAW TIA.

When I was still living at home, I pinned my claustrophobic feelings mostly on her. For having to share everything, for not having a single personal thought untouched by her loud voice in my head. But as I waited on the balcony now, with Didu and Ma giving me the local gossip, I only half-listened to them. I grew impatient to see my sister again. Video and phone calls hadn't been enough. I couldn't wait to see her walk in with hips swinging.

In some ways, Tia was exactly like our mother. She never touched alcohol, had old-fashioned notions about the sanctity of marriage and familial duty, hated the idea of anyone being displeased with her, and was fiercely protective of me.

When we were younger, when I still thought Tia was a goddess descended to Earth, more Kali than I could ever be, she didn't hide her disappointment in my social anxiety. I had trouble finding things to say around people I didn't know well, and she'd nudge me with her elbow or shake her head while I struggled.

Tia, like Ma, had the ability to recall exactly how many children a distant relative had and the history of their physical ailments. She asked for updates, leaning in close, making encouraging remarks.

Baba got frustrated with me once. We had bumped into one of his colleagues in the queue at the bank. He had Parul in his arms and me lingering by his side. Ma had taken Tia and Arjun for haircuts. I hadn't been able to meet the man's eyes, and when he asked me friendly questions about school, I made no response and ended up in tears after he left.

When we were all home again, Ma and Baba were discussing the incident in raised voices in their bedroom. Ma insisted it was a phase I was going through, Baba was concerned I had nothing to offer the world. Didu and Kobita continued their game of Ludo in silence in front of the TV, which was playing a cricket match Arjun was glued to.

Tia and I had been given the responsibility to spoon-feed Parul her dinner. I kept my head down, but could feel Tia's eyes on me and her growing rage. I thought she was cross with me, that I'd finally done it now—proven I was an imbecile.

Tia threw the spoon and it went clattering on the floor, and she hauled her thirteen-year-old self to my parents' bedroom with hands in tight fists.

I could only hear her voice, because my parents had fallen silent in her presence. She yelled at them, telling my father he obviously didn't know me like she did.

"Durga is too smart to waste her time talking to your stupid friends."

It was the best she could come up with but it was enough to make Baba come groveling to me later.

"You don't have to talk to anyone you don't want to," Tia had said.

Tia returned to me, fizzing with indignation. Then she lifted the spoon off the floor and scooped some mashed vegetables off the plate and hovered it in front of Parul's mouth.

"And you need to start feeding yourself," she snapped at our sister, threw the spoon on the floor again, and stormed off to our bedroom.

Parul ate the rest of her meal without a fuss, and there were minimal tussles at mealtimes between her and Ma after that.

* * *

PERHAPS THIS WAS why I was comforted by Joy's loud and animated presence in my life now. I had always needed defending.

On the balcony, we heard the *tick-tick* of Tia's kitten heels up the steps. I jumped off the floor in anticipation, surprised by my own excitement.

Tia came in, in a fog of her signature Marc Jacobs scent. She wasn't one for subtlety, topping up her pulse points several times a day.

I embraced her violently, making her drop the phone from her hand. She huffed and acted inconvenienced when she had to pick it up.

"You said you'd come home twice a year," she complained, pulling me into another hug.

"Why haven't you visited me yet?"

I spoke into her shoulder. My sister was a slight woman with delicate buttery skin. She still had lines on the insides of her forearms, near the elbows. Like a chubby baby.

She was hairy as a teenager, and even though she was meticulous about getting rid of most of it from her arms and legs now, her cheeks were covered in bleached down. I examined her carefully, to make sure nothing had changed.

"If you want us to let you go back to Ireland, you'll have to come twice a year."

"You can't hold me prisoner here."

"You have a duty to your family."

"You won't even be here. You're getting married, remember?"

"Precisely why Ma needs you. In fact, you should move back home."

We were mock-quarreling, holding each other at arm's length.

I rolled my eyes and our mother stepped in. "We can talk about this later. Durga needs to rest. Come on, stop it, you two." She tried prying Tia's fingers off my arms.

"Oh, Meenu, let them be. This is what they always do. It's only play fighting," Didu said, rocking slowly in her chair.

"I'm not playing, I'm very serious. Durga thinks she can just forget her family. Her job is more important to her." Tia let me go and tidied the stray hairs off her face.

She would have said anything to distract us from the tears filling her eyes. Happy tears. I had some too.

"We are very proud of you, Durga, don't listen to her nonsense. You don't need to move back for us," Ma said, if only to temporarily put me at ease now. I knew she'd begin her campaign to bring me back home at a later time.

Tia crinkled one side of her mouth in thought. "I have to show you the jewelry. We got it all out of the bank lockers."

Ma had the family heirlooms safely stored in safes at the bank. It was our annual tradition to go check on them on Ma and Baba's wedding anniversary. The whole family went. One of the bank employees would hand Ma the key, then guide us down long dark corridors to an air-conditioned room. We were left alone in there.

I still remembered the excitement on Ma's and Didu's faces when she'd look for the safe and pull out the velvet boxes. Like in one of those Grand Theft films Arjun watched.

We'd huddle around the table, fingering the gold necklaces, amazed by the ruby and emerald studded bracelets. Ma had received them at her wedding, and she was going to pass them down to us. Between the four of us, we'd probably get two pieces each. Even as a child, they looked dusty and old-fashioned to me. I didn't have the heart to tell Ma I'd never wear them.

Tia grabbed my hand now, tugging me off of the balcony.

"Don't make me come in there and drag you out for dinner. It's in one hour, girls," Ma called after us.

I couldn't suppress a giggle as I chased Tia to our old bedroom. I'd knowingly given this up, having her with me every evening, her warmth beside me every night. What was I thinking?

At our bedroom door, Tia stopped, whipping around to block me from entering. "Don't be mad but you'll have to sleep on the floor tonight. I have all my outfits laid out on the bed. You're not allowed to move any of it."

I wasn't mad at her. I'd craved this. My sister's reign over the household. Her bossing me around. Her turning her nose up at my two-step skin-care routine when she had at least seven. Perhaps it was Stockholm syndrome, perhaps it was love, but I wanted Tia to tell me what to do with my life.

I shook my head. "I'll sleep anywhere. It doesn't matter, Tia. You're here."

She looked at me like she was disappointed in me. She had her eyebrows raised, head cocked, her lips stretching tightly.

"You should learn to put up a fight," she said.

TIA WANTED US to go shopping. The day after I arrived in Calcutta was the only day we had when there were no other wedding-related engagements.

When I asked her what she needed to buy, my sister told me she needed nothing, because all the wedding purchases had been made. But she liked to go shopping to expand her mind. In fairness, if anyone in the family needed a thing, they always asked Tia where to find it.

She knew about the wholesale market where the best priced cushion covers were sold, for when Ma was in a frenzy replacing all the old upholstery in the house. She knew about the locksmith in Gariahat for when Baba wanted to repair the clasp of a pocket watch he'd inherited. Didu rarely left the house anymore, and Tia kept a steady supply of white saris in her wardrobe. They were so perfectly matched that our grandmother had no idea they were being replaced from time to time.

"I just want one last day of doing nothing, of having nowhere to be and no commitments," she told me.

Ma wanted us to include Parul and I supported the idea, hoping to break down her cool exterior with some heart-to-heart, but Tia was adamantly against it.

"She's going to be on her phone the whole time anyway, Ma, and when she's not she'll be sulking."

Ma argued back, about how Parul felt like an only child because her siblings refused to include her in their lives, and could we really blame her for being a strong independent young woman and speaking her mind?

Tia got her way eventually, after she emotionally blackmailed our mother with claims of wanting to spend her last days of maidenhood the way she wished.

We took a taxi to Park Street and went for breakfast at Flurys first.

"I don't want any of this," I said, looking at the menu, which hadn't changed in decades.

An English breakfast, pancakes, omelet—none of these captured my imagination. I was craving mutton rolls and kochuris, against my better judgment. Tia told me I could watch her eat, and ordered baked beans on toast and a fried egg.

She didn't want to discuss the wedding because she was too overwhelmed by it, so we talked about the honeymoon. Apparently she'd convinced Bikram to cancel all the Switzerland bookings and they were going to Japan instead.

"I'm glad he let you have your way," I said. The sooner he learned this about his future wife, the easier life would be for him.

I was drinking a cup of tea, saving space for all the other things I wanted to gorge on later.

"It's a good sign, isn't it? Even though I know his father gave him grief over the money he lost, because some of the bookings were nonrefundable."

"He should have consulted you before booking everything, especially if he used his father's money."

"Durga, he wanted to surprise me." Tia was pouting, to show me how sweet she thought he was.

"I hope he doesn't surprise you with other major life decisions."

"Don't be negative. He's a romantic. He told me he's thinking of buying a flat, in one of those luxury complexes in Newtown. If he does, we can move out of his parents' home."

"You could chip in, then you could afford it easy."

Tia smiled at someone passing our table, as though she knew them. It was one of my sister's curious habits. A determination to make a pleasing impression on every stranger who passed through her life. With her dazzling smile, heart-shaped face, and natural confidence, it was impossible to miss her, even if they were passing by momentarily.

"I'm not an idiot, Durga. I'm saving my money. You know how Ma has to ask Baba every time she wants a new pair of shoes? That'll never happen to me."

Chapter 20

WE WENT TO A FEW CLOTHES SHOPS ON PARK STREET, then to the famous kati rolls that were sold through a nondescript window. Tia stopped to examine the counterfeit wares being sold by roadside vendors. Perfumes, designer bags, pirated books printed on cheap paper, cartons of cigarettes.

"Don't tell me you've resorted to buying this stuff to save your money, Tia. Do not use any of this fake makeup, please."

I was trying to pull her away, but she stood her ground, lifting up a pair of sunglasses that were identical to the popular Gucci cat-eye design. Complete with the gold logo and a cheap plastic finish.

"I'm curious. Sometimes they pass for the original."

She fixed them over her eyes. Tia had shopping bags hanging off the crook of her elbows; she was wearing an ankle-length paisley dress with a wide leather belt cinched at her narrow waist, her hair was held up in a messy topknot. I could picture her walking around Manhattan, in Lily Pulitzer, with not a prospective wedding date in sight. I had yet to submit to the idea of my sister settling.

I had my reservations about Bikram, even when we were much younger and he was a hormonal teenager with a squeaky voice that was yet to break into manhood. I'd pointed out the gummy festival bands he always wore on his wrists, in neon colors with the print rubbed off. Tia told me he used them as conversation starters and this displayed forethought. In my opinion, he was an unapologetic show-off, and like his father: a secret penny-pincher.

Tia put the sunglasses back and we walked away from the man listing out a descending series of price drops.

"You're right, I have a standard of living to represent now. You know, Bikram applied for membership to The Saturday Club. His uncles have nominated him. There's a four-year wait list, but we'll get in eventually."

Tia breezed past the other vendors, smiling at everyone.

I could have spoken about the stench of the post-colonial hangover Bikram's family gave off, but I refrained from it. It was not worth it, telling her how to live her life. Recently, she had stopped ringing to remind me to change my sheets and iron my underwear, even though she was the only one strongly against me leaving home. Even my parents hadn't been as aggrieved for as long as she was. But now she'd accepted my new life, of becoming an individual out from underneath her shadow. I wanted her to make her own choices too. My job was nothing more than to be her support system.

"So, after my wedding, will you meet with some of the men Ma has handpicked for you?" Tia said, as though she'd read my mind about her softening, and wanted to prove me wrong.

"No, I absolutely won't. That's not what I'm here for. I met Surjo like you all wanted. I've fulfilled my yearly quota."

"Just meet some of them. How long will you live like this?"

"I'm happy with my life, Tia. There's no need to feel sorry for me."

"At some point you'll regret it, wasting so much time when you could be building a relationship with a nice man. How can you leave your life up to chance? You know these dating apps people use now? They're nothing more than a glorified Nita mashi."

This would have been a good time to mention I *had* been dating someone. That my ex had died. I wanted to tell Tia because I knew that eventually, she would feel every ounce of my aching loss. But only once she got past my crime of not telling her about him when we first started dating, not calling her straight after I lost my virginity. When we were younger, we used to tell each other everything, and Tia believed I still did. That I was still that reclusive shy girl of fourteen who came to her sister for advice.

AFTER WE'D SPENT the day shopping and eating, Tia texted Bikram to see if he was free for a quick coffee with us. While I would've discouraged her from this before, I did want to see him this time. I couldn't be at peace until I'd witnessed them together, seen how he treated her.

We waited for Bikram at the Café Coffee Day outlet we used to frequent as teenagers. It was the first American-style coffee shop chain to have arrived in Calcutta, before Starbucks and others entered the market several years later. I went old school and ordered a supremely sweet cookie-flavored frappé, while Tia nibbled on a biscuit.

Bikram arrived in his noisy sports car and parked right outside the café doors. I saw how Tia's eyes lit up and that she sat straighter in her chair. I'd seen them together before, when we were younger, but always around our parents. Tia was never not excited to see him, her betrothed, but now she looked more sure of herself. All the plans were made, the flowers were bought and arranged, Bikram was as good as hers.

He strode in smiling, like he owned the place. Maybe he did. I knew his father had a large investment portfolio.

Bikram was all lanky and confident, in loose clothing with a large rock on his left ear. He had a thin mustache and a goatee, like he belonged in a hip-hop music video from the early 2000s.

I knew Tia had better taste than that, but she'd been under his spell for years, and I wondered if he was just a familiar habit for her.

I watched him lean down to hug her. It was a quick, casual embrace but Tia lifted herself up toward him. Basking in the glory of this public acknowledgment.

"Hey, Durga. Good to be back?" Bikram practically threw himself into the peeling leather couch they hadn't replaced in a decade.

"Yeah. How are you?"

"Excited!" Tia spoke for him.

He gave her a chuffed look, like she'd taken the word out of his mouth. He wasn't displeased, which stilled my worried thoughts.

"It's all getting real," he said.

"You won't be a bachelor anymore," Tia chirped in.

I sat in my seat, silent and anxious. I wanted to believe I'd judged him unfairly all these years, but my feelings toward him hadn't changed. He made me furrow my brows—with his fidgety hands drumming the glass-topped table between us, his furtive eyes unable to fix on a steady spot.

"Honestly, I can't wait," he said, throwing Tia a knowing smile.

"What? So I can dress you every day? He sends me a photo every morning for a fit check," she laughed.

I couldn't believe she'd approve of what he was wearing now, that she hadn't already tried to change his style. Since when had my sister become so accommodating of other people's opinions?

But they were looking into each other's eyes with such tenderness that my brain sparked and malfunctioned. This *could* be true love.

"So, you met Surjo." Bikram turned to me again, grinning.

"And heard about Chloe," I said, crossing my arms.

Bikram rubbed the back of his head, smiling, like he thought it was funny. I was certain he'd known about Surjo's girlfriend all along, but he'd allowed the farce to continue, allowed my parents to get their hopes up.

"Surjo didn't want anyone to know about her, so when they were setting you two up, Bikram couldn't say anything. Nobody else knew about the girlfriend, none of his other friends, his family. Even Arjun was baffled," Tia spoke for him again, jumping to his defense. He nodded along.

"And who put him forward as a possible match?" I asked.

Tia blinked twice, slowly, then turned to Bikram with a smile. This time she waited for him to respond. Thankfully, my sister had the sense to not lie for him.

"My mother. Your ma told her she was looking, and you know how much my mother loves Surjo," he said. "I did tell her it wouldn't work. That Surjo isn't ready to settle down." Bikram shrugged.

I got the feeling he wasn't telling the whole truth. I had to wonder if Bikram suggested I meet with Surjo just so he could have a laugh at his friend's expense, maybe even mine. He'd enjoyed putting us in an uncomfortable situation, knowing full well that Surjo was seriously involved with someone else.

I watched Tia closely for a reaction. Her cheeks were flushed and the skin on her forehead was wrinkled with concern. She composed herself quickly and smiled at me. "Anyway, it's all in the past now. We should really be getting home before Ma threatens to disown us."

She stood up with a flourish, smoothening out the skirt of her long, pretty dress. We said our goodbyes quickly and I noticed how Tia wasn't as lovesick leaving as she was coming in. I was sorry if I'd been the cause for the change in her mood this close to the wedding.

"You okay? Do you want to talk about something?" I asked. I knew I couldn't address the problem directly.

We were waiting for an Uber, standing next to Bikram's car. He was still sitting inside the cafe, on a phone call. Even though she was marrying him in a few days, Tia wouldn't have wanted our family finding out that she was meeting Bikram privately. Not that our parents would disapprove, but Tia didn't want to be bombarded with the questions and teasing.

Tia looked up from her phone, which she'd just used to order our taxi.

"What is there to talk about? I'm a blushing bride, can't you see?" Her smile was lopsided and unfocused.

"Tia . . ."

"You need to go easy on him, Durga. You promised you would.

He's a bit of an idiot sometimes, just immature. I'll whip him into shape in no time. You'll see."

All I could do now was trust she would.

WE RETURNED HOME in the late evening, to a state of chaos.

"Tia, we'll have to go to the Rajbari in the morning. The decorators have used marigolds instead of carnations." Ma was flustered, expecting Tia to overreact because of the mix-up.

We were putting our bags down on the dining table.

"It's fine, Ma, I don't mind. Now that I think about it, I like the idea of the marigolds. Retro, right?"

While an overexertion at the gym was a worrying sign, I knew my sister would have mentioned it to me if she was getting cold feet. No, she was prepared for this marriage, and a sense of unusual calm had befallen her.

Ma clearly hadn't been long acquainted with this side of Tia either. I hoped it was a sign of maturity, rather than the sense of acceptance that reportedly overcomes some inmates who are scheduled for an execution. Tia turned to me with a smile, and I nodded, while Ma tried to hide her shock.

Baba appeared in the room, ending his phone call.

"Oh good, you girls are back. Durga, let's take tea together? We haven't had a chance to talk."

We went to the living room with the cups of tea Kobita had made, and bowls of puffed rice mixed with chanachur, which Ma had pushed into our hands. Ma said she knew when we looked hungry, even before we knew it ourselves.

Baba sat on the couch, and I noticed how his belly had grown larger and was hanging over his belt now. His hair had thinned significantly and he had a bald patch expanding on the back of his head. Ma was looking after him the best way she knew how—furnishing a life of leisure.

He proceeded to quiz me on the mechanics of my life in Ireland. Was I comfortable paying the rent? Was my commute not too much of a hassle? Did my flatmate share the load of household chores? Could I really not afford a maid?

"Ma told me about Surjo Sengupta. Don't worry too much, we will find another match for you. A better one. He's a good boy but the girlfriend is a problem."

I wanted to laugh. He was making it sound like Surjo's girlfriend was only a temporary impediment. A hurdle easily resolved if I was willing to be patient.

"It's not a problem, Baba. He wants to marry her, and I'm happy for him."

My father shook his head. "Kids these days think they can decide for themselves. It's a lifelong commitment, marriage, you have to get it right."

"I'm not worried," I said.

"You should be! Durga, how long will you continue to live alone?"

"I don't live alone. Joy is wonderful. I love living with her."

"And one day she will get married and move out, then you'll be all alone in a foreign country."

It made me anxious, thinking about everything I was hiding from him. For his own sake, because he was too far gone in life to begin opening his mind to the idea of a different world.

"I'll get a new flatmate if that happens, Baba."

He threw a handful of puffed rice into his mouth. "Don't be silly, you can't live with women all your life."

He was grinning as he took a sip of his tea, blissfully unaware of the number of ways in which his statement was untrue. I could live with Joy forever if I wanted to. I did want to, if that's what she wanted. If we could get past this bump in our road, if she could forgive me for breaking her brother's heart.

I felt a rush of relief that Jacob had never met my father, that he wouldn't have to endure this, that Joy would be spared for at least another year. Then I felt guilty for having that thought. Maybe Jacob and Baba would have got along just fine, maybe I should have been brave enough to bring Jacob here.

I was embarrassed by Baba, as much as I loved him. He'd been a good father, the best he knew how, with good intentions. Tia was his favorite, his most beautiful and dutiful daughter, but he loved all his children. He honored his mother, respected ours. But he was born in a different time in India, and hadn't had the advantage of being educated abroad. He'd fallen into the cycle of marriage and children and work at a young age. Each day of his life was identical to the previous one.

It would be unfair of me to ask more of him.

Chapter 21

I TEXTED JOY A FEW DAYS BEFORE THE WEDDING, SINCE I hadn't heard from her at all. I asked if she was well and how she'd been spending her days. She replied several hours later, when I was in the middle of watching Tia eat.

The whole extended family and all our friends were at a hotel function hall that was booked for the *ashirbad*. The Bengali version of the token engagement ceremony, when the bride and groom are overfed and the bride is gifted gold jewelry and clothes by her future in-laws.

I had to excuse myself from my sister's side, in order to reread the message I got from Joy.

I'm fine. Are you having fun? I've been hanging with Maeve a lot lately. She's been a big help, Durga. You don't need to worry about me.

I was at a loss for words, and stood in the bathroom stall for several minutes, trying to come up with a response. For the first time since my return to India, I wanted to go back to Ireland. To stake my claim on Joy. Protect her from Maeve, who I was convinced was only temporarily stringing her along. I had been Joy's only source of emotional support for two years.

I gave up eventually, deciding I needed time to compose my thoughts. Just because she told me not to worry didn't mean that I shouldn't.

We all make poor choices in grief. In my desperation to escape it, I'd leaned on Luke. I didn't want Joy to make the same mistake.

I left the toilets, and found a man at the door, about to walk in. He nearly crashed into me and took a step to the side just in time.

"Sorry. Durga?"

I didn't think I recognized him at first, I was terrible with faces. I hadn't expected to see him here, or ever again.

"Surjo? Oh!"

He was wearing a pristine white kurta pajama with a blue embroidered collar, looking entirely different from our meeting in Cork, when I'd seen him in trousers and a loose shirt. The stubble was gone, he'd cleaned up for the wedding.

"Fancy seeing you here." He grinned.

"I was lucky to be invited. You know how hard it is to get on the guest list."

"Don't I know it. I had to call in some favors." His smile was boyish, radiating all over his face.

I was glad to see him, someone I felt comfortable with. As briefly as I knew him, it was like meeting an old friend.

"You're on holiday?" I asked.

"Bikram wanted me here. I hadn't been back home in two years and the pressure was mounting."

"Same for me, and I've been made to feel like a tyrant."

It was nice to talk to someone who understood. Surjo made for pleasant company. He was disconnected from the particulars of my life, so we could keep it casual.

"Nobody told me you'd be here."

"I arrived last night, wanted to surprise Bikram. I hope your family doesn't mind my being here, after us meeting up."

"Shit, sorry. They all know about Chloe."

Surjo shrugged. "It's fine. We broke up before I could propose anyway."

I stared at him with my mouth open. "Surjo, I'm so sorry. Are you okay?"

I was expecting him to be heartbroken, the way I was when Jacob and I broke up. But there was no pain on Surjo's face. He was smiling still, and not in a half-hearted way. This was just life, and he had accepted it.

"I have no intention of changing her mind. Our relationship had run its course."

His positivity was infectious—how he was able to simply move on. For a moment, I allowed myself to believe all was well, that I wasn't burdened by sorrow.

"I should go check on my sister now. Enjoy the food."

"I will. That's what I've come for."

"My mother will be pleased."

"It's funny how we all associate getting fed with our mothers."

I had to smile at that. I was glad I'd have him around for a few days, as much as I'd need to fend off my family's inquisitiveness.

He even smelled good. Pine trees and peppercorns.

"Well, I better let you go. I don't want you to piss yourself," I said.

As I walked away I heard him laughing, and I was smiling too. Surjo was single and I couldn't help but wonder if he was available.

I WAS DESPERATE to find out more about Surjo. But before I could allow myself to ponder this, I needed to confirm his status without asking him directly. As it turned out, Arjun was too occupied by a new love interest to give Surjo and me a second thought.

I spied my brother speaking with a pretty lady on several occasions, seeking her out specifically.

At first, I only caught glimpses of her through the throng of our relatives. She was in a dusty rose silk sari, her luscious hair was stylishly blow-dried and set to frame her face. When she had her back turned to me, leaning in close to speak with my brother, I noticed how low her blouse was cut. Her love handles were deliciously on display, between the blouse and the belt of her sari. They were like glossy soft dough. I understood the appeal.

I didn't recognize her and assumed she was one of Arjun's friends, but then I saw her standing with one of our cousins and his family at one point. They had plates in their hands, heaped with biryani and meat. She had a tender smile fixed on her face while the others spoke around her, but her mind was elsewhere, like she was thinking of someone else.

I found Parul scrolling on her phone, sitting on a chair wrapped in white linen. There was a gold bow tied around its back like a present.

"Who is that?" I said, hovering over her.

"Who?" Parul looked and sounded bored out of her mind.

I tipped my head in the woman's direction. She was with Arjun again, the two of them were smiling about something.

"The one in pink, talking to Arjun."

Parul's eyes roamed the room. "You call that pink?"

"Do you know her?"

"Sharmila? She's Priyam's new wife. You missed his wedding last year."

Parul sighed like I was taking up too much of her time. Like she was tired of having to do all the heavy lifting for the family.

"Is she an old friend of Arjun's? They seem to know each other well."

Parul's sharp eyes were on me, as though she was trying to discern if I was playing dumb. Then she shrugged and returned to her phone. "They met at her wedding, as far as I know. Arjun hangs out with Priyam sometimes, so maybe he knows her better now. Why are you asking me?"

I turned to look at my brother, and all my senses were suddenly attuned to the change in his demeanor. His face shone as he spoke to Sharmila. She was dainty in the way she fiddled with her gold earring. Arjun snuck in a close look when she turned her face from him briefly. She walked away from him in the next moment and he followed her with his eyes. He was filled with disappointment at her leaving, but there was nothing he could do because she belonged to someone else.

To be fair to Sharmila, she didn't proactively engage in any seduction. She remained humbly by her husband's side and only spoke to Arjun when he found her standing alone. It was shocking to me that my brother could get past this—that this woman had her duties, that she officially belonged to another man.

Arjun eventually busied himself with the task of feeding our guests, and I decided to take this opportunity to speak with him. The entire time our guests assembled at the tables to take their seats for the meal, I hung within my brother's peripheral vision. Surjo was keeping to himself, or rather out of my family's way. My gaze drifted to him repeatedly, wanting to know exactly where he was and what he was doing.

BABA STOPPED IN his tracks whilst walking past Surjo, then proceeded to make some joke out of my earshot, which led to the two men laughing and Baba thumping the younger man's back. I remembered how laid-back Baba was about Surjo's girlfriend. Had his prediction come true? Were our families still determined to throw us together?

But my mind drifted quickly away from Surjo when I saw my brother busy with our guests. I needed to speak to him about Sharmila, to get a sense of what he thought he was doing, becoming infatuated with a married woman.

Arjun didn't seem to notice my urgency. Even when I went up and tapped his shoulder while he was scooping biryani from a big hot pot onto a second cousin's plate. Tia had insisted on certain traditional practices to be followed at the wedding, which included members of our family personally serving the food. It had to be one of her attempts to remind us she was head of the household—putting us in a position where we were in service to her guests.

"Surjo Sengupta," I whispered in Arjun's ear, desperate for my brother's attention. I wanted to talk to him about Sharmila, but that would be a difficult subject to bring up.

"Not at all. That's not enough. Here, have some more." He scooped more biryani and covered our cousin's hands, which she had fanned over her plate in an attempt to block it.

"Surjo? What about him?" He finally addressed me.

Arjun moved one space to the next guest at the table, and I followed him closely.

"Did you invite him here today?"

Arjun ignored me in order to chat with the guest he was serving, then turned to me while holding the ladle up in the air. Rice grains fell on the floor between us.

"Yes, I did. He's just got here, to Calcutta. I wanted to catch up with him and he wanted to meet Tia before the wedding," he said.

Not unlike Tia, my brother too made friends easily. While Tia breathed her charm over everyone she met, made strangers feel as though they'd known her their entire lives, it was only temporary, only until she breezed as smoothly out of their range as she had come into it. Arjun, on the other hand, made friends for life. He was convivial in spirit, always had a broad range of interesting topics to bring up in conversation—the desert in Namibia that meets the ocean, the artificial rain generated over Dubai, some books he'd recently bought but not yet read. There was something for everyone. I wasn't surprised that Arjun and Surjo had become friends.

People didn't forget either of my siblings, even after a brief encounter. Tia was remembered for her beauty, for the gentle caring hand on their arm when asking after an ailing relative. Arjun for his sense of humor, his good spirits, for the interesting conversations.

Even Parul had a small but close group of friends she spent all her waking hours talking to. I was the only sibling who didn't seem to have these amiable qualities. I didn't feel the need to text a single friend that I was back in town. I'd posted a few photos on my socials, of Calcutta, wedding preparations, the food I was eating here. All the engagement I got on those posts were general and noncommittal. Nobody I knew from school or college had suggested we meet up. I knew this was entirely my fault. I hadn't bothered to keep in touch with old acquaintances. After several attempts made on their parts over the years—to grab coffee, go to the theater, attend birthday parties—and with my continued absence the invitations stopped arriving. I thought I was happy with my family. Didn't I have Joy now? But a friendly distraction would have served me well. Tia was a bride surrounded by her friends. Who would I invite to my wedding, if I ever had one?

All of a sudden, my wrist was hurting again. It hadn't bothered me in days and now it was back. I was reminded of why I'd wanted to leave Calcutta, the version of me I was trying to get away from.

I checked my phone but there were no more messages from Joy. I regretted not responding to her yet. If I lost her, I'd have nobody.

"Are things going to be awkward between you and Surjo?" Arjun asked.

"No, not at all. We spoke briefly. It's all good."

Arjun paused before he moved to the next guest, who was looking hungrily at us. His turn to be served so cruelly snatched from him.

"Great. I like him, he's a good guy."

Since he seemed to be in a good mood, I tried my luck with the other thing I wanted to say.

"Priyam's wife seems nice, she's so beautiful."

Arjun focused on the food again, ladling a pile of biryani on another plate. I watched him closely in profile, how he kept his eyes turned away from me. His hands didn't shake, not one bead of perspiration appeared on his forehead. I wanted him to tell me everything, to just be honest with me.

"Is she? Yeah, you're right, she's beautiful. Priyam is a lucky man."

He straightened up and our eyes met. He was being aloof, merely stating a fact. He even managed a smile.

"Arjun . . . is there . . ."

"Go grab the kosha mangsho and start serving, before Ma finds out you're slacking and uses that knife she brought from home," Arjun said, and returned to the task.

* * *

MA HADN'T BROUGHT a knife with her, but I'd nearly believed Arjun, and that was saying something.

I did, however, find her in the hotel kitchen, interfering with the cooking and preparations. The staff weren't being rude but the chef looked displeased, like he was moments away from snapping.

"Ma, let's leave them to do their job. Come out with me."

I tugged at her hand but she lifted the lid off a dish to give the food a sniff.

"Did you cook it with ghee?"

She turned to the nearest kitchen staff, who might have been a porter, because he ignored her and continued on his way with dirty pots in his hands.

"They're going to kick you out. Let's go," I tried again.

Ma looked around, attempting to catch someone's eye, but they all kept their heads down or talked among themselves. I finally managed to get her out of there.

"Why don't you try and enjoy the day and stop fussing for a minute?" I suggested.

Ma was tapping the big red bindi on her forehead to stop it from slipping. We'd gone into the changing room, so she could wipe the sweat off her face and check the arrangement of her sari.

"I just want all the events to go smoothly, and these people are always ill-prepared. Do you know we're running low on all the non-veg dishes? There won't be enough time to cook more and feed everyone."

"And you can solve this by taking matters in your own hands?"

"Why aren't you out there helping your brother?" she asked.

Ma was done fixing herself up and now she made for the door. I put my arms around her while she was turned away from me, placing my cheek where the blouse scooped down on her back.

While she patted my hand, I said: "Arjun doesn't need my help." *Actually, he did.* "Do you know Priyam's wife well?"

It wasn't a smooth segue and Ma turned to eye me suspiciously, as though it was ridiculous I would even ask her such a question.

"Sharmila? Yes, why?"

"Just curious. I haven't met her yet."

"Yes, because you missed their wedding. She's a sweet girl, you would know if you came home more often."

At first she sounded peeved, but she softened soon and reached out to stroke the sides of my hair, smoothening out my wispy sideburns.

"She visits regularly. She heard of my cooking and wanted to learn from me. You girls these days are so unprepared for married life. That girl couldn't even boil an egg when she first came to my kitchen, and now she cooks for the family every weekend. Elaborate meals."

"So she spends a lot of time at our home? With the whole family? Tia and Parul and Arjun?"

Ma was watching me closely, sensing I had more to say. But she didn't want to hear it. Whatever I'd observed pass between Arjun and Sharmila couldn't have gone unnoticed by Ma.

"She comes with me to the charity twice a week, to teach the kids how to read. Those poor children," she sighed. "Sharmila is so good with them, so patient."

I could now see why, when the subject of finding Arjun a match was brought up, he vehemently rejected it. He relied on a few tactical excuses. His most successful campaign so far was that he wanted to wait until all his sisters were married before settling in his own domestic bliss. The martyr card. Which worked on nobody other than Ma, who must have been in denial because she too had to have noticed the way he looked at Sharmila. A woman he could never have, because she would never leave her husband for his cousin. Unless she was willing to live through the scandal, to be ostracized by the community and her family.

"So she doesn't spend time at home with the others much?" I probed.

Ma huffed and gave me a look. She didn't want to acknowledge what I was implying. "I don't know, I'm not God, I don't see every-thing. Go see if your brother needs help."

Despite how lightly Ma was taking it, I was going to keep a close eye on my brother, the truth now revealed to me. Of this silent dance he was engaged in. Of looking but not touching. Of laughing to-gether and then parting ways. Of pining secretly for each other and pretending like the world didn't stop spinning around them.

Was Ma really that oblivious? Was she so blinded by her trust in her son, by her friendship with this young woman, that she couldn't see what was happening right under her nose? Arjun was having an affair with a married woman, and one wrong move, one instance of stupidity, could spin my entire family off its axis.

I immediately knew how this would affect my brother for the rest of his life. The niggling what-if wouldn't leave him, even if he settled down with someone else someday.

Chapter 22

THE DAY BEFORE THE WEDDING, OUR HOME WAS FILLED with people. We'd organized for Tia's Gaye Holud ceremony at home so Ma and Kobita could do all the cooking themselves.

Bikram and the rest of the groom's party were scheduled to visit us in the morning with gifts. The Gaye Holud ceremony itself was supposed to be reserved for Tia alone, where female members of the family were going to smear turmeric paste on her face and limbs to prepare her for the wedding day. A sort of old-timey spa treatment.

However, she didn't want to stick to the nuances of this particular tradition and wanted Bikram's family involved too. I suspected it was a cheeky way for her to cover Bikram in turmeric paste, and get physically close to him in front of all our family because now she had that license.

Sharmila arrived early morning to help Ma in the kitchen, and it was impossible trying to get Arjun out of there, even when all the guests began to arrive.

Tia, looking resplendent in yellow, was drifting around the house greeting people. Even Parul had little choice but to chip in. She carried food and cutlery to the dining table. Didu watched from the sidelines, while instructing Kobita what to do with the cushions and tissues and bottles of fizzy drinks.

I observed Arjun and Sharmila at the kitchen door. They were standing close together, smiling and talking in low voices. She was blushing like he'd given her a compliment.

"Where's Priyam and his parents?" I said. I was standing with Tia, keeping a close eye on my brother from a distance.

"They'll be here later," Tia said.

I knew I should have said something to her, tried to find out if she had her suspicions about them too, but this was the wrong time for that conversation. Tia enjoyed nothing more than to keep her siblings in line, and I didn't want to cause a scene.

A cousin came rushing up the stairs to announce that the groom's party had arrived.

Tia hurried to look out from the balcony, joining her friends.

I went up to Arjun and Sharmila, and they stopped talking abruptly, turning to me in unison. My brain was momentarily tricked into imagining them as a couple. He, with his round, good-natured face, her with her angelic looks.

We'd been introduced briefly that morning, before Ma hurried her into the kitchen.

"Is Priyam coming soon?" I asked, chancing a look at my brother. He was uncomfortable.

"Yes, he had to go to work in the morning, but he'll collect his parents from home and bring them here." She had a sweet voice to match her cherubic face, like a bird singing.

"I'm sorry I missed your wedding," I continued, trying to stress on the point that she was married.

"I know you're very busy. Arjun tells us all about you and your work. He's a very proud brother." She glanced at him shyly from under her lashes. "Ireland must be beautiful."

Arjun interrupted us. "Bikram is here."

Sharmila quickly slipped back to the kitchen, to give Ma the news, and also to get away from me. Arjun and I exchanged looks. I hoped he knew I wanted what was best for him, but he most likely didn't. Just like in every instance of a family member getting unsolicited advice, he would take it as me relishing in his misery. That I was worried about what the neighbors thought. It would sound banal if I told him I only cared about his well-being.

He went down to greet Bikram and his family, where Baba and some uncles were waiting. Tia and two of her friends were waving from the balcony, and Ma came out of the kitchen with a tray of sweets in her hands. Aunts and uncles were scattered about, and there was a celebratory chatter in the air.

I took a moment to breathe, to enjoy this moment amidst people I knew and loved.

I WAS EXPECTING Surjo to be a part of the groom's party, and found myself mildly vexed that he hadn't shown up yet. Bikram's group of eight were all in our living area, gathered around the dining table. After a short interval, Surjo finally appeared, supporting Bikram's grandmother on his arm.

She had a sturdy cane, which I'd seen her using for years to help with her arthritic leg. Either her condition had worsened severely since I last saw her, or she was pleased by Surjo's offer of assistance. Arjun rushed over with a chair for the old lady, soon to be Tia's grandmother-in-law.

Bikram's people were now in the process of carrying all their gifts to one of our guest bedrooms. Clothes, jewelry, perfume, boxes of dried fruit and sweets were going to be laid out on the bed for everyone to admire. An obnoxious flaunting of wealth if anyone asked me. It was another one of those old-fashioned traditions that Tia was eager to observe.

Surjo and I acknowledged each other, him with a big warm smile, me by pressing my lips together to suppress mine. As I busied myself helping Kobita with the tea, rearranging the tower of sweets, I sensed his quiet eyes on me. Under his scrutiny, I became very aware of the way I moved, the music my bangles made when they tinkled together. Either I was hungry and my stomach was protesting, or I had butterflies in there.

Once most people had gathered in the room with the gifts, only Surjo, myself, Didu, and Bikram's grandmother remained behind in the dining room. The two older women were sitting together, discussing the details of the next day's events.

Didu spoke with such nonchalance that anyone would have thought she didn't remember what the next day was going to be about. She made it sound like we weren't too fussed, and all the festivities were just being thrown together at the last minute. As though it was a pleasant coincidence that Tia's busy calendar happened to be clear so she could do Bikram a favor and marry him. The other lady put on similar airs, but couldn't match Didu. She made a comment about Bikram not being able to take much time off work because they couldn't do without him at the office, but it sounded forced.

I could have joined the others in the guest room, but I didn't. Surjo could have gone too, but he chose to come stand beside me at the table and reach for a cup of tea.

"So, any thoughts about marriage?" he said. When he saw the shock on my face he corrected himself. "I mean, Bikram and Tia getting married. Not us. Not that I'm saying we could never get married, just asking what your thoughts are in general. You know, about marriage."

Surjo took a flustered sip of tea, which I knew must have scalded his tongue, but he soldiered through it by blinking rapidly.

"I don't know if it's absolutely necessary anymore. Do it if it makes you happy. Tia has always wanted to marry, so I'm pleased for her."

I was enjoying watching him squirm. He'd seemed like such a tranquil person thus far, like the world and its rules didn't have a hold on him. It was particularly refreshing to see this side of him, that he too could experience embarrassment by putting his foot in his mouth.

I selected a fat shondesh from the plate in front of me, dark brown because of the jaggery, and broke it in two. It was stuffed with syrupy raisins and made a mess in my hands.

"I completely agree." Surjo held a fist to his mouth and tried relieving his throbbing tongue with a cough.

"You seem to be everywhere Bikram is. Does he rely on you a lot? Have you made it a habit to provide emotional support to all your friends?" I said.

"I think I have, and I'm proud of it. What are you like with your friends?"

Surjo forgot himself for a second and took another sip of the boiling tea. His face grew red, and he licked his lips bravely.

"Yeah, I have lots of friends," I said.

It was an exaggeration, and I felt foolish to have phrased it that way. Other than occasionally reading at cafés, I mostly spent my time accompanying Joy to places she wanted to visit.

"I'm sure you do. What do you like doing in your free time?"

"Don't get too excited. I spend most of my free time reading or listening to music. Are you one of those people with an obscure hobby?"

There was a long vein that bulged all the way up his smooth tan forearm. The full sleeves of his eggshell cotton kurta were rolled up to his elbows. Now that I was looking closely, it was obvious he worked out.

"Yeah, I collect eighteenth-century steel buttons, which I polish every night."

He was so specific I didn't know whether to take him seriously or not.

"You bought that? No, I read recipe books. I especially love finding old handwritten ones in charity shops."

Surjo put the cup down on the saucer he'd left on the table, giving up on the tea. He wiped his scorched mouth with an arm.

"And you are in fact right about my friends, they do seem to depend on me for emotional support. I don't know how to get them to stop. Now that I'm in Calcutta again, they have me booked for their poetry readings and whatnot," he said.

"I wouldn't attend a poetry reading if my best friend paid me to."

"Good to know you have friends," Surjo said.

"Just the one."

I ate the rest of the shondesh self-consciously, while he watched me. I took tiny bites and dabbed away the sticky granules from the corners of my mouth. I couldn't tell if he wanted one himself, or was simply enjoying watching me eat. Maybe I was imagining it but I could have sworn he looked like a man whose mouth was watering.

I found the strength to hold his gaze, questioningly. If he had something to say I wanted him to take the plunge now. I wasn't made of time.

"I couldn't interest you in an art exhibition, then?" he finally said.

I waited a beat, expecting him to burst the bubble with a joke about how it wasn't a real invitation and that he didn't appreciate art of any kind. Instead, Surjo waited with me, allowing the old ladies' chatter to fill our silence.

"Durga? Do you have that video on your phone? Tia's dance performance from last year's Rabindra Jayanti?" Didu called out to me.

Somehow, the tables had turned between the two women. Didu was the one struggling now, making a juvenile attempt to prove she had the more accomplished grandchild.

I took my phone out and scrolled through the gallery for the video. After I'd handed it to Didu, I returned to Surjo, who still appeared to be awaiting a response.

"I can get you some ice," I said.

"What?"

"For your mouth. You've burned it."

He looked down at the teacup and nodded.

"Ice would be nice. Hey, that rhymes."

"You'll enjoy your friend's poetry reading," I said.

He followed me to the fridge and waited until I'd placed two ice cubes in his hand. He had soft hands, which he used to hold the ice to his lips.

"I don't have much free time, but I'll go to this exhibition as long as you don't expect me to discuss the art," I said.

"I want to go for the free food," he said.

He was speaking my love language.

THAT NIGHT IN our room, the last night Tia would spend in our family home, neither of us could sleep. We'd been talking about the next day. She was excited about the life she was going to have, her new life with a new family. I wanted the best for her, and didn't want Bikram to disappoint my sister.

"I want you to be happy," I finally said.

I was sitting on our shared bed, while Tia sat at the dressing table, brushing her hair.

"Of course I am. This is the day I've been waiting for. And I want you to be happy too. I saw you talking to Surjo today."

"I wasn't expecting him to attend the wedding. We're friendly."

Tia raised her eyebrows. "Everybody knows he's broken up with that girl, Durga. Was it because of you?"

"I don't think he gave me a second thought until he saw me the other day at the *ashirbad*," I said.

Tia put down her brush and turned to me. She seemed so child-like all of a sudden, in the pink floral nightdress she'd owned since she was a teenager.

"I can't say I'm his biggest fan, after what he did, meeting you when he already had a girlfriend. But Arjun and Bikram have both insisted he's a good, reliable man. He's losing his hair but there are transplants for that."

"We've been talking, that's all. I find it easy to talk to him."

We smiled at each other and she stretched her arms up high over her head and yawned, reminding me again of when we were children, how she'd let out this big yawn in the darkness of our room, and be sound asleep seconds after.

"Just keep an open mind, Durga. Don't resist fate."

Chapter 23

TIA WAS MARRIED THE NEXT DAY.

The wedding venue was a Rajbari, an old palatial home passed down through generations of landed gentry. They were distant relations of ours, and Baba was able to strike a reasonable deal.

We spent the morning getting our hair and makeup done, then Tia was dressed in red and gold, and all the jewelry Ma had taken out of the lockers, and then some. She looked beautiful, like the true Goddess Durga from my childhood imaginations of her.

In the late afternoon, the groom's party arrived and they were greeted at the gates by Ma with a tray of incense sticks and sweets. Parul, some of our cousins, and I stood back, watching the reception ceremony.

Bikram was dressed traditionally too. He wore a white and gold dhoti on the bottom, but couldn't bring himself to remain bare on top, so he went with a white tank top instead.

He was joyful, and laughed when the younger cousins wrestled him out of his leather sandals and ran away with them. He'd end up paying a ridiculously large sum of money to bribe them back. The children in the family usually made a good bit of money at weddings.

The ceremony itself was long and slow, and carried on for several hours. It was like attending a large fair; you made your way around, sometimes checking in on the main attraction, which carried on in the background, while you sampled the food and other entertainment.

Parul was appointed as sentry, but Tia engaged more with her friends who surrounded her. The rest of the family milled about the place, making sure all the guests, especially the groom's side, were being fed well and looked after.

The priest sat with Tia and Bikram, around a low-burning pyre, whilst reading from the Holy Scripture. He made them repeat verses in Sanskrit that neither of them could interpret or pronounce correctly. It was mostly the older generation that kept the couple company, making sure all the rituals were being adhered to.

I hovered near her, anxious not about the correctness of the ceremony, but that it was all getting too real. My sister was married. Tia twisted her arm behind her, grabbing the bottom end of my sari and yanking me forward.

"What is it?" I gasped, panicked that she'd changed her mind. That she wanted me to put a stop to the ceremony.

"You're making me nervous. Stop pacing about. Why don't you go find Surjo?" Tia hissed in my ear. She glared at me, while keeping a big smile frozen on her face for appearances.

"I want to stay here," I pleaded like a child.

"This will go on for hours. Take a break and come back later. I'll be fine without you."

Baba had to sit with them for a little while, holding Tia's hand and reciting in Sanskrit. I couldn't leave her side yet and watched our father hug her when his bit was done. My sister had tears in her eyes. Before I could step in, one of her friends brought out a tissue so her makeup wouldn't smudge. She was right, she didn't need me here.

It must have been strange for Tia and Bikram, I thought—going through school and life knowing exactly what this day would look like for them.

We all laughed when Arjun and some of our male cousins had to lift Tia up on a wooden seat and carry her around Bikram seven times. This bound them together for seven rebirths. She had to hold two betel leaves in front of her face and then slowly remove them, which was, in the olden days, the first sighting between bride and groom.

It was a horrible thought, that for generations this was the moment when a couple saw the face of the person they would spend the rest of their lives with. Seven lives. Tia winked at Bikram when they gazed upon each other's faces, and that lightened my mood.

Garlands of flowers were exchanged and more chanting ensued. Female members of the family blew on conch shells, a tricky skill to master.

Everyone gathered around the happy couple to watch them take seven turns around the pyre; locking in the rebirth contract. Some grains of puffed rice were thrown in the fire. Then the marriage was sealed with Bikram smearing vermillion powder along the middle parting of Tia's hair.

I thought this would've been a good moment for applause, but everyone simply drifted away, now that it was done and the food could be enjoyed without distraction.

I overheard Baba telling his brother that his life's duty was accomplished. His brother reminded him it was only temporary relief, since he had two more daughters to worry about. A reminder that my family was still steeped in that mindset. The rest of the world had moved along, freeing themselves of the shackles of duty and tradition, but they hadn't. My father lived by rules from a different time, and I was reminded of Jacob again. What he would have made of this wedding ceremony with all its archaic rituals. If I'd brought him here, would this have been the final straw instead? Watching my family celebrate the giving away of their daughter to a man undeserving of her?

Tia and Bikram were led to the ornate velvet seats set up for them near the banquet tables. Guests would go up to the couple, carrying gifts and taking pictures. It was Tia's time to truly shine and do her magic, while Bikram looked proudly on, having married a woman adored by all.

When I saw Surjo walking toward me, I was relieved. He was dressed for the occasion, in a fawn silk kurta and white traditional dhoti. He looked regal and strong, like an aristocratic poet of old Bengali nobility, descended from kings. The gold buttons on his kurta dazzled in the bright lights, which were strung to form a canopy above us. Some people turned to look at him as he headed straight for me.

I'd been overwhelmed by the air of celebration, the crowds of people I didn't recognize, a sense of doom. But now that I'd seen him I was calmer, almost happy.

"You look beautiful," he said, smelling as divine as ever.

"In this old thing?"

"If my mother were here and she saw you, she'd be hunting all your relations so she could lock down an engagement contract."

I laughed, pleased he would think that, and glad he was only joking. That we *could* joke about this together.

He took the chair beside me and we sat facing the married couple.

"So, I'm leaving for Ireland in a week. How long are you here for?"

"Another two weeks. My parents are thrilled Chloe is out of the picture now. They have girls lined up for me to meet."

Surjo was speaking with the same composure as before, like this was water off a duck's back. I was enraged on his behalf.

"And are you meeting these women? You're just going along with it?"

"You did, didn't you?" Surjo crossed his legs. His leather sandals were new, bought especially for his best friend's wedding.

"I only met you, and I'm not going to meet anyone else. I'm done."

"So I ruined it for all the men who've been waiting eagerly," he said.

"It's not just you, it's nothing personal. I've done my part and it didn't work out."

Surjo smiled at Bikram, who'd spotted us from his throne on the makeshift stage, then he turned to me again. He even went as far as to touch my hand, which was on my lap. As brief as that touch was, and despite the topic of our conversation, I fizzed with excitement. His touch was warm, caring. He'd be a great hugger, I thought.

"I'm here for a short time, I'll meet whomever they want me to meet. I'm doing it to please my mother. They can't force me to marry. But they wouldn't have to put a gun to my head if it's you."

I blushed at that, my annoyance was slipping.

"We hardly know each other, Surjo." I returned to my old habit of clicking my tongue. I wanted him to think his words didn't affect me, that I wasn't foolish enough to take him seriously.

"You're right, we shouldn't skip the fun part of our origin story."

When I didn't respond, Surjo rubbed his forefinger with his thumb, as though making an important mental calculation. "You seem agitated about something," he said.

"This wedding has me on tenterhooks. I can feel the pressure from my family, reminding me I'm next. I hate that I even give a shit what they think. And now you're saying we should just do what makes them happy."

"We don't live at home. It's easier for us to do their bidding, isn't it? Just for a while, just to keep the peace."

"I feel like I'm hiding away in Ireland, but reality is waiting for me here. That one day soon, I'll have to return, to where I belong. They have it all mapped out for me."

I inched my hand toward his, a bold move in my books. He took it and we weaved our fingers together in a strong clasp. I thrilled in his touch. I was aware of a shift in me, as a person. First with Luke, and now with Surjo. I'd never pictured myself as the person making the first move. Perhaps I'd matured, perhaps losing Jacob had instilled a sense of urgency in me.

Surjo kept looking straight ahead, like he didn't want to fully commit and acknowledge the hand-holding yet. He stared at his friend and his new bride. They were accepting a big wrapped box from a group of relatives and doing a good job of keeping up their enthusiasm.

"I think our origin story should be Fake dating. Tell your family you and I have hit it off, that we're hopelessly in love and soon to be engaged. It might keep them all off our backs for a while," Surjo said.

He looked at me and the spell broke, I slipped my hand away. He had a knack of easing my burdens, reminding me it didn't have to lay so heavily on my shoulders alone. I'd found an ally in him.

But I knew I wouldn't be able to carry out the ruse for long, having always been a shifty-eyed liar.

"I'm terrible at pretending," I said.

"Well, I'm open to not pretending."

Arjun appeared, and I was glad to see Sharmila wasn't with him. He sat down in the empty chair on my other side.

"I still can't believe it, I won't have to listen to Tia singing in the shower every day," he said, gazing at Tia and Bikram on their thrones.

Surjo leaned forward to look at him past me. "That bad? I should warn Bikram."

"Or trip over all her shoes scattered around the house," I said.

"She'll be so good for Bikram," Surjo said. I turned to him and he was smiling in a way like he was consoling me.

"Yeah, what Tia needs is a new project. As far as she's concerned, she's done her job with the rest of us," Arjun said.

Ma and Baba were rushing over to us, Parul trailing a long way behind, scrolling through her phone. Ma's face was flushed with exertion and Baba appeared downcast, with pride and sorrow.

"There you two are. Look, it's all done, the guests are starting to leave. Arjun, go stand at the entrance and shake hands. Durga, ask everyone if they've eaten enough." Ma always had orders to give.

Baba sat down heavily beside Arjun to examine his daughter. "Doesn't she look beautiful?"

I became astutely aware of how close Surjo was to me, that he was now in the middle of my family.

"Do you need me for anything, Auntie?" Surjo spoke up.

Ma looked at him, startled, like she was noticing him here for the first time. "Oh, yes, Surjo, how are you? Such a good boy. You mustn't lift a finger. You're with Bikram's family." She smoothened the front folds of her sari and shot a look at Baba.

"I'm happy to help. I'm not taking sides." Surjo chuckled.

I expected Ma to snap at him, as she would have done with one of her children, reminding us to do what we're told. However, she seemed to warm to him, smiling and nodding with him. Surjo's easy charm soothed her, like he'd successfully enveloped her in his soft glow of positivity.

"Yes, we're all family here. Why don't you go with Arjun, see off the guests."

She grinned at Arjun, even though she was giving him a command.

The two men got up and left together, laughing about something, just as Parul finally made her way to us and sat down in one of their seats. Baba had yet to say another word, still transfixed by the sight of this beautiful bride he'd created.

Ma and I were both tracking Surjo amidst the people around us.

"He has a nice way about him, that boy, doesn't he?" Ma said.

I could feel Parul's eyes on me so I dared to look at him.

"Who? Surjo Sengupta?" Parul said, not taking her eyes off me.

"Yes, something very neat about him, so charming and polite. He was sitting with Didu this whole time, keeping her company, fetching her plates of food," Ma continued.

Parul's stare turned into a knowing smile and I begged her with my eyes to not say anything. To not ruin this moment with one of her caustic comments—about how she'd noticed us talking, me laughing or, worse still, blushing, us holding hands.

"Yes, I like him very much," Parul said.

And even Baba turned to gape at her.

* * *

WE RETURNED TO our home that night in eerie silence, all of us. It was as though it had finally dawned on my family that Tia had unwittingly slipped through our fingers.

Ma caught sight of an abandoned pair of slippers that Tia reserved for wearing around the house, sitting by the front door. She broke into tears, stepping backward out of the door. Baba grabbed her shoulders, holding her in place.

"I'll run over to their house and bring these to her. She'll need a pair," she cried.

Ma had withered in size, and Baba held on to her until she allowed him to envelope her.

"If they don't have slippers for her, she'll wear one of her hundreds of other shoes, Meenu. You don't have to go there at this time of the night," Didu said. She was trying to put on a brave face.

"Let's save these for her, yes? So she has something to wear when she visits us," Baba said, forcing Ma's face down to his chest.

Didu looked away, and Kobita covered her face with her hands and ran up the stairs to hide her own tears. Arjun huffed loudly, looking helpless in an attempt to remain calm. He used to cry easily as a child, but I hadn't seen him shed a tear in recent years.

Why did you do it? I wanted to ask them. Why had they arranged this marriage for Tia? Given her no hope for an alternative life? Raised her to believe this was all she had in store for her future. They'd essentially gaslit her into wanting this new life.

Ma and Bikram's mother were pregnant together, and the families often made jokes about how wonderful it would be if their children married.

Baba and Bikram's father had been friends since school and had kept in touch over the years. Our family was middle-class; Baba inherited this house and nothing else, held down a reliable accounting job over the years, and kept us comfortable. Bikram's father was born into wealth and took over the family business of manufacturing car parts. The two men had different qualities of life, but they'd valued their friendship.

In some ways, I'd always felt like the poor relations. Bikram's mother bought us expensive clothes on our birthdays, brought us back fancy toys when they returned from trips abroad. Baba didn't notice, but I watched the embarrassed expression that crossed Ma's face. She had to force herself to thank them for the gifts, to encourage us to be grateful.

Maybe she'd just gone along with the plan. Caught up in Baba and Didu's excitement when Tia was born, three weeks after Bikram. The two newborns were introduced and Bikram's grandmother had declared it was fate. That now our families would be bound forever. Baba and his friend had clapped each other's shoulders, overjoyed. But even when Ma told the story to us over the years, she sounded hesitant, like she regretted it, signing her daughter over to them.

Tia and Bikram were infants, voiceless, innocent, and unaware that their futures were sealed.

I looked over at Parul now, who was on the other side of the threshold, stuck behind the still embracing Ma and Baba. She met my eyes and I noticed her dramatically trembling bottom lip, and I slipped past my parents to reach for her.

There was a chance she would brush me away, but instead, she fell into my open arms. I swung her gently from side to side.

"Oh, Parul. You should text Tia. Tell her you'll miss having her around all the time," I said.

"She'll laugh at me or tell me to get off my phone. I want her to be happy but it feels like they've taken her away from us."

Parul was whispering so our parents wouldn't hear. It was heartening to hear someone else in the family sharing my thoughts.

"Stop it, you two. Tia has a husband now, she belongs in his family. If you want her to be happy then you'll wish her a long and peaceful married life," Ma snapped at us. She'd composed herself and wriggled out of Baba's grasp.

Baba went to help Didu up the stairs, and it reminded me of how Surjo had assisted Tia's grandmother-in-law. How Ma said he'd sat with Didu all through the wedding. I wondered what else the two men had in common, besides coming to the aid of old ladies. Arjun followed them, bringing up the subject of what they would do with the leftover food.

"She will be fine, Durga. Arranged marriages are not as monstrous as you might think they are. I couldn't have found a better man to marry than your father."

Ma was speaking while fixing my hair, dabbing my lips to check for moisture because she worried they dried easily.

Yes, all these years later and I still saw them acting like lovesick teenagers when they made up after arguments, which was nearly on a daily basis. Baba never entered the kitchen, because Ma forbade it, and he gave her foot rubs every night before bed because he thought she worked too hard keeping the household and the charity running. Their duties were clearly defined and separate, but they appreciated each other's roles in the marriage. She was right, it did work sometimes, and I hoped it would work for my sister.

"I know what you mean. Modern dating is as good as an arranged marriage in a lot of ways. You meet someone who fits all your criteria and then you enter a legally binding contract and hope for the best," I said.

"How would you know about modern dating?"

"I've been on dates, Ma. I don't live in a cave."

I had a smile on my face, but it was the same eager one a young teacher has when they meet their teenaged students for the first time. Desperately hopeful for acceptance.

Ma squinted as she stared me down. I began to pray, for the first time since I'd finished sitting for school examinations. The last thing I needed to hear from her were phrases like *hanky-panky* or *funny business*.

"I hope you know what you're doing, Durga. I wouldn't want you involving yourself with someone who isn't right for you."

It was progress. It was a much more acceptable response than the one I was expecting.

"I'm going to an art exhibition with Surjo Sengupta."

She raised her eyebrows in surprise, then looked away, needing a moment to think about it.

"Okay. That's good. If you marry him then you and Tia will remain close for life."

I wanted to tell her I wasn't planning on allowing my sister to grow distant either way, but Ma was already taking the stairs. Tia's slippers were in her hands, she was carrying them lovingly like she would a baby bird, taking them to her nest of precious possessions at the back of her wardrobe.

Chapter 24

I T WAS THE AFTERNOON FOLLOWING THE WEDDING, AND I hadn't left my room yet. This was my childhood bedroom, the one I'd shared with Tia all my life. Now she was gone and had taken most of her belongings with her. All her clothes, her books and shoes, her jewelry and makeup, her old stuffies and dolls, even the pair of scissors and collection of ballpoint pens we used to store in a chipped coffee mug. The only things left behind were the posters of the Backstreet Boys and Jennifer Aniston taped to her side of the room, and the study material from her failed law exams.

I'd spent my childhood longing for a private space, but now it felt too big and worthless.

I was lying on the bed, with my knees folded up, reading an old Archie comic book. Tia had divided up our collection and taken her half. Joy rang me then, probably because I hadn't replied to her text.

"How was the wedding? Have you been busy? Did you see my text?"

I would've been more enthused to speak to her, but I found I was too sad about my sister leaving. Joy had caught me at a bad time, feeling sorry for myself.

"Hi, yes, I saw it. Tia is now officially married and no longer our problem." I could tell the joke made Joy glum.

I pressed my eyes closed and wished I could think of something else to say. We'd both lost a loved one recently, but not in the same way. Was I being insensitive by not being happier for Tia? For the very fact that she was still alive?

"Sorry, I shouldn't have said that."

"It's fine, you're allowed to talk to me about your siblings."

"How's work? How's Maeve?"

Joy's voice changed, she sounded happier. "Work's the same, but let me tell you, Maeve is not the same girl you knew. I don't know what's happened but she's become very attentive to my needs."

"Is this a sex reference?"

Joy laughed in that way she had, with contagious abandon. I could picture her with her mouth wide open, one hand stroking her long neck as her voice became hoarse from the loud laughter. I was happy to hear it, that she maybe felt lighter now.

"I mean, she made me breakfast in bed this morning. She's been picking wildflowers and bringing them to the flat. We now have flowers in the old wine bottles, Durga."

I could feel the full force of Joy beaming through the phone, and I didn't know what to say. I was tempted to tell her about Surjo but it somehow felt wrong to bring up the presence of another man in my peripheral vision. I was afraid of reminding her of Jacob.

"In fact, I took your advice and we're on a strict no-alcohol policy, so we can get all the talking done. I know you'll be surprised to hear this—we haven't argued once."

"That's good progress," I said.

Unlike with Jacob and me, when the three of us lived in our own little world, I knew I wouldn't be invited to be a part of Maeve and Joy's. This fear was in the forefront now and I didn't like myself for thinking it.

"So what's happening now? Are you officially dating?"

"We're taking it one day at a time. Our friendship is equally as important as being in a romantic relationship. Besides, we've known each other so long, I don't know if we could ever go on traditional dates. That would be too weird."

"That's very mature of you. I like the sound of that."

I rolled onto my side and stroked the kitten's forehead. She was the kind of cat who fit well in my life. Not needy or even very attentive, but she was always there in the vicinity, just an arm's length away.

"Tell me about *you*. How was the wedding? Send me pictures."

"There was so much food! Tia is living in a different house, sharing a room with a man for the first time in her life."

"Oh Lord. She's going to get acquainted with the smell of his farts for the first time too. It could make or break her marriage, depending on her pain threshold."

"You know, once Jacob farted so loud and strong that I felt a tremor and it woke me from my sleep. We laughed about it, but it got me wondering if I could live with that smell and the force of it for life. What a dark marital secret I would have to carry," I said.

Toilet humor was my family's way of dealing with uncomfortable situations and awkwardness. Some people giggle at funerals, my siblings and I mumbled rhyming words for bodily excrements at Didu's sister's memorial. Joy knew me well enough to guide the conversation in this direction. The fact that she hadn't broken her phone in fury, or burst into sobs at the mention of her brother was a good sign.

"Speaking of farts, you miss me at all? Sorry I was such a bitch the last few days you were here. I was still processing everything, I think," she said.

"You don't have to apologize, I get it. It sounds like you're feeling more settled now, and that's good to hear. I do miss you, Joy."

"You're going to be back soon. Just a few more days to go."

"Parul and I had a moment, by the way. I think she's sad about Tia leaving. I might have successfully comforted her, because she asked if I'd like to hang out with her sometime."

"Maybe she's not sad about Tia. Maybe she's just been waiting for her to get out of the picture so Parul could have you all to herself," Joy said.

I allowed myself a brief moment to imagine this being true, but the reality was that if Parul sought the approval of anyone in the family, it was Tia's. As did we all.

"It's been nice here. I didn't realize how much I've missed being home, having family around, you know? Not having to think about what to cook, not having to go grocery shopping."

Joy hmm'd like she understood and then stopped abruptly. "Are you considering staying?"

I enjoyed the guilty pleasure of hearing the panic in Joy's voice. I liked being reminded that she still wanted me back.

"As convenient as it would be, I can't live at home. I'd miss you too much."

"Okay, I have to go now but I will hold you to that. Email me your return ticket so I have the flight times at hand."

There was a knock on my door.

"Durga, Ma wants to know if you'll be joining us for lunch. There are leftovers from the wedding." Parul was at my door.

"I have to go too. We'll talk later," I whispered to Joy.

Our call ended but I knew I'd be thinking about her all day.

THAT EVENING I went for dinner with Arjun. We kept it casual the whole time we were eating. I spoke about work, he gave me cricket updates. I told him about the pub scene in Ireland, and he educated me on the correct way to pour a pint of Guinness. When he told me he was thinking of visiting me at Christmas, I was overjoyed. I couldn't wait to have my brother there with me.

But there was something I needed to talk to him about. I hadn't wanted to dampen our dinner, but time was running out. In the car on our way home, while he was driving, I finally said the words I knew would ruin our evening.

"Do you have feelings for Sharmila?"

"Durga, she is our cousin's wife."

"I know the facts, I had a different question."

It was easier to talk about this in the car, when we didn't have to look at each other.

"We get along," he said.

"That still doesn't answer my question."

"Has Tia put you up to this? Has Ma?" He was angry now, tightening his jaw and his grip on the steering wheel.

"I haven't spoken to them about it. Just tell me the truth, please."

"I am trying to be a good friend to her."

"Why?"

"Because she needs friends. She is in a lonely marriage, without anyone on her side."

Uncharacteristically, Arjun made a sharp turn without indicating. He was always the one complaining how other road users flouted the rules. This was how I knew how deeply affected he was by Sharmila.

"Are you more than friends?" I asked.

"They're giving her a hard time, about not being able to conceive. It's not even her fault. They did all the tests, it's Priyam, not Sharmila. But he doesn't want his parents finding out because it would make him less than a man somehow. So he encourages them to continue making snide comments about her health and body. It's horrible. I wish I could do something for her."

I felt equal parts horrified for him and sad for Sharmila.

"Arjun, what could you possibly do?"

It took a few moments for the pieces to fall together.

"Arjun, no. Are you thinking of . . . I don't know . . . goodness! You're not planning on doing the job, are you? You really want them to raise your child? How will you stay away?"

He stared straight ahead, but from his neutral expression I knew he had considered this option.

"And Priyam would know. He would know someone else made the baby with her. He would make both your lives miserable!"

"Will you relax? I'm not going to do it," Arjun hissed.

"Promise me. You need to stay out of it. If anything, encourage her to leave the marriage. Not so she can be with you, but for her own safety and peace," I said.

Arjun had tears in his eyes, but he blinked them away.

"I tell her every day. She's not brave enough. Priyam won't make it easy if she asks for a divorce. He has connections and money. And she won't have the support of her own family."

I felt the urge to go over there, to physically take Sharmila out of that house, bring her to Ireland with me. But that wasn't practical or even possible.

"I'm sorry this is happening to Sharmila, but you need to keep your distance."

"I can't just leave her to deal with it on her own. She doesn't eat or sleep, and they badger her all day about this damn baby. The worst part is Priyam would make a terrible father."

I was never close with Priyam the way Arjun was, but I took my brother's word for it.

"I know you've never wanted to leave home, Arjun, but maybe it's time that you do. You have options," I said.

"But she doesn't. I can't abandon her."

"You will ruin your life for this girl?"

Then he shut up, refusing to speak to me for the few more minutes it took us to get home.

At home, Parul heard Arjun slam his bedroom door and looked at me with a smile. She was in the middle of eating a late-night snack: using squares of chocolate to scoop vanilla ice cream. I'd forgotten about this, until I saw her with a tub of ice cream and some Dairy Milk on the balcony.

She hadn't wanted to tag along with Arjun and myself when we went for dinner, citing the importance of catching up on college assignments. I couldn't blame her for wanting the best results and working hard for it. As I'd been, she too was itching to get away.

The chocolate chunk in her hand had started to soften and smear her fingers. She went in for another scoop nonetheless, and licked the ice cream off. Ma would give her an earful later, about ruining the tub and making the ice cream inedible with all her mouth germs.

"You two had words? You never piss people off," she said.

"I've been doing a bit of that lately."

I sat on Didu's rocking chair and the kitten promptly jumped into my lap.

"Let me guess, you couldn't not mention Sharmila." Despite Parul's façade of indifference toward us, I knew she clocked everything. She was probably the first one to have noticed how intimate Arjun and Sharmila were.

"I couldn't *not.*"

Parul shifted in the chair, folding one leg under the other. She was wearing one of Ma's old chikan kurtas, light white cotton with delicate white embroidery, and black bicycle shorts underneath.

"I would leave him alone," she said.

I turned to her, offended.

"She's married, Parul. To our cousin! He's setting himself up to get his heart broken or his head bashed."

"Surely he has a pretty clear picture of the potential consequences."

"Maybe he needs someone to knock some sense into him. What do you think would happen if Ma and Baba found out?" I said.

"He's justified it to himself somehow. Maybe he thinks he can carry on like this forever, or he has a plan. Either way, your interference will do no more than distance him from us," Parul continued.

This girl was going to be all right, I thought. That air of maturity she carried wasn't pretense, she *did* have it all figured out. I was excited to see the future she had in store. Which global crisis was she going to rescue us all from?

"I had to talk to him, Parul, bring him back to reality," I said.

"And he's going to listen to you?"

"I've done everything this family has asked of me. Isn't it time someone listened to me for a change?"

"Why have you? Followed every command? I don't get it. Is it a competition between Tia and you? Who gets to win the Most Duti-ful Daughter medal?" She licked the chocolate, which was a paste on her fingers now.

"I was in a relationship with someone I didn't think the family would accept," I blurted.

Parul appeared unperturbed, and slowly closed the lid on the ice cream tub, which now had swirls of chocolate mixed in with the vanilla.

I stared at her for a reaction, but she was reading the label on the tub, taking her time. "Did you know that ice cream is a Chinese in-vention?"

"Did you hear what I said?"

"Marco Polo took it to Europe," she continued slowly, while I sat fidgeting in my chair. "I think I prefer gelato anyway."

I was about to get up and go, but first I had to move the kitten off my lap.

"How long were you together?"

"Two years," I replied, blinking rapidly to keep the tears at bay. The fact that she had heard me and processed the information came as the biggest relief.

"You shouldn't have ended things with him, Durga. If this is the guy you truly want to be with."

"He was black. Mixed race, actually. I didn't know how Ma and Baba would react, if they'd accept him. I couldn't bear the thought of cutting off ties with them. Didu wouldn't have known what to do with him either."

"You give them less credit than they deserve."

"And what, spend years trying to convince them to accept him? You know how they are. They'd put him up for inspection every time we visited, and wait for him to trip up."

"You should speak to them," she said.

"I thought you were against talking to the family about personal problems."

"This isn't a problem. You've made it one."

"It doesn't matter, Jacob died. He was the brother of my flatmate, Joy."

I nudged the kitten and stood up. Parul wiped her sticky fingers on Ma's kurta, to further infuriate her. Not only was she wise for her age, she was also brave.

"Okay, that's shit, Durga. What the fuck? Your ex died and you didn't tell any of us? You've come here to Tia's wedding, acting like nothing's happened?"

She was right, and all I could do was wait while she judged me. There was no need for it, but it was her I wanted to apologize to. My little sister.

"I know, it's awful, I feel awful about everything. I don't know how to fix it, how to feel better about it. I can't change anything now because Jacob is gone."

Parul was disappointed in me, I could see it written all over her face. For failing to have a backbone and introduce my boyfriend to the family.

"You're here now, Durga, you can do something about it. Take ownership of your life." She stood up with a sigh, like she was done with this conversation. "Tell Ma and Baba. You owe it to Jacob."

Chapter 25

I N THE BEDROOM, ALONE, WITH THE KITTEN SLEEPING curled up at my feet, I was wide-awake and trying to think of all the reasons why I couldn't have brought Jacob to India. If he were alive, if we were still together, even if I'd told my parents about him, I wouldn't have brought him here, I thought.

I wouldn't have wanted him subjected to the scrutiny, the judgmental stares, the gossiping behind his back. I rolled over on my belly so I could muffle my sobs with the pillow. I was only kidding myself. He would've loved it here.

A scent of jasmine would greet him every morning, from the pots on the balcony. Jasmine oil in Ma's hair. He would have loved the heat, shedding most of his clothes, rejoicing in the cold showers. The people. Jacob would have loved to talk to the people who stopped him on the streets to ask him where he was from. I might have had to translate for him, but he'd have enjoyed their open, inquisitive stares, prepared to answer their prying questions, prepared to keep them engaged for as long as it took them to understand him. To realize he was just like them in different skin. A few shades darker than some of them, lighter than others. He had the same fears as them. We all watched the same news—the world could be ending, we could combust at any moment now, there were wars before and more wars now. Everyone around the world had the same agenda: to keep our loved ones safe.

I missed Joy. I wanted her to stroke my hair while I cried into the pillow, to forgive me for breaking her brother's heart and not being brave enough to mend it. I knew she'd already forgiven me, but I didn't deserve it.

The cat yawned and made a squeak. She was in the middle of a long second yawn when I looked over at her, with her sharp tiny teeth lining marshmallow-pink gums. She opened her jewel eyes, sleepy in her ignorance, then tented her paws over her nose and fell back asleep.

I didn't know where I wanted to be, with my family here in Calcutta, or with my independence in Ireland.

I texted Tia when I was back in my room. I couldn't stand being here, among the ghost of her things. After my conversation with Parul, I needed a distraction.

We'd spoken briefly since her wedding, but she was always too busy to talk, reminding me coquettishly that Bikram demanded her full attention.

She rang when I told her I was going to meet Surjo the next day.

She was bubbling with excitement, but trying to whisper. I heard the muffled sounds of a TV in the background. From childhood visits to Bikram's house, I guessed she was in the little room adjoining their living space, where they stored the cleaning things and the household linen. A room visited only by the maid.

"You're meeting him on a date? How did this happen?"

"We got talking at the wedding."

"Oh, Bikram will be thrilled to hear this. I'm surprised he doesn't already know, but he would have told me if he did. We've made a pact to always be honest with each other, no matter how painful the truth is. I tried it on him yesterday. I told him he has to shave his mustache and goatee because they make his face look fat. He took it pretty well."

"Has he shaved it off?"

"Not yet. He's waiting until after the honeymoon because it might be cold in Japan and his face isn't used to feeling a chill."

"That is ridiculous. He's buying time and hoping you'll forget," I said.

"How could I possibly forget? I'll be looking at his face every day."

It sounded like Tia was pacing. She had a host of red and white shell bangles she'd been wearing since the wedding ceremonies, and I was surprised to hear them jangling. I thought she'd have taken them off by now, since they'd clash with her usual taste in outfits.

"Anyway, yes, I'm meeting Surjo. I think I like him," I said.

Tia took a few quiet breaths, but she sounded happy when she spoke again.

"I'm excited for us, Durga, for you. Surjo is great, from what I keep hearing. A bit of a prude, but you'll suit each other."

"A prude?"

"Bikram always complains he doesn't want to hang out with the group when they go to gigs. Apparently Surjo finds the music too loud, and he doesn't like to drink because he gets bad hangovers. Also, he is a mama's boy, so be mindful of that. Is the girlfriend really out of the picture?"

"He may still have feelings for her, I don't know. We're just hanging out for now."

"I'm excited," she said.

"Will I see you before I leave? Listen, I know you have money saved and you can take care of yourself, but if you ever need anything, please call me. Don't be too proud to ask me for money. I'm your sister."

"Don't worry about me, Durga."

"What are you going to do all day, now that you've quit your job like an idiot?"

"I'm redecorating. Ma said . . . Bikram's mother . . . she said she'll stay out of it, and I can do what I like with our half of the house. That'll keep me busy for over a year at the very least. And we want to start trying for a baby right away."

When we were children, I was the one who played with the baby dolls; cradling them and feeding them from wooden milk bottles, changing their cloth nappies and reading bedtime stories. Tia liked to dance. She obsessed over form and accuracy, and choreographed original routines. I didn't know when things changed, when her biological clock started ticking so loudly.

"I'm happy you and Bikram want the same things."

I heard Bikram's voice just then. He'd come into the room Tia was in. They exchanged some words and I was glad he didn't sound impatient with her. Like with Maeve, I didn't trust him. I was waiting for him to slip up and show his true colors, which my gut told me he was shrouding.

Tia had worked very hard to qualify as an accountant and had risen quickly up the ranks at the firm. To give it all up with the smearing of some powder on her head seemed like a waste. But someone had told me recently that there are many kinds of people in the world.

"I'll see you before you leave, I promise. Bye now. We're watching a movie."

Tia giggled before she ended the call, and I realized I couldn't picture her with anyone other than Bikram.

Chapter 26

THE EXHIBITION SURJO INVITED ME TO WAS LESS ABOUT art and more about ego, or so it appeared to me. But I couldn't claim expertise on the matter.

I didn't recognize the guests, but that was purely a personal failing, because the gallery was filled with notables. The cream of Calcutta's crop. Actors, musicians, business folk, CEOs, models; the social elite. A strata of society quite different from the one my middle-class family mingled with. A world Tia had now entered and was perhaps slowly getting acquainted with through Bikram.

The struggling artists walked around with glasses of bubbly and deadpan looks on their faces. My heart went out to them.

"So, these are your friends?" I said.

Surjo brought me a glass of wine, which I wasn't going to drink, and two cocktail samosas.

"I don't know most of these people personally. The featured artist is an old friend."

We both looked in the direction of the framed abstract painting we were standing beside. The image had a series of intersecting circles and some splashes of color. It made me feel nothing, other than bringing up a vague memory of being bored with Venn diagram homework. I had to admit it would brighten up a room, though.

"It's okay. I don't get it either," he said.

"So why are we here?"

"Because I've grown up with these people. I don't drop my friends because they've turned into annoying adults," he replied with a shrug.

I wanted to say something about Bikram, that it made more sense now why someone as likable as Surjo still hung with Bikram. But I didn't want to be this openly harsh about my new brother-in-law. He was a part of the family now.

"You're obviously kinder and more patient than I am," I said.

"Yeah, just a better human being."

Surjo hid his grin with a sip of wine and I rolled my eyes, and we both proceeded to eat the samosas.

"Maybe some of your goodness will eventually rub off on me."

"So you think a person can change?"

"Maybe I'll be able to put up with incorrigible people in my life someday."

"I wouldn't change a hair on your head," he said.

"That's the first thing I'd change about myself if I could!" I laughed. "I've always wanted curls."

He was dressed in an olive green open-collared shirt, dark trousers, and sandals. The poppy red socks came as a pleasant surprise. He was looking at me like he wanted to say that he loved everything about me, and I chewed my samosa as demurely as I could.

"Want to get out of here, find something to eat?"

He took my glass from me, sloshing wine on the polished marble floor.

"Can we go somewhere we're paying for the food?" I said.

It was a test to see how easily offended Surjo could get. He grabbed my hand and we practically ran out of there. He went flying through the test in his dazzling red socks.

* * *

I WAS THRILLED when he suggested the street-food vendor who was famous all over South Calcutta for being open until the wee hours of the morning. It was only nine, so there wouldn't be a big queue.

We got ghugni, kati rolls, and an assortment of batter-fried vegetables. An eclectic mix, but we wanted to sample as many things as we could manage before we left.

Surjo ordered and waited for the food, then brought it to the car. It smelled of nostalgia as soon as he opened the plastic bag, and my mouth watered.

There were plastic spoons for the ghugni but I dipped my forefinger in it for a quick lick, which made him laugh.

"Don't laugh at me. I've been starved for nearly two years," I said. "What do you cook?"

"Noodles and oven pizzas, and salads on good days. My flatmate, Joy, is a good cook. We also eat out a lot of the time. You're a professional chef, you're not allowed to judge me."

We delighted in the feast. Wolfed it all down hungrily, licking our fingers, sighing with each bite, chewing noisily. It seemed like all the food was gone in minutes, and we sat silently, bloated, in the fumes of our spicy food. We glanced at each other then looked away, red-faced, both slightly ashamed of our greed. Like we'd just had sex.

Surjo cleared his throat. "I want to be as transparent with you as possible, Durga. I was with Chloe for over a year. It was a serious relationship by all accounts. I won't be disrespectful to her and claim it meant nothing to me. I know I should've been more honest with everyone. I shouldn't have encouraged our families to set you and me up. I've spoken to my folks. I'm not meeting anyone else on arranged dates."

It was brave of him to take a stand. I hadn't met his parents, but if his mother was anything like mine, I knew it couldn't have been an easy conversation.

I nodded. "Good for you. I was in a relationship until a few months ago. It was serious, I was in love."

His fingers were greasy from the onion bhajis he'd just devoured and when he touched my hand he left little oily spots on my knuckles.

This was a good time to tell Surjo I was grieving the loss of my ex. I hadn't been completely honest with him either. But talking about Jacob in this moment seemed disingenuous to his memory. He'd been appalled at the idea that my family was trying to arrange my marriage, and I didn't want Jacob to be a part of this conversation. Also, Surjo might have to battle mixed emotions; of feeling relieved that Jacob was out of the picture, and guilt about rejoicing in someone's death. I'd reserve the guilt for myself alone, at least for tonight.

"But it's over now?" he asked.

I nodded and couldn't say more.

"I don't regret them setting us up. I'm glad we met," he said.

Surjo's lips were coated with grease too and they glistened under the streetlight. I would have kissed him but I was thinking about Jacob.

"I'm sure I'm not the first guy you met on an arranged date?" He spoke through my thoughts about Jacob.

"Actually, you were."

"Wow. How did you hold out that long? That's why I left, because my mother was inviting people to our house without telling me. I'd come home from work and find a new family in our drawing room, Ma serving them tea and snacks."

"My parents haven't been as pushy, but they've tried to gently nudge me in the right direction."

"This feels more like my decision. I mean you." Surjo searched my eyes and I nodded.

"Especially because they gave up on us. They think this is a dead end."

He laughed. I put my box of food down on the floor of the car and reached for him, placing my hands on his chest. I felt his heart beating fast under my palm, but I couldn't go further than that. Not with Jacob still on my mind. Not when I could remember in painful detail all the times we'd fooled around in *his* car.

"Will I see you before you leave for Ireland?" he asked.

I wanted to, but I was enjoying the lull, of not knowing where we were headed, if this would ever work. I liked liking him, living in this feeling of not knowing him well enough to perhaps be disappointed by the details of him. Basking in the warmth of his liking me too.

"I don't think I'll have the time, I'm sorry."

"There are always video calls. I can come visit you in Cork some weekend. Soon?"

I nodded.

Surjo covered my hand with his and lifted it up to his mouth. When he kissed my fingertips, I was rapturous. That I was feeling something, anything, made me hopeful.

Chapter 27

I'D RECOGNIZED BABA'S SHAPE ON THE BALCONY, AND when I reached the landing at the top of the stairs, he was standing at the doorway looking unsure.

"Is Ma asleep?" I asked.

"She was very tired, so I told her not to stay up for you. Where did you go with Surjo?"

I hadn't informed him of our date, but I wasn't surprised he'd found out. My parents never kept anything from each other. Although Baba was in the habit of using Ma as his mouthpiece, and preferred to keep an air of distance from his children's personal affairs, I had a niggling feeling that tonight Baba wanted to speak with me directly.

"We went to an art exhibition, and then for dinner."

I didn't want to tell him we'd spent most of our time sitting in Surjo's car talking, because Baba would be uncomfortable with that information.

"Okay, that's good. Have you spoken to Arjun or Bikram about him? We don't know the boy too well, although he seems nice. I've met him a few times, his father is a civil engineer, isn't he?"

Baba relaxed a little, perhaps eager to discuss Surjo with me as a continuing marital prospect. My resentment mounted. If I'd brought up how Tia's new mother-in-law had treated us with disdain for years, he would've balked at that, perhaps even walked away from me. But he was keen to chat about this, assuming I wasn't opposed to the idea of an arranged marriage with Surjo. Another one of his children offered up to the Holy Gods of matrimony.

"I'm not interested in his father. I want to get to know Surjo."

"Yes, good, that is the right way. The modern way. Get to know him before we make any arrangements."

He was so oblivious to how this affected me. I could see the cogs turning—who to get Ma to ring tomorrow to dig up more information about the Sengupta family. I knew Ma parroted his words to us because I'd hear them arguing in their room—about Tia's decision to give up dancing, Arjun's marital prospects, my plans of taking the job in Ireland, Parul's social life and choice of friends.

"Going on one date with him doesn't mean I want to marry him," I snapped. "I don't know if I want to marry anyone ever."

Baba was becoming increasingly anxious, and when this happened, he usually spoke very quickly, and his jowls trembled.

"We want the best for you, Durga. A decent boy from a good family. Look at how well matched Tia and Bikram are, and all because she trusted us. We can help you find a good man."

It was as though he hadn't heard a word I'd said. Ma argued with us incessantly about everything. Why we weren't eating enough, why we hadn't called her siblings, who we wanted to marry. But at least there was an open channel of communication. Baba had as good as covered his ears with his hands, refusing to let me have a voice.

"Who is a good man, in your opinion, Baba? I'm curious."

"You know what I mean, Durga. We don't have to talk about this now. Maybe you should discuss it with your mother instead."

I didn't want to talk to Ma about it. Whatever her personal opinion, she stood guard of what Baba thought anyway. All these years she'd faithfully turned to him for guidance. I needed to speak to the source directly.

Baba was already attempting a getaway, finding this candor too unbearable. We could have stood here and chatted at length about the declining number of newspapers in circulation, no problem.

"No, Baba, I want to talk to *you* about this. Please tell me, who is a good man?"

"A good husband for any of my daughters would be someone reliable, someone who will keep them happy and content. A good match of minds and of the families."

I had a nice evening with Surjo, and I knew my family approved of him, and yet I felt as though they were gatekeeping this decision too. That they had somehow influenced my attraction to him. That I was entertaining Surjo's advances only because he was the safe option. I had left home because I didn't want to color inside the lines anymore, but at the first opportunity to use my own free will I'd scurried back to familiar comforts. I was frustrated by my own weakness.

"I was in a relationship with someone in Ireland, it was serious. We broke up but I'm curious to know what you would have made of him if I'd brought him home."

Baba was stunned into silence. His eyes bulged in surprise. Both my parents were naïve enough to think none of their children were keeping secrets.

"An Irishman?" he asked, when he eventually found his trembling voice.

"Yes, but he was mixed race. Half-black."

"Black?"

"Of African descent, Baba."

He folded his arms, placed a finger on his lips, and huffed a few times as he looked at me closely. As though he'd been tasked with tailoring an outfit for me.

"I don't know what to say, Durga."

"Yeah, that's what I thought."

I couldn't keep the fury from my voice. My worst nightmare was coming true. My father, whom I loved, had lost my respect. I was right in not bringing Jacob here, to be faced with this. He'd always deserved better than me.

"Durga, you misunderstand me." Baba reached for my hand to stop me from leaving. "Yes, I am surprised by this news, but I don't want you to think of me as small-minded."

"We broke up because I thought you would never have accepted him."

"Durga, why would you think that of me? He would be a foreigner in this household, as would anyone from another country. We might have taken time to get used to him, but that is all. Your mother and I are very open-minded people."

He was tugging at me to try and pull me in his arms, but I resisted.

"You keep saying that, that you're open-minded. But you fixed Tia's marriage when she was a baby. You convinced her she couldn't secure a better future for herself. You'd want the same for me, and once Parul is old enough, you'll do the same to her. If you were truly forward-thinking, you would let us make our own decisions."

Baba released me and I stumbled backward. He looked like a man who'd just been struck with an open palm across his face.

"Did you truly end it because of what we would think?" he asked, looking horrified.

"It was complicated, but yes, that was one of the deciding factors."

"All these years, Durga, and don't you know me at all?"

Perhaps I didn't know him. I'd grown up sharing a house with a father who left for work at eight, came home to sit at the table with his family and enjoy a meal cooked by his wife, every day. He asked us about school, took us swimming on weekends, sometimes read us a book when Ma told him to, but he never disclosed to us how he truly felt. He didn't talk about who was promoted at work, if he'd missed out on a bonus, how it felt to be friends with Bikram's father, who took his family on holidays abroad. I didn't know if he'd ever loved another woman, if he'd done his duty and simply settled for Ma.

"Are you terribly unhappy?" he continued.

I couldn't despise him, couldn't even answer him. How could I burden him with Jacob's death now?

A relationship was wasted, and now I knew I was wrong about my father. I was too late, and I should have known Ma wasn't the kind of woman to remain in this marriage if she was ashamed of him. I'd made a big mistake. I should have invited Jacob to India. I shouldn't have hidden him from all the joys and colors of my family.

Chapter 28

THE DAY BEFORE I LEFT CALCUTTA, I SPENT THE MORN-
ing at the wet market with Ma, where we went in search of a
whole rui. She would use it to cook a fish curry for my going-away
dinner that night. I waited for her to bring up my conversation with
Baba. They'd always told each other everything, no matter the fight
it led to. But Ma carried on with her careful selecting and haggling.
Baba was obviously waiting for me to leave the country before he
told Ma about Jacob. As much as I wanted to talk to her about it, I
was grateful to Baba for giving me a peaceful departure.

After the wet market I sat on the balcony with Didu and Kobita,
and disclosed my decision to name the new kitten Kaju, in memory
of my childhood pet.

In the evening, Tia and Bikram joined us for our family dinner.

Ma and Kobita had spent the day cooking, and our mother wasn't
at the door to greet her daughter and new son-in-law because she
had to have a shower. She'd become sweaty from being in the kitchen
all day.

The table was laid out with big serving bowls of hot fluffy basmati,
fish curry, fries cut so fine they resembled confetti string, a potato
and poppy-seed dish, and everyone's favorite—mutton in a puddle

of red oily curry. Later, Kobita would bring out the rice pudding Ma garnished with raisins, saffron, and cashews.

Tia was greeted by the family as though we hadn't seen her in years. Bikram was ignored until Parul pointed out that he looked red in the face. It made him cough into his fist, and Tia lovingly stroked his back and told me she'd already warned him about our sister.

Baba sent Parul to fetch Ma, while Didu took her seat at the head of the table. Bikram would get the chair at the other end.

We heard Ma practically running down the corridor. Parul must have taken the opportunity to slip back to her room because she didn't follow Ma in.

"Tia! Here you are. And our darling son-in-law."

Ma and Tia hugged tightly, but neither of them cried. If Bikram wasn't with us, Ma would've asked Tia if she was being well looked after, but she obviously didn't think it was appropriate to ask in her husband's presence. He was beaming at his bride, and it felt like the best send-off I could have received. I would be reliving every moment of the evening for weeks to come.

Ma sent Arjun to fetch Parul and he went grudgingly, knowing there was a danger of the food going cold by the time he returned.

Kobita and I set to task, serving the food on everyone's plates. Baba and Bikram fell quickly into a discussion about a recent news piece regarding a criminal gang leader's arrest. They were both convinced it was staged and he'd be released soon with no charges.

Tia begged Ma to stop fussing and to sit down. As always, I took the seat between Didu and Tia. I turned to my sister with a smile, satisfied now that I'd seen her and she looked well.

"Do you see? He's shaved off all the facial hair. He didn't wait until the honeymoon," she said, leaning toward me.

I looked in Bikram's direction, having noticed it already. "You were right. His face does look slimmer."

Tia settled in her chair with a triumphant expression.

"How'd it go with Surjo?" she continued, while the others talked.

I still looked around to make sure nobody was eavesdropping. Parul was the only silent one but she was glued to her phone. She could be listening and taking notes, I thought.

"It was good. We'll keep in touch."

"Is that all you're going to tell me?" Tia grabbed my wrist and whispered in my ear, "He told Bikram he's smitten."

I let out a sharp laugh and everyone looked in my direction. Tia picked a potato fry off her plate and popped it in her mouth. "Durga just told me she's moving back home."

Baba stood up in surprise. Ma cried out. "What? Really?" Arjun raised his brows, still trying hard to give me the cold shoulder. Even Parul looked up from her phone. "It would be so wonderful to have you back," Didu said.

Tia covered her mouth with the back of her hand, laughing while chewing her food. I rolled my eyes at her and turned to my family, who were all staring expectantly at me.

"That's not what I said."

"But you're thinking about it?" Ma asked.

In that moment I loved seeing them all beaming at me, knowing I'd been the source of their excitement.

"Yes, I'm thinking about it," I replied. It wasn't entirely a lie.

WE WERE FULL of food.

Once Tia and Bikram left, Ma and Kobita got to clearing and cleaning. Didu had fallen asleep in her chair and Baba had to wake her to help her to her room. She hated admitting to have dozed off, as though it implied a weakness.

"I close my eyes for one moment to think, and you act like I've committed a crime."

"I'm just going to take you to your room. You can think there," Baba said, smiling.

Parul had already disappeared, and Ma was calling for her, her voice ringing through the house.

Arjun went to the TV room to watch the rerun of a cricket match he'd missed. I never watched with him usually, so he was surprised to see me following him.

He'd been avoiding me for a few days, since we talked in his car, and it felt unnatural. Arjun and I had never fallen out before. I sat with him on the sofa, leaving a gap between us. We sat staring at the screen for at least fifteen minutes, until he couldn't bear the silence and turned to me.

"I can't enjoy the match like this, Durga. You got something to say?"

"Nope. Nothing."

I knew I was torturing him, but I didn't want to say the wrong thing again. I didn't want to force him to cancel his trip to Ireland in December.

We fell into silence once more, and a few more minutes ticked by. Then Arjun shook his head.

"Don't worry about me, Durga. You'll be in Ireland, and I hear things are going well with Surjo. We can talk more when I visit you in December."

"I can't help but worry, Arjun. I want you to be happy. I want what's best for you."

"You sound more like Ma every day," he laughed.

He pinched my cheek like he used to when we were children, and I swatted his hand away.

Ma entered the room, wiping her forehead with the loose end of her sari.

"Look at you two. We will all miss you, my darling girl. But you will seriously think about coming back, won't you?"

She tapped Arjun's knee and he moved so she could sit between us.

"I have a lot to consider, workwise. They might not approve the move back," I said.

"So just quit. Your time in Ireland has chiseled out a few abs," Parul said. I hadn't noticed her slink in. She was sitting cross-legged on the rug near my feet. "Your CV now has a six-pack."

Arjun and I laughed at that, while Ma looked confused.

"Think about it. You can have any job you want. Live anywhere you want," Arjun said.

"No, she will live here with me. And I'll cook for you. All your favorite meals. Arjun will drive you to work," Ma said, and held my hand.

It did sound nice, easy, comfortable. The sweetness of not having to think for myself, being responsible for my choices.

"Nobody wants to watch cricket. Put on that game show where the families are pitted against each other," Ma said.

Parul clicked through the channels until she found the show.

The thought entered my mind that my family needed me. With Tia married and gone, Arjun and Parul would need a sister. My parents might need the company. Tia was very good at that, at meeting everyone's needs. Perhaps, if I tried, I could fill that gap in their lives? Be the good daughter in her stead?

I hadn't considered it before, but now I couldn't completely disregard returning home. How ironic that the fresh start I was looking for might begin once I returned to the place I had tried to escape.

Chapter 29

I LANDED IN DUBLIN, WHERE I HAD TO GET A BUS FOR another nearly three-hour journey to Cork. I had a lot to think about, and did very little sleeping.

Green hills rolled by, and I was greeted by a gray day instead of rainbows and sunshine. I missed the Indian sun on my skin. Everyone on the bus seemed to be asleep, having been picked up from the airport, presumably after their long journeys home. The only sound was the driver speaking into his radio from time to time, or of the toilet flushing when someone went into the minuscule cubicle down the steps. They each came out looking embarrassed. Traveling together was an intimate affair.

Joy was supposed to collect me from the bus stop in Cork City, and I'd checked in with her every few hours on my journey.

From the moment I'd said goodbye to my family at the airport, wiping Ma's tears from her face, forcing a kiss on Parul's cheek, giving Baba and Arjun the tightest hugs they'd allow, I felt an extreme exhaustion descend upon me. I became obsessed with the necessity to lie down in my bed. My own bed in my flat, with a heavy duvet covering most of my face.

Even the slightest delay in taking off, or a long queue at one of the transfer check-ins, led to watery eyes. I began texting Joy incessantly, trying to make sure she wouldn't be late collecting me from the bus stop.

When I got off the bus, I couldn't see her anywhere. Until an hour before, she'd confirmed she was going to be on time. I was prepared and had a raincoat out, but even all buttoned up and with the hood on, I felt entirely soaked through. Wet and miserable, I blamed Joy.

At least the air was clean here and didn't hurt my lungs, so I took in a few deep breaths and walked to the taxi rank. I was about to talk to the first driver, when I heard honking from the other side of the street. If this were India, it wouldn't catch my attention, but the sound startled me in Ireland.

"What are you doing? Get your ass over here!" Joy was hanging out of her window yelling at me.

I crossed the street and threw my bags in her backseat. She drove a mint green Nissan Micra that was scraped on the sides and hadn't ever been taken to the car wash. I had to swipe away crisp packets and empty bottles of Mountain Dew off the seat first.

"Did you think I wouldn't show up?" Joy asked.

She was the kind of person who shouldn't have been driving, and reinstated my belief that not everyone is born to drive a car.

Joy barely checked the road before she pulled out and zoomed through a yellow light. The wipers were swiping across the windshield maniacally, unable to keep up with the velocity of the rain. Being in the car with Joy wasn't unlike being a passenger in India.

"You okay?"

"I'm just tired."

She was looking better than I'd expected. Joy was wearing eyeliner again, which was a good sign. She'd even painted her nails and had been looking after her curls, which she'd neglected since Jacob died.

"When are you back to work?" she asked.

"Tomorrow. I need sleep."

"I've made spaghetti bolognese, if you're hungry."

I generally enjoyed Joy's bolognese, but I still had the taste of Ma's cooking in my mouth. All that food. I already missed it. The *thunk-*

thunk of Kobita grinding spices in the old granite mortar, releasing the smell of cumin and cardamom all around the house.

"How've you been? How are things with Maeve?"

"Nothing's changed since we last spoke. I think she wants me in her life, as a more permanent fixture. It feels good. I think I want her too."

I still had suspicions, but I didn't want to voice them, not when Joy looked so pleased. Maeve had a history of leaning on Joy when she needed something—like the time she hadn't paid her bills for months so ESB cut off her electricity. Joy made all the calls, even loaned her money, to get the power supply up and running again. All Maeve did was sit at home and blow her nose into endless tissues, crying over how she'd never learn to be a responsible adult. Self-awareness didn't lead to change, though.

Joy was effervescent in her happiness now, but I had to wonder which life crisis Maeve needed rescuing from this time. But what did I know? Perhaps they had a cosmic attachment. Two erratic nomadic souls, circling each other infinitely through time. Perhaps this was their destiny, what made them happy.

Joy pressed on the brake hard and we came to a screeching halt behind a car stopped at a red light. She turned to me impassively, as though her perception of distance wasn't dangerous.

"Tia happy in her new marriage?" she asked.

"Seems to be. I want her to be. Things seem complicated at home, I'm not sure how to describe it. Everyone's problems seem much bigger. More larger-than-life."

"You're seeing things differently now, with a different eye. You're noticing things about your family you couldn't see when you were in the thick of it."

We were off again, and Joy changed into the lane for oncoming traffic, in order to overtake the slower car ahead of us. We got beeped at by other cars, but she took no notice.

"Maybe. I was happy being there, I felt at peace. But I'm happy to be back here too."

"Is this your way of telling me you're going to move back to India?"

"I haven't made a decision yet."

"I suppose without Jacob around, you no longer have a reason to stay."

She silenced us both with her words.

I kneaded my forehead in pain. I'd been able to distance myself from Jacob in India, but now he was everywhere again.

"I can't believe you just said that. He was my boyfriend, I was in love with him, and I'm heartbroken. But you're my best friend. All I've done since his death is try to support you."

My voice hadn't been shrill like this in years, not since my screaming matches with Tia as teenagers. We fought over silly things like ratting each other out to Ma about trying on makeup. Ma had very strict rules about what we could wear and how much. Lip glosses but no lipstick. Kajal but no eyeliner. Eyeshadow was out of the question.

"Nothing you do will bring him back, Durga. You hurt him. You made him feel like he didn't deserve to be a part of your life. Maybe it would be for the best if you went back home."

Joy stopped the car in front of our house and stared straight into my eyes. I sat frozen, motionless under her glare. Only a few hours ago, I was enveloped in the warmth of my family, who loved me, who were missing me now. What was I doing here? Pretend playing at being a part of Joy's life? Of being this independent young professional in a country that didn't even want me here? The only reason I was allowed to live in Ireland was because I had a particular skill, proven by the letters and certificates I had to supply for the visa. I was being taxed richly and paid an exorbitant amount of rent for this tiny flat.

"You're right. This isn't my home. I don't belong here," I said.

HONESTLY, WE NEEDED a good fight.

Joy stormed upstairs to our flat, but she snatched the bags from my hands first, because she knew I was exhausted from my journey.

"So that's it? You're just going to give up and go?" she hissed, while heating the bolognese in the microwave.

I felt like I was floating between two worlds.

"I'm trying to make a life here, but I'm not doing it right, am I? I'm clearly not welcome anyway. Not in the country, not here with you."

She slowly served the spaghetti into bowls for us.

"You've been here over two years, Durga. It's time you stopped feeling sorry for yourself because you miss your mother."

I scoffed at that, ready to continue, but the bowl of spaghetti made me realize how hungry I was. I picked up a handful of slippery spaghetti and stuffed it in my mouth. Using a fork seemed like a waste of time.

"That's not fair. I do miss her, I miss all of them, but it's not just that. Sometimes it doesn't feel like home here."

Joy followed my lead with the spaghetti, and pinched a portion with her fingers.

"I'm sorry. And I'm sorry about what I said about Jacob."

"I did hurt him. It was my fault. You're not wrong."

"He reacted poorly. He should have given you a chance and talked to you about it months before it escalated, instead of shutting you out completely. We're all carrying baggage."

I jumped off of my barstool and nearly stumbled on my way to reach her. Joy caught me by my elbows and pulled me into a hug.

"I'm going to stop being a bitch about Jacob. I miss him, and I know you do too," she said.

I'd never had this before. The breathing space to let it all out, speak my mind freely, to hold nothing back and still be forgiven. With Joy I felt seen and heard.

"Jacob loved you. So much," she said. She put her palms on my cheeks and squished them hard, so my crying turned into laughter. "He'd kill me if he knew I said anything to hurt you like this. He was so happy with you."

"I miss him. I wake up every morning and remember he's gone and I can't breathe."

She nodded, because she knew. "Colin and the lads have found someone to take his room. It was going to happen, they need the rent money. Anyway, they want me to come get his things. I don't want to go alone." Joy's lips trembled and I squeezed her arm.

"I'll go with you."

Chapter 30

WE WENT FOR BRUNCH ON SATURDAY, AS PER USUAL. I asked Joy to invite Maeve. Now that they were taking each other more seriously, I wanted to get to know her better.

We were at the usual café, eating Eggs Benedict and pancakes. Maeve ordered the same pancakes as Joy and they took bites off each other's plates. They were at ease.

I saw it in the way their fingers brushed, how Maeve held her body half-turned to Joy, how they looked to the other for approval when one of them made a funny remark. All that talking had done them good. Past errors were forgotten, misdeeds forgiven. They were living in the moment, which I needed to do more of.

Maeve looked like she'd just woken up, fresher than usual, with her face devoid of decoration. She'd tied her strawberry blond hair in a plait, which was coming undone, and her fringe was messy. Her hair was full of split ends, and I remembered Joy mentioning she had an irrational fear of scissors.

She flipped the plait off her shoulder at the café, and gave me a smile like she knew what I was thinking. Like she knew Jacob always had her back.

She had very good posture, and her ramrod-straight spine hadn't wilted once since we sat down.

Her smile turned into one of wonder, and I now recognized in her a longing for approval too. She wanted me to endorse her presence in Joy's life.

Maeve used a tissue to wipe around her mouth, and I noticed how her gloss still perfectly coated her lips. She'd barely touched her pancakes, only taking a few nibbles from Joy's plate. She was nervous. My demolished eggs looked like a greedy indulgence now.

Joy was nervously digging at her nail polish as her eyes swung from my face to Maeve's. The pregnant pause in the conversation was disconcerting to her. She wanted this to go well, for us all to get along.

"Joy tells me your novel is coming along. I'd love to read it," I said quickly.

"I don't want to waste your time. It's probably not your vibe anyway."

"You should send her the manuscript. Durga spends all weekend reading. She'll be able to appreciate it better than I can," Joy said.

Maeve slowly sipped her coffee and wiped the foam from around her mouth. "I'll send you some links. I've published in a few literary journals over the years. Maybe see if you like the style first, before committing to a full novel."

"Yes, please. I'm sure I'll love them."

I'd finally broken through her exterior and Maeve became comfortable enough to reveal more about her writing. She told me about the novel she was working on, which was about a woman who lived on a small island. This woman, Arabella, travels to the mainland one day to visit her estranged family, then returns to the island carrying a virus that has sparked an epidemic on the mainland. One by one, the people in her small community die excruciating deaths. Only Arabella survives, because she's immune to the disease.

Joy looked confused by the end of the plot narration, while I nodded in appreciation. I felt the need to live up to the high literary expectations Joy had set.

"Fascinating. Can't wait to read it," I said.

"It's taking me a while to finish. I can't decide how to end it. Would Arabella take her own life from the guilt? Or would she continue her lonely life on the island and turn into a mad old woman?"

She was looking expectantly at me as though I might give her a breakthrough idea.

"Or she could return to the mainland to make peace with her estranged family, only to find they are all dead too," I suggested.

Maeve nodded, deep in thought, and Joy gave me a look like this was good. I was doing well.

"You'll figure it out when the time is right. You're a genius," Joy said.

I watched them exchange a light kiss. It was sweet, to see this uncynical, uncritical side of Joy. Love did make putty of the heart.

I checked my phone and saw I'd missed a call from Surjo. We'd scheduled a video call for Sunday, our first.

"I'm going to make a call. Family. I'll be back in a bit," I said.

Maeve and Joy were holding hands under the table and barely noticed me leaving. I would have felt envious of Maeve before but I didn't anymore. I wanted this relationship to work, so I'd have to worry less about Joy if I did indeed decide to leave eventually. I was slowly coming around to the idea that this experiment—of me living away from my family—wouldn't last forever.

Chapter 31

"HELLO, YOU," SURJO SAID ON THE PHONE. "Sorry I missed your call. I'm out for brunch with some friends. How are you?"

I was standing outside the doors of the café, tightening the scarf around my neck.

"I'm back in London, back to the rain. I forgot how cold it is here. I'm on my break now and thought I'd try you. Hope I'm not interrupting."

"No, I'm glad you called. I'm with a couple and feel a bit like a third wheel."

I wondered if Joy had ever felt that way around Jacob and me. Or perhaps we were a perfectly balanced tricycle.

"I can't remember the last time I had brunch on a Saturday. It was probably with you that time in Cork. I usually sleep until eleven and then it's time to get to work."

"Busy at the restaurant today?"

"Always busy, but I've been thinking about you," he said.

This made things awkward for me. In reality, I hadn't been thinking about Surjo much. The luster of romance had rubbed off with the distance between us.

"How nice," I said. Not an appropriate response.

He gave it a moment, probably to allow me to correct myself, but I couldn't.

"How's work?" he asked.

I didn't want to talk about work, and I realized then that he knew nothing about my life to ask specific details. He didn't know much about Joy, nothing about Jacob or Maeve.

"Yeah, good. Boring. How were Bikram and Tia when you last saw them?"

I knew they'd hung out a few times before he left, and Surjo supplied me with little tidbits about their new married life. Bikram was partying less, not staying out as late, ringing Tia when he was partying without her.

"He's being a good husband, don't you worry about it," Surjo said. "Anyway, I just wanted to hear your voice, you should probably return to your friends."

We said a quick goodbye, and when I ended the call I saw a text from Luke.

I was surprised because he was never the one to reach out first.

Heard you're back from India

I hadn't realized he knew I was gone. Joy or Maeve must've been talking about me to their friends.

While I sat with Joy and Maeve at the table, still deciding how to respond to him, whether to respond at all—Luke texted again to say that he would like to come around. This conflicted me.

I was excited and guilty at the same time. Especially now that Surjo had entered the scene. I didn't yet feel I owed him my loyalty, but I was hesitant to sleep with someone else after we'd left things the way we had in Calcutta. In limbo.

I left Luke hanging for a while, chatting with the others, paying the bill, hugging them outside. Joy was going to spend the night at Maeve's.

I was keeping my involvement with both men from Joy. At this point, I was hiding so much from Joy and my family that making amends seemed impossible.

I didn't know Surjo well enough to anticipate his reaction. We hadn't discussed exclusivity, since it was all a bit new and casual between us.

But Joy looked so happy with Maeve, so peaceful, that I was now beginning to wonder if I too deserved a change.

I eventually replied to Luke when I got home. My mind needed clarity but my body needed proof that pleasure was still possible.

He arrived empty-handed to the flat this time, with his hands stuffed in the pockets of an oversized hoodie. Had I thought about him when I was in India? Yes. Looking exactly like this, in fact. Tall, broad-shouldered, with that boyish grin on his face, already undressing me with his eyes.

"Howya?"

"Joy's not here," I said.

At the threshold, he leaned toward me and kissed my lips like he'd been thinking about me.

"Come in?"

He pulled a charging cable from his pocket and helped himself to the outlet in our sitting room when we entered. I studied his bent body while he plugged his phone in. The elastic band of his Jockey underwear was sticking out from above his joggers. When he walked around, his black sneakers made a squeaky sound on the floorboards. He brushed a hand over his velvet scalp.

"So, howya?"

I detected some nerves. He was either not paying attention because his mind was elsewhere, or he was concentrating hard on saying a particular thing to me.

"You okay, Luke?"

He looked around the room and then appeared relieved when he spotted the couch, which he'd been standing beside this whole time.

"I am, yeah. You?"

"My sister got married, did I tell you?"

I sat down on the coffee table in front of him, crossing my legs and cradling my chin in one cupped hand. Luke sat with his hands on his knees as though sitting on a throne.

"No, didn't know you have a sister. Maeve said you went to India to visit family."

"I've got two sisters."

He reached for my leg and gently stretched it out to place my foot on his knee. He rubbed the sole of my foot through my sock, while keeping his eyes on me.

"I've got two brothers," he said, more at ease now.

My eyes drifted to the way he was pressing my toes, and I was curious where he'd learned to give a foot rub like this.

"Do you live with your brothers?" I asked.

Luke ignored my question and kept his eyes on his hand working my foot, pressing the arch, which I didn't realize was sore until it got some attention.

Then he expertly pinched the nerves at the back of my ankle and I let out an involuntary moan.

"How are you coping with the Jacob situation?" he said.

I pulled my foot away, feeling immediately unclean. "I'd rather not talk about him."

"Okay, if that's what you want."

"It's still raw, and I talk about him all the time with Joy."

Luke nodded and reached for my other foot. When he cupped my thigh, I slid off the table and onto his lap, wrapping my arms around his neck.

"I'm sorry for bringing it up. I was thinking about you and thought maybe I'd been too abrupt or cold the last time I was here. I don't want you to think I don't give a shit how you're feeling. We're having a bit of fun here, but you're a human being who just lost someone."

His serious face made me want to giggle, and I stopped it by kissing him. He lifted me up, cradling me like a firefighter carrying a survivor through a burning house. Because we were still kissing and he wasn't watching where he was going, he bumped his knee on the corner of the coffee table, but that didn't slow him down. Heroically, he carried me to my bedroom and threw me on the bed.

As I watched him peel his clothes off, I wondered when he'd lose this. Thirty-five? Fifty? At what age would he stop having sex like this? When he was too exhausted from being a parent? When he'd been having sex with the same woman for years? When would he become disenchanted with foreplay and want to get the task done so he could move on to cooking dinner?

Luke, naked now, slid over me, covering the length of my body with his. I was glad I had this version of him, and wouldn't have to dwell on who he'd turn into.

Chapter 32

THE NEXT DAY, I TOLD JOY ABOUT SURJO BECAUSE I wanted to stop keeping things from her, and also because I caught her looking at me suspiciously a couple of times over the weekend. We'd gone shopping for groceries, and there in the fresh fruit aisle, Joy held up a box of raspberries and gave me one of her funny looks.

With her mouth she sounded the words: "Might go well with the overnight oats?"

With her narrowed eyes she seemed to say, "Are you a liar?"

I had a shopping basket in the crook of my elbow and I put it down. It was time I came clean.

"I met Surjo Sengupta at the wedding and we've been talking ever since."

She was bewildered, and then amused. The raspberries were left behind and she came over and lifted the basket off the floor.

"Okay, but doesn't he have a girlfriend?"

"They broke up."

Joy nodded and wandered off to the vegetables, studying the leeks and cauliflowers with interest. I stood beside her, trying to study the changes in her expression.

"I'm not mad. Did you think I'd be mad? Jacob is dead, Durga.

You guys broke up before he even died. You're allowed to move on, have a life. Is he nice, this Surjo?"

"He's nice. We have a lot in common." I could feel the tension release from my body.

"But he lives in London. How will that work?"

"I don't know yet. I don't even know if I want something serious with him."

Joy nodded. I knew she was glad I was taking my time, not jumping into things. I should have told her much sooner.

"And Luke. I've been seeing him on and off. He's come over to the flat a few times. I'm sorry I didn't tell you. I thought I couldn't."

The smile melted from Joy's face and she assessed me closely. It was one of the hardest things I've had to do—hold her gaze and stand my ground. I needed her to see I was taking charge of my life. I hoped that's what she saw. When she smiled I was relieved.

"Luke and I have always got on really well. I'm sure you know what you're doing," she said. "I'm not going to judge you for enjoying yourself."

I WENT TO the gym that evening. I felt like the shackles had loosened a bit from around my ankles. The pain in my wrist was gone. I was experiencing a lightness of spirit, which manifested as me pushing myself on the treadmill even when I was out of breath and sweating from all my pores. After I'd showered and changed, I felt renewed, capable of facing the world now that I was concealing less from Joy.

Ma rang on my walk back home. She was in the habit of ringing me often, but her calls rarely lasted longer than a few minutes. She usually called me to inform me of something inconsequential—a passing thought she'd had about growing her own basil so she could make homemade tea for the next time Baba caught one of his chesty coughs. Or to tell me Didu needed to visit her sister who lived at the other end of the city, so they were going to employ a car and chauffeur for the day because Didu wouldn't manage with taxis. Ma seemed to not have lost that toddler sensibility of voicing every sub-conscious thought, and when there was nobody around she could tell it to, she called me.

"There's a big bubbling purple gash on my palm, you know. I only tapped it against the pot while it was on the stove, and now I have a serious burn." She couldn't wait to tell me this, as soon as I answered the call.

"Call your doctor, Ma. He'll give you a cream or something."

"I don't have the time. I'm on my way to buy some books for Parul. She needs them for her exam."

"Okay, call the doctor when you're back."

"Anyway, listen, Nita mashi has found another boy for you to meet."

I stopped in my tracks and had to apologize to the man who'd bumped into me. "I thought we were past this."

"You must keep all your options open."

Baba had to have told her about Jacob, they all knew I was still in touch with Surjo. It upset me that she knew how emotionally bur-dened I was, and yet was choosing to hound me with marital pros-pects.

"Stop it, Ma, please just stop."

"Stop what?"

"Pressuring me into a marriage. I am not like Tia. I have other priorities. You know I've been talking to Surjo."

"Are you going to marry him? Have you two spoken about it?"

"No. And I'm not going to marry him until I'm ready and I know he's the right choice. I mightn't marry him at all."

I was walking in circles around a public bin on the side of the road. Its black plastic body was dotted with burn marks from ciga-rette stubs. It stank of damp garbage but I didn't want to move away or head home, refusing to bring this conversation into my safe space.

"If you're not sure about Surjo, then why don't you meet some other boys and see if they're the right fit?"

"Do you even hear yourself, Ma? I'm not shopping for an outfit."

"Aren't you?" She had a laugh in her voice, and like an elastic band, I was stretching. "Even your baba seems to have given up. He told me he doesn't want to be involved in your matchmaking. But I'm your mother, Durga, I have to keep looking."

"Surjo isn't the only man I'm seeing."

"Yes, Baba told me about the other fellow. You should have told us. I would have liked to meet him."

"There's someone else in Ireland now." Ma was silent, so I continued. "And I'm not serious about him, or Surjo. I'm having fun, keeping my options open."

"Durga . . ."

"What will you do? How will you stop me?"

I was giddy on adrenaline and the support I knew I had from Joy now. I felt free and wild, imagining myself wielding a glinting sword like Kali, snapping off shackles and heads. But then I heard my mother say my name again, this time more softly, like she was choking up. Ma turned to rage in the face of a hurdle, rarely tears.

"Durga, I can't stop you. It's your life. I'm disappointed in you, that's all. I thought I'd raised you differently, to not take your life so lightly." She spoke through tears and I gulped down the cackle that had risen in my throat.

"I'm not. That is exactly what I'm not doing, Ma. Don't you see that I'm trying to make an informed decision about what I want my life to look like?"

My mother sniffled and steadied herself again, firming up her voice.

"Durga, come home. I think you should come back home. You need to be with your family. This boy you were close with has died, and you didn't even tell us. You are not yourself."

I was silent for a few moments, and Ma allowed it. I hated that she thought I was considering her suggestion.

"No, Ma, I'm not the girl I was, you're right. I'm someone else, more me than I was when I lived with you."

I ended the call and threw my phone in the bin before walking away.

* * *

"EVEN I WOULDN'T put my hand inside one of those bins," Joy said.

She was still in her shiny chrome puffer jacket, dripping rainwater on our floorboards. I'd spent hours pacing, waiting for her to return from Maeve's place. I couldn't text her even though I'd wanted to, because I didn't have a phone. Eventually, I'd resorted to sending Maeve an email from my laptop, because Joy didn't have it on her phone. She'd rushed home.

"But I need it back. I'm so stupid." I covered my face with my hands.

"You can buy a new phone. Just call Vodafone and they'll restore your number. It's all good."

"It's such a waste of money."

"You'll get a company discount. It won't cost you that much."

I sniffled pathetically and she came over to cradle my head as I sat on the couch, resting it on her stomach.

"But did it make you feel good? Chucking it in the bin?"

"For a moment, yes. But I feel like an idiot now." I wrapped my arms around Joy's hips and clung on. "And now I'm going to have to turn celibate. I can't possibly have sex again, knowing my mother is picturing it and cursing me."

Joy shrugged and scratched a spot on her hand. "Maybe go off the grid? Don't get another phone. A cleanse might do you good."

"My family is in another country. They'll call the embassy if they don't hear from me by tomorrow."

"Email them, write them a letter, send them a postcard." She began taking off her jacket and unlacing her Doc Martens.

"I'm never telling my family anything again. I swear to God, something bad happens every time I open up to them," I said, dragging my fingers down my cheeks, leaving stripes of yellow on my skin.

"Don't be silly, Durga, there is no God."

THE IDEA OF God stuck with me for the rest of the day. I hadn't given it much thought in years.

My family wasn't religious. We observed the annual Durga Puja rituals, but that was more a cultural celebration for us. We went to look at the art and sculpture installations around the city, bought new clothes, received gifts, and ate out.

God wasn't featured in our everyday lives. I wasn't made to pray during exam season like other children in my class, who visited the temple every morning before a test.

Didu had a framed portrait of Kali in her room, which sat atop her cupboard. An artist's interpretation of what Kali looked like, with her four arms and cobalt blue skin, her tongue sticking out in shame and rage for having accidentally stepped on her husband's body in the middle of her world-destroying rampage. To me Kali was gorgeous, and flawed like me.

Every day after washing herself, Didu lit a few incense sticks and circled them in front of the portrait, while mumbling chants under her breath. We weren't involved in her daily routine, and neither did we ask questions. For many years I assumed religion was practiced only by the elderly, since Didu was the only person in our house who seemed to give it some thought.

But I did think about a Higher Presence today, while we drove to Jacob's house. I could see how easily it became an explanation in the absence of one. What other possible reason could there be for his death? Where else could he be now if not somewhere safe and eternally temperate? In another life, re-birthed as a monk.

Jacob had had two housemates and they'd left the key under the mat, so we could let ourselves in. They didn't want to be here because they didn't know what to say to Joy, would have probably been embarrassed to see me again. They'd avoided me at the funeral.

The last time I was at this house, I'd stood at this door, begging Jacob to let me in. I didn't want to be here now, to be reminded of how we'd ended things, how I'd behaved, and what I'd lost.

Joy and I held hands as we walked through the door, unsure of what to expect. I realized I was holding my breath, as though anticipating Jacob to greet us with that half smile of his, to tell us this was all a big joke. I released the choke hold on my lungs the same time as I released Joy's hand.

With Jacob gone, the other two hadn't been keeping the house as clean. It still looked as I remembered it, except for the muddy shoe prints on the carpet, an intense trapped smell of cooked meats because nobody had opened a window here recently.

Joy hadn't made it past the front door yet and when I looked at her she had her nostrils flared. Her eyes were fixed on Jacob's car keys, hanging off a hook by the door. I didn't know where his car was, which was usually parked outside.

"I can't do this. I need to get out of here. Please, Durga, I can't."

So we decided that she would wait outside while I took care of her brother's belongings.

Inside Jacob's room, everything looked exactly the way I'd left it the morning I was last here.

Double bed with plain white sheets and two fluffy pillows. He never left the house without making sure his bed had tight hospital corners. The sheets were tucked in with military precision.

I ran my hand over it.

On my last morning here, I was blissfully unaware of its finality. We'd gone for dinner and drinks at a tapas bar the previous night. We held hands on the walk back home. We talked about the holiday we were planning for the next summer. Because of the food we'd just eaten, Spain was a top contender.

After two years, the sex had slowed. Both in frequency and intensity. There was no urgency to discover each other's bodies anymore, and we'd returned to his house, got ready for bed, and pulled the sheets off together. I used to struggle with undressing his bed for sleep, with those unyielding sheets and stiff folds. He was so warm beside me.

Jacob spooned me. We were like two layers of an onion, stuck together for the rest of the night, neither of us moving. We'd fallen asleep laughing over the noises coming from his flatmate Colin's room, next door. He used to lift weights in the middle of the night.

With his earphones in and loud music blaring in his ears, Colin wasn't aware of his own full-throated huffing and grunting. With every metallic clanking drop of the weights, our floor reverberated.

In the morning I awoke to the sound of Jacob's electric shaver. I took a quick shower while he prepared our coffees and we drank them in his kitchen. We made plans to go to the cinema that weekend, for a river walk in Crosshaven. We drove in his car in companionable silence, listened to the radio, smiled. Then he dropped me off at the bus stop closest to our office premises so I could walk in separate from him. Even that day, after two years, Jacob asked if it was time we came clean to our colleagues. He made a joke about how he wanted to "claim" me because I'd been asked out on dates a couple of times. I'd walked away from his car, laughing, teasing him with no reply.

We broke up that weekend. He brought up my sister's wedding on our walk in Crosshaven, and that was it.

IN HIS ROOM today, I found bags in his wardrobe, the ones he would have packed for our holiday to Spain. I packed his clothes, his shoes, his underwear. They didn't all fit, so I had to get bin bags from under the sink in the kitchen.

His books, his socks, his belts and toiletries from the bathroom. The clock off the wall, cuff links in a box, his speakers and books off the bedside table.

I lifted the small framed photograph he still kept of us. It was a selfie I'd taken at the beach. The sun behind us, so harsh that our faces were underexposed and inky. I never knew why he'd chosen that photograph to frame, probably because it had been a perfect day. We got ice creams and read on the beach for hours, dozed, kissed, read some more. I missed him, and pressed the frame to my heart. If he were here, he'd have taken my hand in his and encouraged me to cry, to release the grief I was hiding from everyone else. Jacob was good at that kind of thing—expressing emotions, talking things through, giving personal feelings the space they deserved. I'd always thought he would have made a good dad.

I was rubbing my eyes before the tears even appeared. I'd found a gem, and now he was gone. Everything seemed empty, strange, pointless. I sobbed, releasing the pain I felt from the loss of him. I had to wipe the frame with the sleeve of my blouse.

I slipped the picture into my tote with shaking hands.

I knew I would live with regret, wondering how I could have better spent the time I had with him. But I accepted it, at least in that moment. I was glad that I'd come here, that I'd had the chance for this quiet farewell.

I CAME OUT of the house pulling the stuffed bin bags. Joy was waiting in the car and she jumped out, wiping her swollen eyes. Hers matched mine.

She helped me bring the rest of the bags outside and we managed to fit them all in the boot and backseat of her car. We hadn't said a word, didn't speak at all as she drove us back to our flat, with the bulging presence of her brother behind us. It was pressing on the rear of our seats, making it impossible for her to get a clear view of the road in her rearview mirror.

Jacob will always be with Joy, behind her, beside her. Just a shadow, a voice in her head, in the faces of strangers who remind her of him.

Chapter 33

NALEDI INVITED US TO DINNER THE NEXT WEEK AND I couldn't refuse.

I asked Joy why she wasn't bringing Maeve with us, and she told me she didn't want to complicate things tonight. I suspected it was because she wasn't ready for it. They'd been friends for years, her parents would immediately detect something was different when they saw them together.

Joy also warned me not to mention Jacob unless one of her parents brought him up themselves.

We took a box of chocolate truffles and a bouquet of yellow roses with us. Joy didn't want to bring wine because she wasn't going to be the one encouraging drinking in the house.

I hadn't seen her touch alcohol since Jacob's funeral, but she did have a pack of smokes in her glove box. She parked the car a few houses down the road from the Cronins' and lit up.

"You nervous or something?" I said.

"I don't know how to describe what I'm feeling. I'm concerned when I'm not around them, but I lose my patience within minutes of being home. I wish something were different. Them or me or Jacob."

Joy finished her cigarette and crushed it in the ashtray, which would stink up the car for days. We drove to the house and took turns checking our makeup and hair in the rearview mirror.

"You know, I feel like Jacob's death has brought them closer. Daddy is concerned she's not looking after herself and Mum thinks he's about ready to explode any day now if he doesn't express his grief. He wants her to eat, she wants him to cry. He used to be able to cry easily before Jacob died," Joy said.

I watched her dabbing her lips with a shimmery balm. I suspected she'd borrowed some of Maeve's makeup; I'd never seen this metallic blue eyeshadow on her before either.

"That's a good thing, isn't it? That they're concerned for each other," I said.

"No. I was hoping this would cause the final break in the marriage. They're terrible together."

ERIC CRONIN GREETED us at the door in an apron that read *Hot Stuff Coming Through*. His nearly all-silver hair looked even lighter, almost chalky white now. The bags under his eyes were heavier. He smelled how I imagined Austria did—of cheese and beer.

"You're cooking, Daddy?" Joy asked, handing the chocolates to him.

"Your mother gave me the recipe and instructions. I'm making bobotie."

He gave me a small wave moments before Naledi appeared at the end of the hallway.

"Sorry, girls. I was just having a bit of a lie-down. Don't worry, I've sautéed some mushrooms, and there's potato gratin, and I also picked up focaccia from The Bread Basket. We won't go hungry even if Daddy's mucked up the bobotie."

Naledi took turns hugging us. When I gave her the roses she said they were her favorite and lifted my hand up to her mouth to kiss it. I was conflicted between feeling sorry for Eric's public humiliation and gushing with pride from Naledi's appreciation of my gift.

She led us to the sitting room and Eric returned to the kitchen. Joy wasn't exaggerating about Jacob's posthumous presence in the house. His skateboard was framed in the hallway. The bookcase, which used to be filled with books, was now stacked with memorabilia, including the medal he'd won as a young gymnast.

There were photographs of him everywhere. On the mantel, on the walls, on the tables either side of the big velvet couch, where lamps used to sit. The lamps were on the floor now. They'd even commissioned an artist to sketch a portrait of Jacob, with one foot on a skateboard, his hair more frizzy than I remembered it. It was impossible to not experience his loss all over again, and I couldn't imagine how Eric and Naledi got through the day.

I could picture Jacob standing beside me, his hand grazing mine. When I'd visited this house for the first time with him, I'd imagined a day in our future when I'd be a comfortable presence, a part of the family. Helping Naledi in the kitchen, knowing my way around the house and all the rooms, gently removing an empty glass of whisky out of Eric's hand.

Joy and I sat close together on the couch, while Naledi drifted around the sitting room, absentmindedly lifting up photographs of Jacob and then putting them down again. I wanted to go over and grab her hands, to still her, because I was feeling the same way: restless.

Joy gave me a look, like this was exactly what she'd been talking about.

"Mum, what's for dessert?" Joy said.

"I made peppermint crisp tart," Naledi said. "It was Jacob's favorite," she added. We all knew.

"Wine? Beer? Eric could whip up some cocktails?" she offered.

Both Joy and I said we weren't in the mood for a drink, and she sighed and decided she'd pour herself a glass of something, as though we'd twisted her arm.

"I want to leave," Joy whispered, after her mother was gone from the room.

I leaned my shoulder against hers.

"It's just dinner and dessert. They seem happy to see you."

"Maybe I should have brought Maeve. That would have given them something to talk about after we leave."

WE SAT IN the sitting room for a bit, all four of us, but there was a heavy silence between each attempt I made at conversation.

I asked Naledi about her knitting group, and she said she'd stopped going since Jacob's death. I asked Eric if he preferred his new hybrid car, and he responded with a shrug. I inquired if Naledi had read any good books lately, and she said she had a pile of overdue books from the library, which she didn't have the heart to return because then she'd have to talk about Jacob with the librarians. I offered to return them for her when I went on Saturday, and she told me not to bother. Eric eventually stood up and declared it was time for dinner.

We sat around the dining table, in a kitchen that was too warm from the range being used all evening for the cooking. Both of Joy's parents kept replenishing their glasses. Naledi shared the bobotie recipe in detail with me, and talked about how she wanted her children to grow up with as many South African staples as she knew how to cook. Joy and I ate, while her parents continued to drink.

I looked up when I sensed Naledi's eyes on me. She was at the head of the table, smiling with her wine-stained mouth. She was dressed in an elegant cream satin skirt and a black blouse.

"Jacob loved you," she said.

Everyone stopped moving and I turned my eyes to my plate. Some of the mince was left over because I hadn't been able to eat much, as delicious as it was. I gripped the cutlery in panic.

"Mum, please," Joy spoke up.

"I loved him too," I cut in. I had to give his mother that.

Naledi dabbed the corners of her eyes with the napkin from her lap. "But it's time for you to try to forget him, Durga. You have a whole life ahead of you. And I'm so happy *you* two found each other. At least we don't have to worry about our Joy."

I returned her smile but Joy snapped at her. "What do you mean?"

"You know what I mean, my love. Isn't it wonderful to find someone you share so much in common with? It's always a relief when the search is over."

Eric cleared his throat gruffly, followed by the clang of Joy dropping her spoon on the plate.

"The search? What bloody search?"

I was confused too, but I didn't want this confrontation to play out. However there was no way of avoiding it. The train carriage was already shunted.

Naledi's eyes flickered over her daughter as she clutched the bowl of her wineglass. "You said over the phone that you have some news. That you've started seeing someone."

I didn't know Joy had broken it to them and I turned to her in surprise.

"I think I'll get more bread." Eric stood up and grabbed the bread basket.

"And you immediately assume it's Durga? My brother's ex-girlfriend? My best friend!"

Naledi looked at both our faces and then her lips turned down. "You said you liked her," she murmured.

Joy jumped up and banged a hand on the table. "That was two years ago, Mother. I made a passing comment. It meant nothing."

I kept my head down, and the intensely umami flavors of the meat dish made me nauseous.

"Well, I didn't know, because you don't tell me anything."

Naledi was already sobbing. When Joy stepped toward her I thought she was going to console her mother, but instead, she walked past her chair and through the kitchen door to go into the garden. She slammed the door behind her.

"I'm sorry, Durga. I didn't mean to make things awkward between you. I never know what to say to her."

"It's okay, Naledi. You haven't. Joy's in pain, just like you."

I GAVE HER a few minutes before joining her in the garden. She was sitting on a cast-iron chair next to a rusty barbecue, smoke in hand.

I sat down on a step by her feet and she offered me her cigarette. I took one drag and returned it to her.

"I had a fleeting crush on you when we first met. It lasted literally one week, and it was never anything serious. When you and Jacob got together I was happy for you both. I was never jealous of him, Durga. I want you to know that," Joy said.

There was a time, a few weeks after Jacob and I broke up, when Joy found a house on a property website that she fell in love with. The property market was on a steep and steady decline in Ireland. The cost of houses had become so inflated that it seemed unrealistic for people our age to ever afford a home. Also, she was still too young, and despite her decent income, she wasn't close to having saved the deposit for the purchase of a literal mansion.

Nonetheless, we drove to the house in Farran several times that month. She was right, it *was* a dream home.

Large gates, a long driveway, and sprawling grounds kept it secluded and secure. Joy cared about things like mature gardens, which the property boasted acres of.

We only ever saw the inside of the house through photographs online, and it looked like the current owners had recently renovated— giving the old country mansion a modern finish and top-of-the-line conveniences.

We gushed over the cherry blossoms shading the house, the stone fountain, the gazebo and the rock pond, the conservatory at the side, which got so much sunlight it could have been a greenhouse. There was space for a polytunnel, some chickens, and a couple of big dogs, if Joy fancied. And she did fancy it all. She couldn't help herself from imagining summer barbecues, inflatable pools, a fire pit for winter nights.

"We could pool our money together and put the deposit down?" she'd said.

"I do want to live with you forever," I'd replied.

But it had soon sold to the highest bidder, and our dream of buying a house together seemed too distant now.

"Remember when we wanted to buy that house in Farran?" I said in the garden, smiling.

"That wasn't because I was in love with you, Durga. I wanted us to buy the house together because we'd be able to afford it that way, because I like living with you. It works."

"I know, you don't have to explain."

Joy bumped her knee with mine and we smiled at each other. I wanted her to know this didn't change anything. I knew all about fleeting feelings.

"We're so much better off as friends. Not to mention, you're straight," she continued.

"And you're in love with Maeve."

She scoffed and crushed her cigarette under her shoe.

"Maybe Naledi is right, you should talk to her more? Sounds like she wants to get to know you better."

"It's difficult talking to someone who always thinks they're right about everything. I don't need her advice, or for her to point out all the ways I'm doing my life wrong."

"Come on, let's go inside," I said.

We tried helping each other up, and I lost my footing and landed back down with a *thump*. Joy grabbed me under my armpits and I made myself go limp, so she dragged me to the door like a corpse.

We entered the kitchen and silenced our giggling when we heard soft, muffled voices coming from inside the house.

"Think they're talking about me and my temper?" Joy asked.

I followed her and we both stopped at the doorway to the sitting room. Naledi and Eric were standing by a tall window. They weren't looking out because the curtain was pulled close, but they had their backs to us, like they didn't want us seeing their faces. Eric's shoulders were shaking and when he turned to the side briefly, we saw him crying. He rubbed his eyes with the heel of his palm. Naledi was stroking his back, the wineglass was in her other hand.

Joy walked slowly to them. Naledi looked at her daughter and then they embraced. Joy held an arm out for her father and Eric joined in for a group hug. I stepped out of the room quickly, before one of them felt the need to invite me to participate in the moment.

We left the house soon after, with Joy sniffling. Naledi had given us boxes of leftover bobotie and all the peppermint crisp tart.

"Why does everyone always end up crying when you're around?" Joy asked.

We were sitting in her car, seatbelts on, ready to go.

"I just have one of those faces," I said.

Chapter 34

I HAD TO GET A NEW PHONE. JOY'S IDEA OF GOING OFF the grid was tempting, but I didn't last three days without feeling anxious when I couldn't keep my hands and mind occupied.

Waiting in the queue at the coffee shop without scrolling through my phone felt like a tragedy. A complete waste of time when I could have spent it learning a life hack from a quick video. How does everyone keep cereal from going soft in the box? There had to be a simple trick to it I wasn't aware of.

I was cognizant of it, and yet helpless against the grip of this addiction.

When I finally had a phone again, I saw all the texts in the family group chat. My parents were carrying on as normal. I didn't participate in the conversations and nobody, not even Tia, urged me to. Ma had told everyone what I'd disclosed to her, it was obvious. I had openly admitted to *having fun* having sex, which was information that was best ignored.

Joy insisted I didn't need to tell Surjo about Luke, that he hadn't yet earned my loyalty. So I continued to take his calls and chat through texts. He was the connection with India I was craving, while my family gave me the cold shoulder. But most of our conversations revolved around food. He described in minute detail the flavors and

textures of the food he cooked, and gave me London's weather re-
ports. I had to be honest with myself, he was beginning to bore me.
I didn't need a long-distance friend, what I needed was to make connections here, in Ireland.

When Surjo asked me to describe my day to him, I left out important details—like how much I missed having Joy to myself. How
much I daydreamed about Luke in bed with me.

It wasn't a good sign that I was thinking of Luke while on the
phone with Surjo.

"Is it raining there?" he'd ask.

I'd lie and say it wasn't, just because I was annoyed at him for
snapping me out of picturing Luke's fingers trailing a path down my
spine.

"But I can hear the rain. Are you in your bedroom?"

I didn't want him to go there. If he asked me what I was wearing,
I'd have to hang up on him.

Joy and Maeve, meanwhile, were living out the slow-motion
montage from a romantic comedy. They held hands everywhere,
dressed in cozy jumpers in an autumn palette, shared hot chocolates
whilst walking through parks. Maeve had even convinced Joy to
start riding her bicycle again, which I was glad to see because it
meant fewer chances of Joy totaling her car.

Maeve spent a few nights of the week at our flat, and Joy had
started staying the weekends with her. She encouraged me to go out
with them, inviting me every time they made plans. I usually just
met them for brunch and left after that, giving them the space they
obviously craved.

I was barely coping though, and these days even before Friday arrived, I was paranoid of the bad choices I'd end up making out of
sheer boredom and loneliness.

It was becoming apparent to me that Joy was subconsciously preparing to leave. I hadn't asked her outright because I wanted to delay
it for as long as possible. I didn't want to give her ideas. But she
spoke often about the changes Maeve had made to her place to ac-

commodate Joy. The plant they'd bought together. How they'd written up a chore list to divide duties, because Joy couldn't stand the mess. I was waiting for her to give me the news any day now—that she was moving in with Maeve, that it was time.

It was only now that I realized I hadn't made an effort to expand my social circle. Because I'd become close with Joy and Jacob almost as soon as I'd moved to Cork, I hadn't felt the need to shop around for more friends.

There were a few people I was still friendly with at work. But most of them had grown up in Cork and had friends who kept them busy.

I hadn't relied on their friendship before. Now, with Joy's impending departure, I was beginning to see them in a different light. Maybe one of them would be good enough, even if nobody could ever replace Joy.

I'd been ringing Arjun for days for an update on his situation with Sharmila, and he finally answered while I was shopping for groceries one evening.

I stopped in the condiments aisle when I heard his voice, with a trolley filled with fresh fruit and vegetables. I'd decided to make healthier choices this week—fewer precooked meals and more wholesome snacks. By Wednesday evening, when there was nothing but a banana to eat between meals, I'd no doubt be cursing this wiser Sunday version of myself. But that was midweek Durga's problem.

"Arjun! Where have you been?" I practically screamed into the phone.

It was late night in India and the house sounded quiet. Even Kobita must have gone to bed because I couldn't hear the TV in the background.

Arjun was unconcerned, repeating the joke that I sounded more like Ma every passing day.

"I haven't spoken to anyone in the family in nearly a week, you could have called me back," I interrupted his laughter.

"I've been busy."

"Has something happened? You're still visiting me over Christmas?"

"I'll keep you posted."

I didn't like the sound of that. I wanted my brother here, and I solemnly stood facing a variety of mustards in jars. Dijon, coarse grain, the bright yellow American kind. A wave of emotion knocked me back at the realization that I needed someone here with me, someone I trusted and loved, to tell me what to do with my life. I was prepared to follow their directive. I thought Arjun could help me, but now he wasn't going to come. And all this because my parents were scandalized by my love life?

"How can you change your plans? Nobody has visited me in two years. Not even Tia. You promised you'd spend Christmas with me. You promised we'd book an Airbnb and spend a weekend away. I've used up all my savings so I can't even go to India if I wanted to."

Arjun listened to me in silence, and when I stopped berating him, he gave me a few more moments to start up again, but I didn't.

"I've left home, I've left Calcutta," he whispered.

So this wasn't about me at all.

"Wait. What? Have you got a new job? Where are you?"

I was reminded of myself as a child, when Arjun, four years my senior, had the more interesting life. I'd follow him around the house, bursting with questions about the films he was allowed to watch, the places he was allowed to visit without adult supervision. The mall, a recent addition to the city, was the pinnacle of my dreams. Hanging there with Arjun's friends was what I aspired to.

"No, I haven't been looking for jobs yet. Only Parul knows, so she can tell the others when they find out. I don't want them to worry."

I didn't at all like the sound of this. I nearly laughed when the thought crossed my mind that he may be running away.

"Have you run away? With Sharmila?" I giggled nervously.

"She can't live like this anymore. I don't want her to," he said.

I left the trolley in the aisle and ran out of the shop so I could yell at him outside.

I told him he was insane for risking his life and future. Priyam would most certainly go after them, and find them, and when he did, what if he took matters into his own hands? Or worse still, handed matters over into the hands of a heavily bribed sleazy cop. What about our family? Our parents, Didu, everyone would be affected by this. Their lives, their peace of mind, their every waking minute would be torture. Even Tia's new family would want to have nothing to do with him.

I asked him how far he was willing to go. Not just the distance, but how far into the future he'd planned. Was he foolish enough to think that they could ever live a normal life after this?

Arjun once again allowed me to rage. He wasn't expecting any less than this. I was getting soaked in the rain outside because I hadn't had the time to open my umbrella. My raincoat was flimsy and only covered my torso, and I hadn't even pulled the hood up.

"Are you done, Durga?" he finally said.

I couldn't respond to that, because in actual fact, I *wasn't* done. I hadn't even broached the subject of what they would do for money or for a roof over their heads.

"We don't live in the olden days anymore," he added.

"The olden days aren't long behind us, Arjun. Even twenty years ago, eloping with someone else's wife could result in serious life-threatening consequences. She's your cousin's wife. Hell, they could still stone you to death in some villages," I said.

"We are in Delhi. We took a flight here this morning. Ma and Baba think I'm on a work trip in Bangalore."

"You went to Delhi? Sure, the seat of modernity and social advancement. How many women get raped in Delhi on a daily basis? On buses, on the streets." I was close to crying.

"Durga, relax. We are staying with one of my friends. For a few weeks, until I find a place to rent. I don't have a new job yet, but I'll find one easily. You know how many times other companies have tried to poach me in the last five years? I don't like to boast, but my qualifications are in high demand. I went to the Indian Statistical Institute, for God's sake."

"Do you realize that landlords care about marital status? They're going to ask if you and Sharmila are married."

"And we'll lie. They don't all ask to see marriage certificates."

This wasn't what I wanted for my brother.

"She's going to ask for a divorce, eventually, when they call off the search. Priyam's parents wouldn't want their son married to a woman who has run away," he said.

"And what about Ma and Baba? Would Ma want a daughter-in-law who was married to her brother's son?"

It was astounding how unbothered Arjun was, and this was how I knew his mind was made up. I knew I sounded like my mother now, emotionally blackmailing him into doing what the family considered to be the right choice.

"Ma and Baba love her already, like a daughter. If, all of a sudden, their feelings for her change, I will lose my respect for them. Then I won't care what they think of us," he said.

"Please tell me you haven't been stupid, Arjun. She's not pregnant, is she?"

"Nothing's happened between us. Durga, believe me, we've never done . . . it. We've only ever just talked. I love her, but I've never so much as held her hand. Not before today."

I needed some distance from this. Someone, unbiased and unrelated to me, was required to assess the situation. Well against my better judgment, Arjun was beginning to warm me to this idea. If for no other reason than to make him feel less alone. If everything went pear-shaped and he lost contact with our parents and Tia, I hated to think of him as alone, without even me to lean on.

"I want you to seriously consider every possible scenario, Arjun, before you go so far you can't come back," I said.

"How about this? How about I give you an analogy that might simplify it for you?"

"What kind of analogy?"

"A food analogy," he said.

"Arjun, you don't need to remind me of my unhealthy relationship with food."

He was laughing again, which was a lovely sound to hear. It meant his soul was unencumbered and free.

"Remember when Tia went on that portion control regimen? She said all her friends were doing it, which I find hard to believe, because the concept is entirely Western and it would never work with an Indian upbringing."

I knew what he was talking about. Tia was in her late teens, and one of her old jeans didn't fit her anymore. It probably shrank from repeated washes, but she was convinced it was Ma's fault for overfeeding her.

"Anyway, she tried really hard, didn't she? She'd sit at the breakfast table and only eat one piece of toast. But Ma would be frying puris for the rest of us and she'd lose control and ask for one. Then a second and a third, because they were so freakin' delicious," he said.

"And she'd eat all her masala potatoes and some of mine too."

"Yes, and she hated us for it. She blamed Ma and the rest of us for not supporting her. I don't ever want to blame Ma or Baba or any of you for my unhappiness. I know this is not ideal, and it could end in disaster, but it's on me. I want to take full responsibility for my life. No portion control," he said.

Arjun was right. Funnily enough, I did understand him better now. If I were to go on a lifelong diet, I would lose my mind too. As a family, we were not built for restraint.

"Okay, Arjun. I just want you to know you have me. No matter how stupid you are and how mad I am at you, please don't disappear on me."

He was laughing without restraint, like a man who knew what he wanted and was doing something about it.

"I'm only able to do this because of you, Durga. You left home. You know you could have told me about him, right?"

"I know, it's just—complicated."

"I understand complicated, believe me. What I'm trying to say is that you did this. Paved the way for the rest of us. I wouldn't even dream of going after the life I want if you hadn't done it first."

I burst into tears, sobbing like a lost child who'd just been found.

Chapter 35

THE NEXT EVENING AFTER WORK, I MADE MYSELF A ham and cheese sandwich. The bread slices had dried out because I'd forgotten to tie a knot in the bag, and the edges of the crumbed ham had hardened to the consistency of seashells from being in the fridge too long.

But I had to feed all the feelings inside me. So, I ate the sandwich, chewing each bite for a long time to make it palatable. I washed down the unpleasant experience with a can of Coke. Joy had spent the previous night with Maeve, and I hadn't seen her in over twenty-four hours. I wasn't sure if she was coming home today, and I didn't want to text and ask. It was selfish of me, to want her here, to want her all to myself. Maeve had been good for her these past weeks, even I could admit that.

When my phone rang it startled me, and I realized there was no music playing in the house, and I was surrounded by only silence. The other sound, apart from my phone, was the boiler warming up the radiators with that distinctive metallic scraping sound. It could have been mice, but I didn't want to think about that possibility.

As soon as I saw Tia's picture on the screen, I knew it was bad news.

We'd been communicating through emails while she was in Japan, and I wasn't sure if she was back.

It was possible that our conversation had motivated Arjun to come clean to Tia. She wouldn't be as easy to convince as I was. I had a dreadful thought that she'd told Ma where Arjun really was, and the house was in an uproar. Did Didu have a heart attack?

Tia sounded hysterical as soon as I answered the phone, and all of my worst fears quickly rose to the surface.

"What's happened? Is Didu okay?"

I abandoned the remainder of my sandwich and rushed to my room to start packing a bag.

"Didu? Yeah, she's fine. I mean, she wants us to call the police, but what's the point in that?"

"No, Tia, don't involve the police in this. It has to remain within the family."

Tia had been whimpering, but she stopped abruptly. "What the fuck, Durga? You're taking *his* side? How do you even know about this? Who told you?"

"Arjun told me himself. We were speaking just a while ago. I'm not taking anyone's side, I'm trying to be supportive of our brother."

"Arjun? What does he have to do with this?"

We were both caught in a moment's awkward silence.

"I'm talking about Bikram. He hit me, Durga. I'm back home be-cause I'm not going to be that woman," she said.

UNLIKE OUR PARENTS, Tia was comfortable relating all the details of unpleasant experiences, no matter how excruciating they were. All my instincts about Bikram were now proven right.

The first six days of their trip to Japan had gone swimmingly. It wasn't cherry blossom season, but the mountains were covered in powdery snow. They went on a day trip to Mount Fuji, walked through beautiful gardens, went to see the temples, and tried strange new flavors of KitKat. They were eating sushi at every meal.

At the end of the week, Tia wanted to go to Kichijoji for the shops, while Bikram said he'd heard about the famous ramen stalls at Sugamo Jizo-dori and wanted to go there instead.

It began as a silly argument. Tia was getting dressed while they quarreled, as lovers do, and she didn't think much of it. Bikram was lying back on their luxurious hotel bed, with silken pillows under his head. A king in his hired castle.

Tia suggested they divvy up the day; hit the shops before lunch and go for ramen after. Bikram finally admitted that the real reason he didn't want to go to Kichijoji was because he worried she'd spend too much money there.

Then he asked her about her savings. Apparently they'd spoken about using some of it to buy a flat, but now Bikram wanted to know what she was going to do with the rest.

"He wants me to invest in his business, Durga. Some new app idea he's come up with. He's obviously had an eye on my money for a while. When I said I wanted to keep some of my savings for myself, he had the audacity to tell me to ask Baba for extra cash. He wants our father to loan him money for his stupid idea. Why would I do that? His father is the one with the money, not mine. I reminded him of it and he sniggered at me. He told me, to my face, that he'd always known this marriage was all about his money. That my parents had pushed us together so I could live off his family money for the rest of my life."

Tia had been in the process of applying lipstick. And upon hearing her husband use those words, she threw the lipstick in his direction. Admittedly, this was wrong, because throwing an object at someone, no matter its size, is an act of violence.

The lipstick, which was without its lid and pushed up for application, landed on the bed near Bikram's crossed ankles. The white sheet now had a burgundy smear.

Bikram's reaction to the mark was extreme. He grew furious about the laundry charge the hotel would add to their bill. He said that Tia was already costing him more money than he could keep up with.

That she needed to find a way to make a bigger contribution to their lifestyle.

My sister, feeling sheepish for having thrown the lipstick at him, but also hostile, stood up from the chair at the dressing table.

"I told him I'll pay for the hotel. The honeymoon. All the costs," Tia told me.

She had gathered her coat and began putting on boots. Bikram continued badgering her about the money. How he didn't need her to pay for the honeymoon. He needed money for his app.

"What exactly is this app?"

"Don't even get me started on it, Durga. He has this idea for a liquor delivery service. So they'll bring alcohol to your home like groceries."

"Isn't there an app for it already?"

"Exactly. I'm sure there is. It's ridiculous. Which is exactly what his father told him and refused to invest, which is why he wants our family's money instead."

When Tia tried to leave, he situated himself in front of the door. She told him to move out of her way, but he grabbed her arm and pulled her sharply away.

Tia said she still had a purple bruise to show for it.

They didn't speak to each other at all for the rest of the day. Tia remained in the room, mostly on her phone, uploading photographs she'd taken around Tokyo to her socials. Bikram lounged by the hotel pool, not keeping account of the money he spent on the whiskies he was ordering.

Tia didn't sleep that night. She was beginning to wonder if she really knew the man she had married, snoring loudly beside her.

The next morning, while Tia was at the hotel restaurant, trying to enjoy the breakfast spread, Bikram joined her at the table with a blue velvet box.

He told her he loved her and urged her to open it. Inside, she found a garish brooch. It was in the shape of a bow, studded with crystals and pink rhinestones. Tia was alarmed, sure that he hadn't purchased this here in Japan.

Bikram explained it was an antique brooch belonging to his grandmother, and he'd been waiting for the right moment to gift it to her. Tia probably wouldn't have minded it so much, even though she couldn't picture herself ever wearing it. But he felt the need to point out that the brooch should successfully satisfy her shopping cravings—now that she had something pretty and precious in her possession. Like she was an addict who needed a small, harmless dose to tide her over.

"He makes it sound like it's me, but he's the one obsessed with money. I never planned on asking him to pay for my shopping. But clearly he didn't want me to spend any of my money either."

She'd stormed out of the restaurant and gone up to their room. She was already packing her bags by the time Bikram came through the door.

He challenged her, claiming she couldn't go home since their flight back wasn't for another two days. She responded by sharing with him the exact amount she had in savings in her bank account, thereby being fully capable of paying her own way back.

That figure must have incensed him because that was when he slapped her. Right across the face, with full lip-splitting force. He fell on his knees almost instantly, begging for forgiveness, but Tia was already out of the door.

Instead of heading to the airport, she checked herself into a different hotel. She wanted time to think, away from him, from his family and ours, before she fell back into the dangerously comfortable routine of domesticity.

She took a flight the next day, arriving in Calcutta a day early, and went to a friend's house directly from the airport.

"I struggled with telling Ma and Baba at first. I didn't want them to be afraid or disappointed. This marriage hasn't lasted even a month," she said.

I'd listened to the story sitting stock-still on my bed, unable to move a muscle until she arrived at the end, when I was sure she was safe.

"Tia, I am so proud of you," I said.

She wasn't crying anymore. She was seething, boiling, hopping mad.

"Don't be. I've spent my whole life waiting to marry this man, live my dream, and he turns out to be a wife-beating miser. What a joke."

"You walked away. You didn't give him a second chance."

Tia laughed a wet laugh, which turned into a soft sob, but she gathered herself quickly.

"I had to tell Ma and Baba eventually, of course. They've been so good about it, so supportive, angry on my behalf. Baba is blaming himself. He's the one who really wanted this marriage, really pushed for it from the moment we were born."

I knew what Baba was thinking, why he felt so guilty. My conversation with him about Jacob must have triggered this. The realization that he'd held both his daughters' hands and walked straight into high tide.

"Baba will speak to Bikram's father tomorrow and they're going to work out the best way forward. A quick divorce. Ma said she's not keeping it under the radar, she's telling everyone so that if they try to set him up with some other poor woman in the future, they will know what kind of man he is."

"I hope he lives a lonely life," I said.

"He won't be *that* lonely. Now he's free to pursue all the female friends he's had dalliances with. I wanted to marry him, but I was never blind. Everyone knew, of course. I bet they all laughed at me and what an imbecile I am for still marrying him."

"You're not. You just wanted to make everyone happy, Tia," I said.

"And look where that got me."

* * *

JOY, IN HER infinite wisdom, returned home with burritos.

I was glad she was alone and Maeve wasn't going to join us for the night. As much as I loved this for them—the cuddling on the couch and the whispering sweet nothings—I was going to treasure my time alone with Joy.

She knew something was wrong when I didn't immediately pounce on the food.

"My family is falling apart. Arjun has run away with our cousin's wife, and Tia just fled an abusive marriage. My parents are being very supportive of her, but they're devastated. And I've only eaten a cardboard sandwich since lunch."

Joy squeezed my shoulders and we sat down on the barstools at the kitchen island. I told her as much as I could before I was out of breath, and she said I needed to eat.

She said she was growing really fond of Tia, even though they hadn't met yet. Arjun was in a tricky situation, and in her opinion, we just had to let it play out.

It all sounded more reasonable, coming from her. Tia was safe and free. Arjun was headed toward happiness, even though I couldn't conceive of it now.

We both wished there were some alcohol in the house, so we sat and chain-smoked her remaining six cigarettes instead. After this, I felt violently ill and tried throwing up in the toilet, while Joy held my hair back.

"It's your throat seizing. Don't bloody smoke, Durga. Here, I'll make you some rooibos tea."

The tea didn't help much, other than warming me a little. I didn't have the same nostalgic relationship with it that she did.

We sat on the couch but neither of us wanted to endure the process of finding something to watch. Joy picked a playlist for us to listen to, and I watched her dancing around the room for a bit. She was a good dancer, I thought, much better than Maeve. I told her so, and Joy asked me to never tell Maeve that. Eventually, I drifted to sleep.

I woke up on the couch the next morning. Joy had already left for work and I was going to be very late. I checked my phone for updates, and there were a couple of messages from my siblings.

Parul: *Don't know if you're panicking. Don't panic. Everything is under control. Ma and Baba are calm.*

Arjun: *Ma and Baba know where I am. I have their support. Don't panic.*

Tia: *I think I want to come see you in Ireland*

Chapter 36

AFTER WHAT HAPPENED TO TIA, I WANTED TO SPEAK with Surjo. I rang him during my lunch break at work, while he was still home.

I would have liked to be outside for this phone call, for the sake of privacy, but we were well settled into winter by now and nothing was worth braving the cold. Worse than that was the rain and the wind, which would have blown the cold directly at my face.

I locked myself in a bathroom stall and hoped my voice wouldn't carry far. Surjo knew what was coming, because he greeted me with a boring *Hello*.

"Do you know what happened with Tia?" I asked.

"Bikram told me they argued and she left Tokyo a day early."

"They didn't just argue. He hit her, Surjo. She was injured."

He made a mewling sound, like a child whose lollipop had been snatched from his hands.

"*If* that's what's happened, then Bikram needs to do some serious groveling," he said.

"My sister is not lying. She has a split lip and a bruise on her arm. What story is he telling everyone?"

"He's not telling much. He's mad because Tia is refusing to pick up the phone and talk. They're married, Durga, they need to speak about this."

"There is no use groveling. Tia is leaving him."

There was another groan from him, as though he'd just watched that lollipop being crushed under someone's boot.

"They need to talk this through. I'm sure Bikram can explain," he said.

"What possible explanation can there be? He used his hand to slap her face. That's what happened. No matter the circumstances, or the argument, these are the facts."

I was expecting something other than this weak attempt at defending his friend's actions. Shock, fury, disgust—they would all be acceptable reactions. He sounded more like a mildly vexed father whose son had stolen another kid's lunch box at school and he didn't want to degrade himself by apologizing for his offspring's actions.

"Okay, let me talk to him. I'll try and find out what he's thinking. He's really upset, Durga. He loves her."

"He's upset because everyone is going to find out what he did. Not because he's sorry, Surjo. Would you recommend that my sister remain married to him, and hope he never hurts her again? Are you willing to vouch for your friend and carry that on your conscience?"

"I don't know what you want me to say, Durga. Bikram is one of my best friends. He needs his friends right now, he needs me."

That was all I had to hear from him. I had no intention of wasting my time trying to change his mind. Not if I had to *convince* him to hop the fence to my side about domestic violence. I'd completely misread the kind of man he was.

"Bye," I said, and ended the call and blocked his number.

I ENVISIONED MYSELF as Kali. I saw myself wielding an axe and using the wooden handle to knock on Bikram's door. When he opens it, Kali smashes the axe on his head, demolishing him into thousands of blood-red pieces like a broken vase. Then she wipes the splatter off her face and gets in her mint green Nissan Micra and drives away. Swerving around potholes, overtaking other cars with the wind in her hair.

I really did want Bikram dead.

Tia, on the other hand, had adopted a cool exterior. I rang her several times a day, and the few times she answered she told me to stop bothering her so she could get on with her life.

Four days after she'd returned from her honeymoon, Tia applied for a job at a multinational company. She already had an interview set up for the following week. If she got the job, she'd be moving to Singapore. I knew she'd get it, not only because she impressed everyone who met her, but because she was capable and worthy.

Arjun was with Sharmila now, and knowing my brother, he would have wanted to stick around and look after Tia. But he knew, and I knew, she didn't need anybody.

When Tia was eight, Didu had fallen down the stairs and severely injured her ankle. Tia was the only one home. Even Kobita was out, doing the shopping. Tia had run out of the house to flag down a taxi, then screamed until the neighbors came running out. But she only wanted them to help her carry Didu into the car. My parents found out what had happened because Tia had left a note to let them know she'd taken Didu to Apollo Hospital.

She didn't need Arjun to comfort her now, and she certainly didn't require me acquainting Bikram with an untimely death.

I was the weak one. Spending my days wandering around grocery shop aisles, trying to plan healthy meals. Then resorting to ordering noodles from the nearest takeaway because Joy wasn't around enough to provide me with the emotional support I needed to consume a salad.

On a particularly quiet Wednesday night, when Joy had been missing from our flat for three days straight, I ended up texting Luke.

We hadn't spoken for weeks, but as usual, he was quick to respond. When he arrived we skipped the niceties. I didn't even offer him a drink, and we went straight to my room.

It was the kind of sex that could have broken the bed. I knew what I was trying to overcome—all the feelings of rage and regret I wanted to obliterate from my system. What was he trying to suppress?

It got me thinking. My mind wandered into the dangerous territory of speculating if this was the kind of sex he had with other women.

After, while he watched videos in bed beside me, I thanked him for coming.

"No pun intended," I said.

He laughed, briefly looking up from his phone to give me a kiss on my bare shoulder. The gold-plated chain around his neck gleamed in the screen's light, and I noticed he hadn't shaved recently. His stubble was flaxen and soft-looking, a darker shade under his nose and lower lip. And I thought—I could do this forever. Perhaps this was enough. Good sex and silence. Kali would have been satisfied with just that.

I remained still beside him, scrolling through my phone, unfocused. I was waiting for him to leave, which I knew he would, soon. Not that I wanted him to go, just expected him to.

The company was nice, having a warm body beside me. But I became anxious from the waiting.

I said, "So, any plans tonight?" at the same time as he said, "What are you doing for dinner?"

"I could cook us some pasta," he said, putting his phone away.

"We don't have any."

"Ah, gotcha," he said.

"No, I didn't mean it like that. I'm not trying to get rid of you. We genuinely don't have pasta. Joy used it all up."

Luke smiled as he got off the bed and began gathering his clothes, not at all shy of his nakedness.

"Joy cool with us?" His voice was muffled as he slid on his T-shirt and then the hoodie.

"I think so. She says she is, says she had a feeling."

"What feeling?"

Joy's exact words to me had been: *I knew you weren't going to ride him just once.*

Telling him this would be impossible. I hadn't planned to let on that we'd spoken about him at all. Luke waited a beat and then seemed to have changed his mind. As though he didn't want to know what Joy thought after all.

He was pulling the zip up on his jeans while gazing out of the window, and I saw a smile stretch across his lips.

"What?" I said.

"There's a cat on that roof."

Luke went to stand at the window and I got out of bed to join him. I'd bunched the duvet around me as best I could, unwilling to stand naked at my window in broad daylight.

There was a jet black cat on a neighbor's roof. It had a sleek tail and the tips of its ears were white. It was walking on the sloping slats, with not a care in the world. Beside me, Luke's face was over-taken by the kind of radiance that comes from a place of enjoying the simple pleasures of life.

"You like cats?" I said.

He never took his eyes off it, and whistled with distress when the cat slid down a tricky bit. We watched with bated breath as it skid-ded to a stop just before falling off the edge.

"They're so smart. Real personalities," he said.

The cat had now decided to settle down for a nap in the gutters, just to bake in the elusive winter sunshine while it lasted. It had to stretch out all four limbs to mold itself to the shape of its new bed.

"And so freakin' cute," I said. "Is that really the most comfortable spot? Maybe it is, what do I know. I wake up with a backache most mornings, maybe I should try sleeping in the gutters sometime."

Luke laughed. "I feel like I can trust you now."

I nearly told him about Kaju, my old cat and the new one, but Luke seemed suddenly in a rush. He took my face between both his hands and planted a kiss on my lips.

"Gotta go," he said.

"Yeah, go. Of course."

I found that I was relieved. Those sticky feelings I didn't expect to have with Luke were pasted all over me this time. I became suddenly terrified of him, and what else I was capable of experiencing if he stayed even a moment longer in my room.

"You should wear this more often. Looks good on you."

He looked me over, in my duvet dress, with his blue eyes glittering. We kissed again, as though he was only leaving to get coffee for us from the shop. Then he was gone.

KALI HAD GOT from this day what Kali wanted, but Durga was alone again.

Chapter 37

I T WAS THE WEEK BEFORE CHRISTMAS WHEN TIA ARRIVED
in Ireland. It worked out well since Arjun already had the tickets
booked, so Tia used them instead. The visa had taken time to sort
out, and she'd also got that job and became busy making plans to
move to Singapore in the new year.

It was good timing since Joy had as good as moved out of the flat,
spending more than just the weekends with Maeve now. I tried to
not let it get to me. When she did check in, it was usually for a night,
or for a few hours to do the laundry and pack a new bag. I noticed
how she hadn't been bringing back the things she took with her the
previous times.

I assumed I wouldn't be seeing much of her over Christmas since
she said she was happy to lend Tia her room.

"I know I shouldn't blame Maeve, but I do," I said.

Tia and I were on a bus to the Marina Market. My sister was
swathed in layers too. A jumper, coat, scarf, hat, leg warmers, boots.
She kept mentioning how the cold weather suited her and like a
child she enjoyed making foggy puffs with her mouth when we were
outside, pretending to smoke a cigarette.

"Of course it's that girl's fault, but it was inevitable, wasn't it? How
long would the two of you live together? You can't eat junk and

watch Netflix forever," Tia said, clicking a blurry picture of a church from the bus window.

I'd always felt like a tourist in my sister's life—following her everywhere, waiting for direction, relying on her to tell me where to buy shoes. In Ireland it was different. Tia struggled to pay correctly with the foreign cash, and had to ask me to take her shopping.

"I could live with Joy forever. She even wanted us to buy a house together. Completely her idea," I said.

Tia rolled her eyes. "It wouldn't work. It's better this way. You need your own life, Durga."

Tia snapped another picture, which appeared to be of nothing significant, but she told me it was the clean quiet streets that astounded her most.

"I've been thinking of going back to India."

Tia put her phone down and turned to me. "You can't be serious. All of us are leaving home. Parul is going to scram the first chance she gets, and you want to come back?"

"It doesn't have to be *home* home. I could move to a different city, maybe even Delhi if Arjun's there."

Tia sighed as she looked out of the window. The bus slowed and then stopped, making its heavy hydraulic huff before the doors opened. She followed me out and we wrapped our scarves around our necks in preparation.

"I feel more at ease here. Nobody's in a hurry, I haven't been pushed once while walking," she said, as we headed toward the open quay.

"Not a good enough reason to make a life here."

Tia smiled at a little girl who walked past us, holding her father with one hand and a teddy in the other.

"Your best friend is here, Durga. You've got your independence, a good job, clean air, tap water you can drink, the mountains, the sea, art and culture, those taco chips we ate last night. You're even thinking for yourself. If you're not lying about your conversation with

Surjo, this is the first time you've stood up for yourself. The old Durga would have tried to change his mind, given him the benefit of the doubt, assumed his heart was in the right place. And Baba! You finally had it out with Baba, after all these years. He needed to hear it. Ireland has been good for you." Tia squeezed my hand. "You should learn to drive, that'll set you up."

The river ran on our side along the market's car park and she walked right up to the edge. There was no wall, no bollards, just free temptation to take the plunge. Some gulls were fighting over a burst paper bag of chips and we watched them in silence.

"I miss the noise, and the people I know, and the smell of Ma's kitchen, and being able to speak in Bangla," I said.

"Come home when it gets too much, just for a break. You'll always have that." She smiled and waved at a man who was working on a yacht bobbing on the bank. "What you miss about home is our childhood, Durga, and that's over. Ma is not going to braid your hair every morning if you live at home. Didu sleeps all the time. You won't have the smell of khichudi in the kitchen if you're renting your own place in a different city. Arjun isn't going to drive you to the mall at your every whim. *This* is your life now, get a cat."

THE MARINA MARKET was a capsule of canopied energy, keeping us all warm and sheltered from the cold and rain. At the center was a vast expanse of distressed couches and picnic benches, thronged with people, well-behaved dogs, and fairy lights. Freshly prepared mulled wine and hot chocolates were on every table, with paper plates of iced donuts and churros. A band was playing covers of Christmas songs at the back, and it smelled of warm food and happy spirits.

I followed Tia as she examined the menu at each food stall, still thinking about all she had said. There were burgers, pizzas, stews and curries, macarons, poke bowls, hot dogs, and loaded chips. I was overwhelmed by the choices but she wasn't. I admired her for it, how she basked in the glory of new experiences, and I knew she was right. Change was good. I had to make this new life my own.

We got strong Italian cappuccinos and cream-filled cannolis and wandered over to the stall where a young woman sold handmade sea glass jewelry.

I held Tia's coffee while she tried on a few rings for size. Then I heard my name being shouted. I looked around, trying to distinguish a familiar face in the undulating crowd of people around us.

"See, you're practically local now. Someone you know is here," Tia said.

"Everyone in Cork City is here."

I thought I'd misheard and Tia went back to looking at the rings when I felt a hand on my shoulder.

"Hey, you."

I turned to find Luke beaming at me, a half-eaten wrap in his other hand. He was in a set of matching gray sweats, and looked lean and athletic. I couldn't stop picturing him naked.

He must have been trying to grow out his facial hair because that stubble was a lot thicker now, and had taken on a more ginger shade, which suited him. With his delicate chin hidden, his blue eyes were sharper.

Three people joined him: two men and a woman. Friends I hadn't known the existence of.

"This is my sister, Tia," I said.

"Didn't you just get married?" Luke held out a hand for her to shake.

I hurriedly handed the coffee cup back to her, trying to catch her eye, unsure of how she would react to the reminder.

"Didn't last. He is an abusive bastard," she said and shrugged.

"Shit," said one of Luke's male friends.

"Hope you're okay," Luke added.

"I am, he won't be. My family is making his life hell."

She turned to me with a smile and I giggled nervously.

"Great vibe here," Luke said.

The other friend held up his can of energy drink and whooped in the direction of the band. Tia smiled at the guy and they both made a sultry sway to the tune of "Santa Baby."

I looked at Luke the same time he glanced at me. It was strange to see him in this context again, the way I'd first known him—fully clothed, among friends.

His friends had roped Tia into a conversation and she'd moved closer to them, leaving Luke and me to the side.

"Your sister seems to be coping well." He leaned in close to my ear to make himself heard, and I ached to touch him, to remind myself how intimately I knew him. I'd nibbled on that lower lip and made him growl with desire.

"My sister is coping better than I would. I'm sorry, there's always some drama in my life."

"Well, I'm getting kicked out of my place because the landlord's selling. I'd be homeless if Mikey didn't give me his couch to sleep on. Yeah, there's always something."

"Are you looking for a place?"

"Yeah, but I'll be grand. You know what it's like with housing right now. Give me a shout when you're free?" he said, then took a bite of his wrap, licking the mayonnaise off his lips.

"I'll text you," I said and reached for Tia's elbow, tugging her away from the others.

They disappeared into the crowd quickly.

"I think I'm going to try some of that Venezuelan food. Those arepas look nice," Tia said, walking away. I followed her closely, afraid of losing her. I stood beside her in the queue, looking around frantically to see if I could observe Luke from a distance.

"He seems nice. Is he the one you told Ma about? I'm sure you've had a lot of *fun* with him."

There was a look of curiosity mixed with concern on her face. My sister had a new lease on life, but she hadn't lost all her moral sensibilities yet. She couldn't condone my sexual exploits without reservation. She hadn't experienced that kind of freedom yet and didn't know if she would like it.

"It was never serious. We've kept it casual."

Tia was watching me closely and it made me self-conscious. I could sense she was picturing us together.

It was Tia's turn and she ordered a pulled beef arepa with black beans and plantains. I said I wasn't hungry and forced myself to finish the cannoli I was still carrying around.

We couldn't find a place to sit so we went closer to the band, and stood there with the music loud in our ears. Neither of us wanted to talk for a while.

I caught sight of Luke with his friends just as we were making our way out of the market. They were sitting at one of the picnic benches, with a whole table full of food between them. He seemed so at ease, laughing with his friends. His neck was strained as he shouted over the music and noise. He wasn't thinking about me, I was already forgotten. I found it curious that he'd even come up to speak with me. Good for him, I thought, that he was able to pause and acknowledge and then carry on.

I'd laid my cards on the table for everyone to see, and it was now my turn to play a fresh round with a clean hand.

This was how we were going to end. Seeing Luke today had humanized him. The illusion was burst, the one we'd crafted so carefully in the darkness of my bedroom. As though it was just the two of us in the world.

But Luke was one of the good ones. He didn't deserve to be used as a fidget spinner for my anxious hands.

Chapter 38

JOY AND MAEVE WERE LEAVING FOR DINGLE THE NEXT evening, for a quick two-night getaway before they became tied to their respective families over Christmas.

"Mum wanted me to tell you she's returned the library books, by the way," Joy said.

I was standing at her bedroom door, we were chatting while she packed. Maeve and I obviously shared the same concerns regarding Joy's driving because they were taking Maeve's car for the trip. Tia had gone out for a walk.

"I'm glad to hear it. Baby steps," I said.

Joy went into our shared bathroom and collected her toothbrush, toothpaste, and makeup bag.

"She was looking well the last time I saw her. Daddy says she's been eating again."

Joy had a blue hard-shell suitcase which was already stuffed with clothes and shoes. I'd seen her sit on it before to try and zip it up, but it looked impossible this time.

"How is Eric?" I asked.

"Daddy is fine, never been much of a talker, so I don't actually know. They will never fully recover."

"Neither will we," I said, and she nodded.

She threw in one last pair of boots, shut the lid of the suitcase, and then sat on it. But the two parts were nowhere close to meeting, she would never zip it all the way around.

"Why do you need all this stuff for two nights?"

She continued tugging at the zip and then called me over to do it for her while she hunkered down.

It didn't work and she returned to the bed with a large duffel bag and began throwing things in it from the suitcase. I didn't know why she needed four coats, several pairs of jeans, and all her boots for this trip, and I had a dreadful feeling she wasn't coming back.

With her bags packed, she sat down beside me on the bed. When she hugged me I noticed that her hair didn't smell of cigarettes anymore. A pleasant improvement.

Before I could say anything Joy began tidying up around the flat. I was relieved that she still cared enough to do this. I helped her load the dishwasher and dust down the surfaces.

Soon after, Tia and Maeve came up the stairs together. Joy and I were on one side of the door, Maeve and Tia on the other. We hadn't introduced them yet, but they were chatting animatedly about a moisturizer they both used, singing its praises.

"You know each other?" Joy asked, after we'd waited a while for them to take a pause.

Maeve leaned in to drop a peck on Joy's cheek. "We obviously know everything about each other since you two can't keep anything to yourselves. Tia, how many times had Joy and I kissed before we started dating?"

My sister scrunched her brows in thought. "Five? Give or take."

"Close. Four. See?"

"What does my soon-to-be ex-husband do for a living?" Tia asked Maeve.

"Gets his ass kicked by all your friends," Maeve said, and they laughed together like it was a big joke.

Clearly, Maeve matched Tia's ability to make light of serious situations. Joy and I exchanged looks of horror.

"Aren't you late already?" I said, while trying to shove Joy out of the door.

Maeve took Joy's duffel bag and we said our goodbyes before they finally left.

A playlist of pop-song covers were playing through the speakers. Tia headed to the kitchen carrying the bags she'd returned with. She said she was going to cook rice and a curry for us, and I knew it would be a disaster. Arjun was the only one who had ever paid attention to Ma cooking in the kitchen, and only because Sharmila was often in there with her.

TIA AND I spent the next two days mostly at the flat. Eating, talking, sleeping, watching TV, looking through old photos on our phones. We both needed this seclusion from the outside world, and in it we thrived.

I got acquainted with a side to my sister I didn't know well. A slower, more observant version of her, behind the exterior of quick temper and strong opinions. She questioned our parents' willingness to hand her over to strangers, to have trusted Bikram and his family so blindly. She said she disliked Sharmila and believed wholeheartedly that she had led our brother on. I urged her to give Sharmila a chance, to try and see what Arjun saw in her. She admitted Sharmila dressed well, which was a good starting point.

Tia was going to begin a new life in just a few weeks and I saw she was nervous about it. She had never lived by herself before, and wasn't too proud to ask me for advice.

We discussed our complicated feelings toward our parents, laid it all out. Every horrendous sentiment we'd harbored since our childhood, but had been too ashamed to share with each other before. She told me they were upset with me for sleeping around, but they were going through a lot. All their children were putting them through the ringer, but thankfully, my sexual exploits were the least of their concerns for now.

"Talk to Ma. Call her. She's waiting for you to make the first move, Durga."

It brought tears to my eyes, because I missed my mother. I wanted her to tell me I'd be okay.

My family was doing better with Arjun's elopement than I'd expected. Maybe we'd all grown this year.

Arjun and Sharmila were still living with friends, and he also had a new job lined up. By now, our family knew everything and so did Sharmila's mother. Baba said he could help them find a more permanent accommodation, because he knew a colleague with an unoccupied flat in Noida.

Arjun told me Priyam and his parents didn't know where they had gone, but they were well aware who she had gone with. The whole neighborhood had found out, and so had our extended family.

Ma was calling me frequently now, just to keep the phone engaged because our relatives were ringing her all day. I was happy she was speaking to me again, like our recent uncomfortable conversations had never happened.

"I hope he knows what he's doing," Ma said on the phone.

It was the middle of the night for me and it was nice listening to her, with the sounds of our home in the background. The TV, Didu's droning lectures to Kobita while she mopped the floor around her feet.

"He does, Ma. Arjun is more grown-up than you think."

We both laughed, because not so long ago he ate what was given to him and showered when Ma reminded him to.

"You all are," she continued with a sigh. "In fact, other people I thought were mature enough to leave our family alone are acting like little bored children looking for entertainment."

People were turning up at my parents' door with a range of moral agendas, berating Arjun for what he'd done. Ma didn't falter once. She knew her son had rescued a vulnerable woman from a dangerous situation, and she was proud of him. Ma was angry with her brother, ashamed that he'd allowed this to happen. He had made his daughter-in-law feel unwelcome and unworthy for not becoming pregnant quickly enough. Sharmila had told Ma everything. There was verbal abuse, ultimatums, strict rules and regulations she had to adhere to in that house.

"How is Sharmila doing now?" I asked.

"I cannot believe how they treated that poor girl. I didn't know my own brother was capable of this. All over wanting a grandchild. They should just let her go, let her live her life in peace since they were so unhappy with her."

"I feel better now, knowing she's with Arjun."

"Yes, he is such a good boy."

Ma had given Arjun the cold shoulder for weeks, until he was finally able to convince her that nothing sexual had transpired between them. The phrase *hanky-panky* was used frequently, and the atmosphere in our home was arrested by severe discomfort, Arjun told me. But it had eventually passed. Above all else, our parents wanted their children to find happiness.

"Ma, I am proud of you."

"Me? Why me? What have I done?" she giggled.

"You have shown more faith in your children than most other parents would."

"I have always had faith in you. If there's one thing your baba and I did right, it's that we've raised good children. But we've made some mistakes, with all three of you. We made some wrong decisions. That Bikram. That bastard."

An unbelieving laugh escaped me. Hearing Ma speak like this was a joy. To know she'd always had this in her.

"And I shouldn't have spoiled Arjun so much. Given him a bit more independence. Maybe if we didn't try so hard to get you to follow in Tia's footsteps, you would have told us about Jacob sooner. That Surjo was no good anyway. Anybody who takes Bikram's side is a bastard. All bastards."

I laughed harder, and wanted to tell her other choice words she could use to describe people she despised.

"You've done well with Parul," I said.

When Ma had tired from answering the door and speaking to the neighbors and family members who were showing up unannounced, Parul took over. My sister was quick to send them packing. Her approach was simple. She told them to mind their business, and if they continued to talk over her, she shut the door in their faces.

"She is a gem, but she's watched and learned. She's the best version of the three of you," Ma said.

Arjun still had a tedious road ahead of him. We all knew it wouldn't be smooth sailing for him, not until Sharmila's divorce was finalized. Then Didu told him her family hadn't approved of our grandfather because he was legally blind in one eye, but she'd married him anyway. She said she was only truly happy when she stopped holding herself responsible for other people's feelings.

I begged Ma to persuade Didu to speak to me on the phone. She'd never trusted technology. Baba used to laugh about how she insisted on knocking on a door when he was a child, rather than use the electric bell.

Didu had lectured my parents when Ma bought a blender; about how the mortar and pestle had served her well enough to make ginger and garlic paste all her life. Baba had one of those rotary telephones when he was growing up, but Didu rarely ever used it. So a mobile phone was practically out of the question.

Ma went away for a few minutes and returned with Didu on the phone. I didn't know what she told Didu, but the first thing she said when she got on was "Stop worrying about your siblings. Everything will be all right."

I couldn't respond to that. I thought I was prepared but my breath rattled at the sound of her voice. She reminded me of everything

good about my childhood, my home. Of long afternoons and summer holidays. Of sitting still while my hair was braided. Puffed rice
and mustard oil. Sleeping without blankets on warm nights. Ceiling
fans.

"Durga, I want you to be free of us. We are nobody's keepers other
than our children's. But only until they are old enough to grasp all
the ways they are capable of hurting other human beings. After that,
they are out of your hands too," she said. "So as long as you're not
hurting anyone, you should do what makes you happy. Other people's feelings don't count. Dash those."

Tia wasn't wrong that I'd slowly changed since I left home, but so
had they all.

TIA STAYED WITH me for Christmas, and we spent it with Maeve
and Joy, at her parents' home. Jacob's designated chair remained unoccupied at the dining table, and Eric placed a paper crown on the
empty plate Jacob would have eaten from.

Naledi made a speech before we ate.

"Our first Christmas without you, my darling boy," she began, ad-
dressing his empty chair.

Eric sat at the head of the table with his head down and eyes low-
ered, still unable to face the reality staring at him from the other
end.

"We all miss you so much," Naledi continued. She reached for
Joy's hand.

Maeve had a hand on Joy's back too, rubbing her gently.

Joy was looking at me as I sat across from her, and I wondered if
she could feel his presence here too. Jacob would have smirked at
this scene, at all of us sitting solemnly at the Christmas table. There
were no decorations this year, no tree, not even presents. He would
have sniggered at Joy, elbowing her when she wiped her tears, reminding her how this was her penance for when she wore his precious white sneakers and left them muddied.

The food was consumed in near silence. Tia and Naledi were the only ones who spoke at all, chatting about the garden like old neighbors.

Eric stood up as soon as he cleared his plate, desperate to get away from this stark reminder of his loss. Naledi was still nursing her glass of wine and she looked up at her husband with a sad smile. He came to stand behind her and placed one hand on her shoulder and the other on Joy's.

"Thank you for that meal, my love. You've outdone yourself," he said. Naledi patted his hand, looking up at him with adoration. They'd found strength in each other; the superhuman muscularity that was required to get through each day since the death of their son. They were living for Joy, and she understood that now. The weight of that responsibility, to find contentment in her own life for the sake of her parents.

"Yes, Mum, Jacob would have really enjoyed the food tonight," Joy said, looking up at her father.

The fact that Eric could bring himself to smile in that moment told me that he would make this new life work. The way Naledi and Joy were.

Then he looked at me, taking me by surprise. "We are so glad to still have you here with us, Durga."

NALEDI AND ERIC went to sleep early. The traditional game of charades was skipped, and Maeve and Tia were in the sitting room, deep in conversation. My sister's approval of Joy's girlfriend warmed me even further toward this relationship.

Joy and I sat alone for a while in the garden. We brought blankets with us outside, and bowls of Christmas pudding.

"Someone forgot a fifty-euro note at the cash point in Centra today," Joy said.

"What did you do?"

I'd made a hood with the blanket over my head. Unless my ears were covered, I could never be completely warm.

"Kept it. If I didn't, someone else would. I doubt the rightful owner would ever get it back anyway."

I nodded. I would have checked for cameras and probably done the same.

"You good?" she asked.

"Yeah. You?"

"Really good, and fifty euro richer. I was going to buy Maeve some flowers and wine, but I'm going to use it to get my nails done."

"An excellent use of funds," I said.

"Never underestimate the power of a good manicure. There's nothing you look at more than what you do with your own hands," she said.

Chapter 39

IN THE NEW YEAR, EARLY IN JANUARY, WHEN EVERYONE remains mostly indoors so as not to spend any more money, Joy and I went to brunch alone. Finally alone. Lately, it had felt like we were always surrounded by other people.

I sat in our usual corner at the café, waiting for her. Maeve was staying at a writing retreat in Monaghan for a week, having won a residency from The Arts Council. She told us she was completing the final edits on her novel, which Joy was certain would be an instant success. After some gentle nudging, Maeve had sent me the manuscript, and I'd stayed up all night reading it. I'd texted her as soon as I'd finished.

It's so chillingly gothic—this woman's downward descent into madness. I could relate in so many ways. Maeve, it's wonderful!

She'd replied with an emoji of that face blowing you a heart-kiss. Maeve was one of those people, but so was Tia. I had nothing against emojis.

Joy had officially moved out of our flat and in with Maeve, and they were both happier than ever before.

Maeve was going to keep her sage green walls and Nordic flower art prints, and they were buying a replica of Dalí's lips sofa, which Joy had coveted for years. Their relationship was perfectly balanced, and I watched them with admiration when we were together. How much they'd grown, how intrinsically connected they were.

The day before Joy moved out, we'd spent the evening watching stand-up together on the couch. Joy told me the box room at Maeve's place, where the single spare bed lived, was to be mine.

"You can stay whenever you want. Hell, move in!"

We'd hugged with tears in our eyes, and no answer was required from me. She knew I loved her, and because I did I was going to give her the space she needed so this relationship could flourish without me. I'd never exploit the room she was offering me.

"I think I'll like living alone," I'd said.

At our flat, *my* flat now, where I lived alone with seven new plants, where I regularly thought I heard Joy's footsteps in other rooms. Every time I switched off the hairdryer, my ears still ringing from the loud noise and hot air, I'd hear the phantom sound of Joy calling out for me from the kitchen. Perhaps it wasn't Joy's, but Jacob's voice I heard. I was prepared to listen out for him for the rest of my life.

WHILE I WAITED at the café with a cappuccino, I resisted the urge to drum my fingers on the table. They were playing "Ignition (Remix)" loud enough to drown out people's conversations. I mouthed "gimme that toot toot" silently, and Joy appeared beside me. When I looked up she joined in and mouthed "beep beep."

Chapter 40

AFTER WORK, ON A FAIRLY WARM THURSDAY IN LATE April, I walked to the park where I'd met Niall and his dog, Dusty.

But I wasn't going there for him. In fact, I hadn't thought of him in months.

The park was blooming today. The cherry blossom trees were lush in pastel shades of pink. There was birdsong, children riding bikes, dogs off leads bounding in the grass, a food truck selling crepes and ice cream.

Nothing compares to a late spring day in Ireland. When there's that *long stretch* in the evening. You're expecting sunset any minute now, but it never seems to arrive, lengthening the day in such a way that you don't remember what it feels like to go to bed in darkness. The grass is golden and alive with bees and butterflies. The air smells surprisingly of coconuts, from the yellow gorse-covered hills around us. Every year, despite what the winter brought—overcast weeks, the frost, the decay, the misfortune—in spring the wildflowers blossom anyway.

I'd fought it for so long, caught in the tug-of-war between who I was in India with my family and who I was now, how I wanted to be. But I could be both, this was what I knew now. That I could curse in

Bangla when I stubbed my toe, and eat black pudding for breakfast on the same day.

I walked to the Fairy Trail—a narrow, shaded path where all the old tree trunks were made colorful by fairy doors nailed on by local schoolchildren. They'd got creative with it. Some fairy doors were decorated with Lego, some covered in sequins, there were designs made with beads. Most had their names painted on. Ellora. Agata. Aria. Rory. Clodagh. Cian. I stood and read them all.

I glanced at my watch and when I looked up I saw a familiar figure sprinting down the path in my direction.

He was in running shorts and a gray T-shirt, with a damp V patch around the neck. His stubble had grown into a full-blown beard now, thick and trimmed neatly.

He slowed down and then stopped in front of me, pulling earpods out and panting lightly.

"Howya?"

"Hi," I said.

I was smiling with a flutter in my belly. From the sheer exhilaration of setting eyes on him again. I had missed him, more than I'd even known. He brought with him the feeling of simple hours, unworried evenings of lying in bed together, the excitement of getting to know him—a whole new interesting person.

Luke stood with his hands on his hips, looking flummoxed. He was bathed in sunshine and smelled of earth. Of sweat and the outside. He even had some dirt under his fingernails, which I now knew came from spending the day with animals.

I'd asked Joy questions about Luke I should have asked him, and much sooner. She told me he worked at the CSPCA, a nonprofit animal shelter. I could picture him rolling in the dirt while a litter of puppies licked his face. I wanted him to introduce me to his houseplants.

"You look beautiful, Durga," he said.

"Thank you."

I had now learned to take a compliment. I looked him straight in the eyes and accepted it for fact. The old Durga would've assumed he was only being polite. The new Durga knew Luke was an honest person.

"I've moved to Ballincollig, you heard? One of those flats near the shopping center. Moved in with my friend Mikey."

I did know. Joy had told me. She also mentioned that he had early shifts on Thursdays and Fridays, and that he'd taken up running in the park. I wasn't intending on lying to him either. Kali was brutal but sincere.

"Joy told me I might find you here. I'm sorry I haven't texted you. I needed some time to work through things. I wasn't fair to you before."

Luke combed closely through every angle of me, as though this was the first time he was absorbing what I really looked like. Or perhaps he was in disbelief that I could be this direct. The Durga he'd been briefly acquainted with would have blushed profusely, stared at her feet just to avoid looking at him. This was his first time meeting the other me, the rendering of me I wanted Luke to have.

"I haven't stopped thinking about you, but I wanted to give you space."

"I did need space," I said.

He was more than my plaything. Luke was a whole person. A man with freckles on his arms and kind blue eyes.

"I've missed you," he said, and awkwardly held out a hand. He was struggling too, the way I had struggled in the past in moments of profound realization. Something significant was happening, and we could both feel it.

Luke had been waiting for me, to come to him.

I reached for him and weaved my fingers with his, and now that he had a grip he pulled me close. I wrapped my arms around his neck and he kissed me.

I swayed and he leaned in, pinning my hips to his body. Tongues, teeth, my nails on his nape.

"When will you cook me pasta?" I whispered in his ear.

* * *

I WALKED BACK home, with the flush of Luke still coursing through my veins. The tingle of the first flushes of a new romantic entanglement.

Luke had said yes. To cooking me pasta. To us getting to know each other better. To taking it slow. I was determined for us to spend some time fully clothed. I'd been afraid before, of being consumed by another man the way I'd been with Jacob, but I was ready now.

I was completely housebroken too, and even had a plant-watering schedule pinned to my corkboard. I was cooking more and had a fully stocked spice rack. I went to the library with Naledi on Saturdays, and then we had brunch with Joy, at which Maeve made an appearance sometimes. I didn't need music to fall asleep, too exhausted from the gym to have my thoughts wander. I had flights booked to India for autumn, when the weather would be cooler. I sang ghazals in the shower, badly, and had cooked khichudi a few times. I started a book club at work and spent time alone with Joy at least once a week. She still deep-cleaned the flat when she came over, and buying a house together wasn't completely out of the question.

I was ready to begin living here. In my own personal space. As this new person. Each voice in my head had its own room, and I was learning to live with them too.

Acknowledgments

My most heartfelt gratitude goes out to the artist Gio Swaby. Her exhibition titled "I Will Blossom Anyway," which explores dual identities experienced by immigrants, are themes similar to the ones I explore in this novel.

Endless thanks to my agent, Marianne, an angel in disguise. She has believed in me from our first "hello." My editors, Jenny and Mae, who had faith in this novel and gave me the space and time to write it. Everyone on Team BLOSSOM: Megan, Jean, Taylor, and Emily.

As most writers will attest, our craft is a solitary pursuit. I'm a loner on most days, and entirely a recluse when I'm writing. The people I'd like to thank here are the ones who understand this about me and have stuck around when I've been most quiet and inward.

Dominique, for slipping in the mud with me in Kinsale, and for raising our daughters together.

Fran, for sitting with me in companionable silence for hours.

Anjana and Krisselm, who have never held my long absences from the group chat against me.

My hype squad through the years: Nayantara, Proma, Priya, and Priya.

Ellora, who tells the best stories.

And Richard, who knocks on my office door without expecting a response.

I couldn't have written this book without all these people in my life.

About the Author

Disha Bose is the author of *Dirty Laundry,* which was a *Good Morning America* Book Club pick and named one of the best books of the year by *Harper's Bazaar* and *Elle.* She received a master's in creative writing at University College Dublin, where she was mentored by Booker Prize winner Anne Enright. She has been short-listed for the DNA Short Story Prize, and her poetry and short stories have appeared in *The Incubator Journal, The Galway Review, Cultured Vultures,* and *HeadStuff.* Her travel pieces have appeared in *The Economic Times* and *Coldnoon.* Bose was born and raised in India and now lives in Ireland with her husband and daughter.

dishabose.com
Instagram: @dishabossy
X: @dishabossy